I0685301

JONATHAN BRADFORD;

OR, THE

MURDER AT THE ROAD-SIDE INN.

A ROMANCE

BY THE AUTHOR OF " THE HEBREW MAIDEN," " THE WIFE'S SECRET," &c., &c.

LONDON:

PUBLISHED BY E. LLOYD, SALISBURY-SQUARE, AND SOLD BY ALL BOOKSELLERS

JONATHAN BRADFORD;

OR, THE

MURDER AT THE ROADSIDE INN.

A Romance of Thrilling Interest.

CHAPTER I.

THE PROJECTED JOURNEY.—OMENS OF MISFORTUNE, &C.

"NAY, my dear husband, I wish you would not laugh at my warning, and call my fears groundless, for there is a terrible presentiment in my mind, that if you persist in going this journey you will never return home alive. You disregard my warning because it is grounded upon a dream, but how many times have I heard of dreams being realised, and of persons falling beneath the hand of an assassin when the terrible calamity might have been prevented had the prognostication been attended to. Do, therefore, oblige me this once, and relieve my mind of its alarm by postponing your journey till to-morrow.''

Thus spoke Mrs. Hayes to her husband, and the earnestness with which she gave utterance to the entreaty, proved how much reliance she placed in the superstitious feeling that had taken possession of her mind. Mr. Hayes was not altogether unmoved by her words, but throughout his life he had been a man of strict business habits, and as the matter he had in hand was of considerable importance, he felt that he was for once compelled to make a firm stand against the entreaties of his wife.

"My dear Katherine,'' he said after a little deliberation, "you know how willing I am always to yield to your slightest wish, but in this instance I cannot do so without making myself ridiculous in the sight of all my friends. To-morrow morning I have to complete the purchase of the Oakdale estate, and unless I keep the appointment, I shall not only forfeit the money I have already paid down, but shall lose the property I so much covet into the bargain. And all through a foolish dream of yours, that you would yourself laugh at if you would only give the matter the slightest consideration.''

"I have tried to drive it from my thoughts,'' answered the lady, "but all in vain, for still do I feel as much assured as ever that if this course is persisted in, some heavy affliction will befal us.''

"Then, for goodness sake, my dear, don't tell your fears to any one, or we shall be the laughing stock of our fellow citizens of Oxford.''

"Their derision would not last long," again sighed the lady, "if my fears should be verified. Besides, a letter might be sent to postpone the appointment till some other day, and no one need be informed of the cause of the brief delay.''

"But I shall have friends with me on the journey, so there can be no reason for apprehending danger.''

"Who are the friends you speak of?''

"My solicitor, Mr. Doxey, is one, and the other is Mr. Rodpole, who is about to make a survey of the estate. Then, as good luck will have it, my honest friend, Jonathan Bradford is in our city of Oxford to-day, and he will accompany us to his inn, where we are to sleep to-night. So you see I shall have plenty of protection on the road, and there is very little fear of being attacked by highwaymen.''

"But you will have a large sum of money with you to complete the purchase of the estate,'' answered Mrs. Hayes, "and even though you may not be attacked by highwaymen, there may be others who would not hesitate to take your life for the sake of that which you have about you. Reflect, then, before it is too late, and think of the misery that would fall upon myself and our poor daughter if you should become the victim of your own blind obstinacy.''

"Does Lucy entertain the same fears as you do?''

"She does,'' answered Mrs Hayes, "but respect for her parent has restrained her from giving utterance to them. Her lover, too, Henry Dornton, would have added his remonstrances to mine had he not been afraid of giving offence to his future father-in-law.''

"He has acted wisely,'' exclaimed her husband, "for these superstitious fears may be excusable in females, in men they are ridiculous, and should not be encouraged.''

"Will nothing prevail upon you to postpone this journey for a short time?''

"If any sufficient cause could be chosen for changing my purpose, I might perhaps yield,'' he replied. "I can, however, see no reason for the delay, and the more especially as the person from whom I am about to purchase this property would have sufficient justification for turning round and declaring that, as I was not there at the appointed time, I had forfeited the money which had been already paid down.''

"But it may be guessed that you travel with a large sum in your possession, and that would prove a temptation too great to be resisted by an evil-disposed person.''

"Ay, but you forget that I shall have three companions on the road.''

"The road,'' answered Mrs. Hayes, "is not the only place where danger may be looked for. You will sleep to-night at an inn, where people of all descriptions congregate, and if your business should be known, it will at once be surmised that you have money in your possession."

"And what if there should be such a notion?" asked her husband. "Have I not often before now slept at the house of Jonathan Bradford, and is there a more respectable inn to be found in the whole county of Oxford than the one that owns him for its master?"

"Yet amongst his numerous customers—many of them strangers too—he cannot answer for the honesty of all."

"I see how it is," exclaimed Mr. Hayes, "this dream of yours has made so deep an impression upon your mind, that you cannot eradicate the fear it has left behind. For this once, however, I must have my own way, and you will therefore oblige me by not sayinganything more to change me from my purpose."

"But it will be dark before you reach the place of your destination."

"Th at matters not," he replied, "since I shall travel in good company, and highwayme n almost always take the road singly. As a precaution, too, all of us will be armed, so that even in the event of an attack we should be able to put a bold front upon the affair."

"Alas!" said the lady, "then you are resolved to go?"

"I have shown you that there is no help for it," answered her husband, "and as for any alarm that you may feel during my absence, that will very soon be dissipated, for the business that takes me hence will not occupy me more than a couple of hours in the morning, and as soon as it is finished, I shall mount my horse and ride back with the pleasant intelligence that the long-coveted estate of Oakdale is ours. That accomplished, the union of our daughter Lucy and young Dornton shall take place without delay, and we will then retire to our newly acquired property, and enjoy ourselves in ease and comfort, after spending all the prime of our lives in the cares and turmoil of business. So now, wife, do try to drive away these melancholy thoughts of yours, and learn to treat dreams and omens with the same contempt that I do."

"If I happen in this case to be wrong I will never place my faith in them more," replied Mrs. Hayes.

"If!" Can there be any doubt of it, do you think?"

"My dear husband," she replied, "you know my weakness, and it would be in vain to argue with me upon a matter that has taken such entire possession of me. I will, however, since you are determined to go, endeavour to compose my mind, and should you return safe. I may then be forced to acknowledge that I have fallen into a great error."

"At all events," answered her husband, "you must feel more satisfied, now that you know I shall travel in good company?"

"That is my only consolation," exclaimed Mrs. Hayes, "but still the worst part of the omen remains, for, in my dream, I thought you were stabbed to the heart in the bed-room of an inn."

"Ay," exclaimed the old gentleman, "that was because you had been thinking [of all sorts of danger during the day, and nothing could be more likely that the thoughts should haunt you in your sleep. But you forget that the house of Jonathan Bradford is a most respectable one, and I shall be as safe from danger there as beneath my own roof."

"Alas! you know not what strangers you may meet with there."

"There's no accounting for that certainly," answered her husband, "but it don't follow that because we meet strangers they must needs be robbers and cut-throats. Such persons would find no harbour beneath Bradford's roof you may be assured, and therefore you may make yourself perfectly easy during the short time I shall be absent."

"I will endeavour to do so," exclaimed Mrs. Hayes, "but I shall know neither rest nor happiness till you return safe, which I am afraid is not destined to be the case."

"Psha! this superstition almost makes me angry with you."

"Nay, I hope you will not leave me in anger," cried the sorrowing lady "for that would only serve to increase the bitterness of grief which your departure occasions. If this is an infirmity, bear with it a little while, and should events take a more fortunate turn than I have anticipated, I will endeavour to cure myself of the weakness in future."

"Well—well, my love," exclaimed Mr. Hayes, "you and I will not quarrel just as we are about to part for a short time. All I wish is that, you may banish from your mind these notions, that only serve to make you unhappy, and my safe return home will convince you that dreams and omens are based on fallacy and weakness. In all other things you are willing enough to listen to the voice of reason, and I feel quite certain that when we meet again to-morrow, you will laugh as much as I do at the superstitious fears that you have indulged in."

"Ay," she replied, "let me but see you again, and I will then freely acknowledge that I have been guilty of a great folly."

"And during my short absence from home you will not suffer yourself to become a prey to unfounded fears?"

"As it is your wish, I will at least endeavour to calm myself," answere Mrs. Hayes "Our daughter will be my only companion, and she will, I know, exert herself to expel from my mind those thoughts which have filled me with so much uneasiness."

"But I am afraid she has imbibed some of your notions."

"There is no doubt of it," answered the lady, "but with more resolution than I possess, she affects to laugh at them as being the mere offspring of a distempered brain. You will, however, see her before you go, that your confidence may impress her with some of the cheerfulness with which you set forth on this journey."

At this moment Lucy entered the room by accident, and having been briefly informed of the nature of the conversation that had taken place, she earnestly joined her entreaties to those of her mother, that the business might be postponed for a few hours. But Mr. Hayes, though generally of a yielding nature, most positively refused to give way in this instance, and as the time for his departure had now arrived, he bade farewell to his wife and daughter with a light heart, and having deposited in his pocket a bag of gold for the payment of the remainder of the purchase money, he left his home, and proceeded to the Vine Inn, in the corn market of Oxford, where he found his three friends anxiously waiting his arrival. Sitting himself down at the table at which they were drinking wine, he, after a few prefatory observations, enquired at what hour they intended to start on their journey.

"Directly," answered Bradford, "our nags are all ready saddled in the yard, and we were only waiting till you came."

"Shall we reach your house before dark?" asked Mr. Hayes.

"In the present state of the roads I hardly think that possibie," replied Jonathan, "but it will be a matter of little consequence, since there will be so many of us in company."

"Are the roads in your neighbourhood pretty clear of highwaymen?" demanded the old gentleman.

"Humph! there are not more of them than usual, I believe."

"I don't see that it matters much whether there are any or not," observed Lawyer Dozey, "for they never venture to attack more than two persons together, and as we shall be double that number we may consider ourselves tolerably safe."

"On the road we may," exclaimed Mr. Hayes, upon whom the words of his wife had —in spite of himself—made some little impression; "but I have heard of these fellows disguising themselves, and taking a lodging at an inn as travellers, to rob those who may happen to be possessed of money. Now I," he added in a whisper, and looking round to see if anybody was listening, "have, as you know, a large sum of money with me to pay away to-morrow, and I was thinking it would be awkward to fall in with such a customer at the house of our friend Jonathan Bradford."

"I have never yet been honoured with the company of any of them," answered Jonathan, "and I have a notion that they are aware of the sort of reception they would meet with if any of them should ever be found under my roof. Nay, more, if you feel any apprehension of danger, Mr. Hayes, I, or some of my people, will willingly sit up all night in your chamber, rather than a robbery should be committed upon a gentleman who puts up at my house as a guest."

"Oh," returned Mr. Rodpole, "what occasion can there be for that; when I'll be bound my friend Dozey and I shall be sitting up to drink punch, long after the rest of the house are in bed. We are neither of us very early boys when we meet together socially, and as we have important business to transact together to-morrow, I don't know that we can do better than sit down and drink success to our undertaking."

"And so," observed the old gentleman, "go to work in the morning with brains muddled and confused."

"Psha!" exclaimed Rodpole, "what's the use of a man that can't take a glass or so without unfitting himself for business? I could make a survey of a farm better after a good drinking bout, than I could do without it, and I'll undertake to say that you will have nothing to find fault with me about, when we get to business."

"By the by, Mr. Hayes," observed the lawyer, "I'm sorry to see that you are a cup too low to-day. You are as dull as ditch water, and I wouldn't mind wagering a trifle that you would be glad to give up this journey of ours for a little while if you could."

"There's no denying it," he replied.

"What has been the cause of it?" asked Dozey.

"It would only cause a laugh at my expense if I was to tell you," answered the old gentleman. "However, I suppose the affair will get wind some of these days, so I may as well confess at once that I have been listening to a foolish dream, till I'm ashamed to say it. I would have been glad if any excuse could have been found for postponing our journey till to-morrow."

"May I ask who had this dream?" asked Bradford.

"My wife."

"That's just what I expected," chimed in Lawyer Dozey, "for women have a remarkable habit of dreaming, and what is more, they always expect them to come true. My wife was as bad as the rest of them, but I never paid any heed to the nonsense, and at last she got tired of annoying me with the recital of them over the breakfast table."

"I have as little belief in such nonsense as you or anybody else can have," exclaimed Mr. Hayes, "but one don't like to be cross with a wife, when she believes she is acting kindly in endeavouring to prevent the mischief she imagines. Now Mrs. Hayes has a firm impression that some fatal mischief is about to happen to me, and my resolution to make this journey to-night, against her advice, has occasioned more uneasiness than I ever saw her give way to before."

"Well," replied Rodpole, "at all events her uneasiness cannot last very long, for you will have returned home by this time to-morrow, and convince her by your presence of her unnecessary alarm."

"But she for one don't think so, I can tell you."

"What in the name of fortune does she think, then?"

"That I shall be robbed and murdered."

"A mere nervous feeling that she will by-and-by laugh at as heartily as any one." observed the lawyer. "Some people are, I know more superstitious than others, but if you only leave them alone long enough, they are sure in the end to see that neither dreams nor omens can ever come true except by mere chance. Women, however, are more prone to these notions than we of the rougher sex, and I suppose that is to be accounted for in one great measure by their having more leizure to think of them."

"And to their having more susceptible nerves," observed the old gentleman. "But bless them, say I, for their alarm is generally most excited when they fancy those they love the dearest are in danger. At any rate, I speak from experience, for I am well assured my wife would not have mentioned her dream to me, but from a feeling that has taken possession of her mind that some imminent peril is impending over me."

"Yet a moment's reflection would convince her that no reliance ought to be placed in those sleeping fancies, that originate in impressions for which we cannot possibly account. Perhaps you think I look at it in too serious a light, but the truth is, I was always sceptical upon the subject, and have no patience with those who pin their faith upon such fantastical notions."

"Ay, ay," exclaimed Rodpole, "we never expect much feeling from lawyers, and therefore Mr. Hayes will easily pardon anything that you say upon the subject. Not that I have any more belief in dreams than you have, nor have I any doubt but that our friend here will return home safe and sound, to give a flat contradiction to that which has occasioned so much consternation."

"We must soon think about starting then," observed Mr. Hayes, looking up at the clock, " or we shall not reach the end of our journey before these rascally highwaymen begin to infest the roads.'

" I am at your service whenever you please to start," said Bradford, "but I may perhaps be allowed to say once more, that there is not the slightest danger to be apprehended from these gentry. People travel too well armed for them now-a-days, and they never venture to make an attempt to stop passengers, but when they are almost certain of succeeding in committing a robbery easily."

"But," whispered the old gentleman, "the attempt would be worth making if it should be known that I have a large sum of money with me."

"And who is to know that besides ourselves ?"

" Very true," answered Mr. Hayes, " and yet it is well known that I have been for some time in treaty for the Oakdale property ; and should it be known that I am pro-ceeding that way to-night, it might easily be imagined I am going to complete the bargain."

"I see," laughed Mr. Dozey, " you have made up your mind that the dream will come true."

"Indeed, I have done nothing of the kind," he replied, " or I should have yielded at once to the earnest solicitation of my wife. On the other hand, however, I am free to confess that I shall be heartily glad when all this money is out of my possession."

"Which will not be long first," observed the lawyer, " seeing that the affair is to be brought to a conclusion the first thing in the morning. You will then be the lord ot the manor of Oakdale, with, I hope, many years of happiness and enjoyment before you."

"By the bye," exclaimed Redpole, " are we entirely to lose your society here when you become the owner of this new property ?"

"I shall very rarely visit Oxford afterwards, I can assure you," replied the old gentleman, "for my whole life has been passed in the bustle of business, and I now mean to enjoy the pleasure of a country life. My daughter, as you know, is about to marry young Mr. Dornton, and as they will occupy the house I at present occupy here, I shall sometimes visit them, but never for more than a day or two at a time."

"Then, in my opinion, you will soon grow heartily sick of your dull, monotonous country life."

"You judge by your own feelings, perhaps, Mr. Dozey ?"

"I believe you are right, there," he replied, " and I know of nothing better to judge by, for we have both been active men in our time, and these sudden changes, though pleasant enough at first, soon begin to grow wearisome and unbearable. However, that's nothing to me, and, as I said before, I hope you may experience all the enjoyment you anticipate."

"But it seems you scarcely fancy I shall ?" laughed the old gentleman. " Well, well, experience will let us into th e secret of that, and for my own part, I can see no reason why I should not be as happy as a prince [in] the new station I am going to occupy."

"At all events, you will leave behind you your only child, to whom I know you are fondly attached."

" That's true enough," answered Mr. Hayes, " but I shall leave her with the husband of her choice, and surely that will be all the consolation I can possibly desire. Besides, scarcely twelve miles will separate us, so that at any time a couple of hours will unite us, if either should be so minded. But now, gentlemen, I must again remind you that it's high time we should be moving, for the shadows of evening are already setting in, and we must not forget that we shall have no moon to light us on our way to-night."

This suggestion was immediately acted on, and the reckoning having been discharged, the four travellers proceeded to the street, where their horses were waiting ready for them. Having bade good-night to their host, they rode slowly up the high street till they reached the limits of the city, when they proceeded some little distance at a trot this, however, they could not continue far on account of the darkness, and drawing themselves as near to each other as possible, they sought by conversation to dissipate the dreariness of their way."

"This is rather an unpleasant journey of ours," observed Mr. Dozey, looking dismally over his shoulder to see that his companions were near him, "and I now begin to think, with Mr. Hayes, that it would have been much better to leave our start til the morning."

"Ay," answered the old gentleman, "but it's too late now for our regrets ; so, under the escort of our worthy friend Bradford, we must push on as fast as we can, and enjoy ourselves over a bottle of his best wine, as soon as we find ourselves comfortably seated in his chimney nook. By the bye, Jonathan," he added, presently afterwards, "do you happen to have much company at your house just now ?"

"Very little indeed, sir," returned the other, " for the weather has been bad ; and business very dull, so that we have hardly seen any of the London or Birmingham travellers for the last month."

"So much the better," exclaimed Mr. Hayes, "for of all the insufferable bores that find their way into decent society, your bagmen are decidedly the worst. Egad, I would rather run a mile any time than throw myself into the way of one of them, and nothing but such a dark dreary night as this would ever induce me to pass the next few hours under your roof, if I thought there was a chance of meeting with any of the gentry there."

"And yet," observed Bradford, "they are pleasant fellows enough in their way, and I find that most of my customers are pleased with their company."

"That may be," answered Mr. Hayes, "but the people you speak of must be some of those who like to hear all the conversation engrossed by one or two men. These commercial travellers seem to think themselves superior to every bodyelse in a room, and for that reason I have always taken care to avoid being in their company."

"You are rather too hard upon them, I think, sir," observed Mr. Dozey, " for I dare say there are all sorts of dispositions among them, and some, perhaps, are pleasant, good-hearted fellows. At all events, I should prefer meeting one or two of them tonight at Bradford's house, to finding suspicious-looking persons there who might turn out to be highwaymen."

Psha ! what's the use of talking about highwaymen at such a time and place as this ?" exclaimed Rodpole, terribly alarmed at these words. "This would be a very awkward place to meet any of them in, and for my own part, I believe the sight of a pistol, and those dreadful words, 'Stand and deliver !' would frighten me out of my life."

"Don't think of it, my good sir," exclaimed Jonathan Bradford, "for we are proceeding on our way comfortably enough, and shall arrive safely at the place of our destination if you will only keep up your courage. We have met no one upon the road yet and I'll be bound we shall be equally safe if we only put a bold front upon matters, and proceed on our way without appearing to be frightened."

"Wh-a-a-t's that I see a-head of us yonder ?" stammered the surveyor, pointing with his aiding-whip towards an object that he saw a little way in advance of them.

"Nothing but a direction-post, as I'm an honest man !" answered Bradford, laughing outright at the alarm of the surveyor.

"Ah !" returned the other, with a groan, " this may be fine fun for you, Mr. Bradford but I am not used to travelling by night, and the dreams and omens we have been talking about this evening have made me feel quite nervous."

"Then let us move on a little more rapidly," exclaimed Jonathan, urging his horse into a trot. "You needn't be afraid of following me, gentlemen, for I know the way very well, and the road for the next four or five miles is excellent."

Thus assured by the man who had volunteered to act as their guide, the three gentlemen followed his counsel, and for the next hour they proceeded at a pace that promised to bring them speedily to the end of their journey. Not a word was spoken by any of them, and they were within a mile of the inn kept by Jonathan Bradford, when the horse of Mr. Hayes suddenly shied at some object near them, and the old gentleman would have been thrown, had not Lawyer Dozey seized his rein, and thus checked the animal in time to prevent the mischief.

"Who goes there?" demanded Bradford of two men who had drawn up by the road side to let them pass.

"Travellers, like yourselves," was the reply.

"Whither are you going?"

"That we hardly know," replied the one who had spoken before, "but I suppose we shall stop at the first inn we come to, if, indeed, we are lucky enough to find one this dark night."

"Are you for London?"

"Yes."

"I don't much fancy these men," whispered Mr. Hayes to Bradford. "Let's put spurs to our horses, and leave them to find the way as they can."

The suggestion was not a very kind one, but Jonathan was not much inclined to offer any opposition to it, and with a sullen "good-night" to the two strangers, our travellers once more put their horses in rapid motion. They remained silent, and kept their ears open, to ascertain if the men they suspected were in pursuit of them; but nothing occurred to increase their alarm, and by the time they reached the hill, on the top of which stood Bradford's house, the fear which had urged them on began to evaporate. Jonathan then checked his horse, to proceed the rest of the way more leisurely, and addressing himself to his companions, he said—

"This adventure of ours turns out to be nothing after all, for the two men we saw just now are only travellers like ourselves; and I dare say we shall see them at my house soon after we reach it ourselves."

"I hope not," answered Mr. Hayes, thoughtfully.

"And so do I," exclaimed the lawyer and the surveyor at the same moment.

"Ah, let them come if they like," said Jonathan Bradford, "for I shall then have a good look at them, and may perhaps be able to discover who they are, and what business brings them this way to-night."

"But I hope you will not give them shelter," observed the old man.

"Why, as for that," answered Bradford, "my house is an open one, and I am compelled to receive all persons who are not known to be disreputable characters. These men may be as honest as ourselves, and in that case it would be hard to refuse them a lodging when there is not another to be found within a half a dozen miles from my inn."

"Very true," returned Mr. Hayes, "and I must confess my own selfishness for offering such a suggestion."

"I suppose, if the truth was known," laughed the lawyer, "the dream you have been telling us of has made no impression upon your mind in spite of all your efforts to drive away the remembrance of it?"

"I believe you are right there," he replied, "for though I laughed at the fears of my wife I have since thought more of what she said than I wished to have done. Those men, too, that we passed just now gave rise to fresh suspicions, though, if asked to do so, I could not give a satisfactory reason for believing them to be dangerous characters."

"The fact is," answered Mr. Dozey, "you have a large sum of money about you, and every trivial circumstance fills you with alarm for its safety. However, it will be out of your possession early in the morning, and then your mind will be at rest."

"And when that is the case," exclaimed the old gentleman, "I shall return home without an instant's delay and appease the terror of my wife, who I know will not be at rest till she has ocular proof that her dream had no foundation in reality."

"But she knows where you are going to sleep to-night," observed Jonathan Bradford, "and surely that ought to convince her that no harm is likely to happen."

"I told her that and a dozen things besides," answered Mr. Hayes, "but the impression made upon her mind is too powerful to be easily eradicated. Nor could I find it in my heart to be angry with her, for the warning was kindly meant, and I should have yielded to her entreaties to postpone this business for a short time, had it not been for the certainty that advantage would have been taken of my want of punctuality by the person of whom I am about to purchase this estate."

"Ay," exclaimed Mr. Dozey, "I know the sort of person you have to deal with, and he would have insisted upon your forfeiting the deposit money if you had not kept your appointment with him to the very moment. But yonder, I see the inn; and now having almost reached our place of destination, I believe we may pretty well consider that all danger is over."

A few minutes more served to bring them before the door of Jonathan Bradford's house, and the four travellers dismounting from their horses, proceeded to the stables to satisfy themselves that their faithful steeds would be properly taken care of for the night. Bradford had soon performed his part of the duty, and then leaving his fellow travellers to finish theirs, he went to make preparations for the reception of his guests.

CHAPTER II.

A WIFE'S FEARS AND ANXIETIES.—A PAIR OF LOVERS.—BRADFORD'S RETURN HOME-
THE TRAVELLERS.

No sooner had the shades of evening began to show themselves than Mrs. Bradford manifested her anxiety at the prolonged absence of her husband. Till the present occasion he had always returned home at an early hour in the afternoon, and now every moment seemed an hour to her, for she thought that nothing but a serious accident could have detained him, and in the restlessness of her alarm she left the house to look for him from the summit of a hill which commanded a long view of the road from Oxford. Still, however, was she doomed to disappointment, for the darkness of night soon came on, and yet he for whom she was looking presented himself not before her. More alarmed than ever, she returned to the house'; and then her faithful servant, Sally, volunteered to go out and listen for the clattering of a horse's footstep, promising to give the earliest information of any news that might afford a hope of the anxiously expected arrival. In the yard at the rear of the premises Jack Rackbottle was occupied in cleaning boots, and occasionally keeping up his spirits by singing snatches of various songs with which he was wont to amuse the visitors of the tap-room in long winter evenings.

"Ah!" he exclaimed, communing with himself, "its just half a year to-day, by the notches I cut in the horse-trough, since I had the honour of becoming boots to the George Inn—the very best house of entertainment all the way from London, and kept by Mister Jonathan Bradford, who, I will say, is as honest and warm-hearted a landlord as ever poured out a noggin of ale, or d ove cork into a bottle. There's no double-scoring here; no short measure ; no adulterated liquors : none of your London tricks upon travellers, but everything fair and above board. Money's-worth for your money is my masters maxim—ay, and mistress's too, for that matter, for I always notice that when she measures out the gin and brandy at the bar she likes to see the glasses run over, just as if she set it sparkling by her own eyes. Then as for the boots of the establishment, where will they find a fellow that understands his business better than I do? Why, no where to be sure, for I'm civil and obliging to everybody, and have a light heart that sets the world and all its troubles at defiance."

Upon this he burst forth with another song, which was, however, soon interrupted by the aproach of Sally, who was returning from the mission she had undertaken."

"Heigho!" she sighed, "upon my word Mr. Rackbottle, you seem to be uncommonly merry this evening."

"To be sure I am, Sally," he replied ; "and in my opinion its a bad conscience indeed that makes people melancholy without a cause. Why aint you as merry as I am I You have a nice easy place of it here."

"That's very true," answered Sally, "but it makes me dull to see poor missess take on so about master's being absent longer than usual. Besides, did'nt I lose my husband scarcely six months ago? and if that's not enough to take away one's spirits, I don't know what is."

"Ah!" exclaimed Jack, slily, "and the worst of it is that to do the think genteelly you must remain a widow six months longer before you think of taking another husband."

"That's the worst of it," again sighed Sally, "that is—I meant to say——"

"That it's a great pity, having lost your old Boots, you cannot immediately take up with new Boots—meaning myself."

"Indeed, Mr. Jack, I meant no such thing," she replied tartly; "and though my husband was old, and we were not united above three months, I fret about him a great deal more than I'll ever let anybody know. You shall never know how I think of him in the night, and what dreams and apparitions frighten me almost out of my senses! Would you believe it, it was only last night that I thought he was jealous of me as usual; and there he was, raging and stamping, and running after me with an old boot in his hand round the room as if he meant to kill me. Ah! you needn't laugh a me, for I was terribly frightened at the dream, I can tell you."

"Well, then," replied Jack, "the sooner you change your dream for a reality the better."

"What do you mean by that, sir."

"I would only ask you," he replied, "what is a woman by herself? Isn't she a boot without a foot—a brush without a back—a currycomb without a horse—a——"

"You are right enough there Jack," she exclaimed. "I feel that I am a miserable lost woman; but how can I help myself?"

"Why, think about marrying, to be sure."

"To confess the truth, I have thought of it very often," answered Sally, "for there's that little bit of money that my poor dear husband left me—it's mouldering away, as I may say, in my keeping, when it might serve to set up an honest, industrious couple in some snug little business."

"To be sure it would," replied the other. "Now, there's the little public-house on t'other side the common to be let, and with an active little body, something of my figure, and a genteel, pretty landlady, something of your figure, the house could hardly fail to do well."

"Come, come, Mr. Rackbottle, none of your insinuations I desire, for I never give any encouragement to such foolish notions as you are speaking about. Consider my situation—a widow only six months, and you talking as if it was likely I should so far forget myself as to marry again for a long time to come."

"Why, you ain't offended with me, are you?"

"No, I'm not offended wtih you," she replied, "but it wouldn't be right, you know, to listen to these sort of things without taking you down a bit. However, if, when the children are in bed, you like to come into the kitchin, and advise me for the best, I'll ake it very kind of you, and perhaps——"

"Will you let me talk about love, Sally?"

"That will depend upon circumstances," she replied, "for I am very unhappy, though I don't choose, as I said before, to let everybody know it."

"Then the best way that I know of, to cure yourself of this melancholly, is to take another husband."

"I'll think of it, Jack," she replied; "but between ourselves I can't think of marrying till after the first twelvemonth of my widowhood has been completed. The world would call me a good-for-nothing creature if I did, and one must not lose a good character through being in too great a hurry to be married again."

"And what, after all, has the world to do with it?" asked Jack. "People are not to pine and fret themselves away with melancholy; and I should advise you to follow your own notions, and not to think of what anybody may say of you."

"Well," she replied, "I don't know but you are right, and perhaps upon a little farther consideration I may consult you again upon the subject. But don't speak a word to anybody about it, or I shall forbid you to come into my presence any more."

"I'll not give so much as a hint about it," answered Jack; "but in return, I hope you'll not throw cold water upon my love."

"You must be very cautions, then," she replied, "for I wouldn't have master or misses know of it for the world."

"Why not?"

"Because they'd think it very hard-hearted and cruel to forget my last husband so soon."

"But he was old enough to have been your father."

"True."

"And was jealous of you without a cause."

"That's very often the case, when there is such a difference in years between husband and wife. But I believe he loved me, for all that, and the least I can do in return is to treat his memory with respect."

"That's right enough," answered the other, "and I like you all the better, Sally, for saying so. All I want is, that you will look kindly upon me, and then I promise not to ask you to become Mrs. Rackbottle till the year of widowhood is up."

"And all I want," she replied, "is that, you will give me time for consideration. Husband's are not to be chosen at a moment's notice; and I should like to see a little more of you before I give any encouragement to your addresses."

"Manyn't I ask you a few more questions upon the subject when I see you by and by?"

"You can ask as many as you like," answered Sally; "but I may perhaps think proper to leave you as much in the dark as ever."

"Then I suppose I'm to understand that you don't care about me?"

"It will be time enough for you to understand that, when I have told you as much, she replied. "If the truth must be told, I have not a very bad opinion of you, Mr Rackbottle; but you must prove yourself worthy of it, or you will never get m y consent I can tell you."

"Ain't I honest and industrious?"

"I believe you are."

"What more would you have, then?"

"I must be convinced that your temper is a good one."

"Well, it ain't for me to sound my own praise," exclaimed Jack Rackbottle; "but I believe there's not a living soul that can say they ever saw me in a passion."

"Very likely not," answered Sally; "but people's disposition very often change after they are married, and I am not going to run the risk of making myself unhappy through not taking care in good time. So have a little patience, and I dare say by and by everything will be as you wish. But hush, here comes our mistress, and by the look of her she's more uneasy than ever about the long absence of her husband."

"Well, Sally," exclaimed Mrs. Bradford, "have you seen or heard anything of your master yet?"

"No, ma'am," she replied, "but I have been up to the top of the hill, and though I listened there for a long time."

"Then, alas! I fear there can no longer be any doubt that some evil hath befallen him," sighed her mistress.

"What do you think may have happened to him?"

"I have thought of many things," answered Mrs. Bradford; "but my chief fear is that he has been met by a highwayman on his road."

"But I think you said he took very little money with him."

"The sum was only sufficient to defray the expenses of his journey," answered her mistsress; "yet that serves not to remove my fears, for I know his resolution and daring and wereany ruffian to stop him on his way he would resist and perhaps lose his life in the conflict."

"Heaven forbid," exclaimed Sally; "and yet why should you give way to this alarm when it is to be hoped he will soon return home safe and sound."

"But he is so much beyond his usual time."

"Which I dare ay there is a reason for," replied the other; "he may have met with a friend and stayed with him longer than he intended, or a dozen other thing may have happened that he will be able to explain to your satisfaction when he comes back."

"I know not of any friends that he is likely to have met with, in Oxford," replied the mistress, "and if he had it is scarcely probable that he would have remained with them so late when he knows how the road is sometimes infested with highwaymen."

"Don't you think it very likely that he has waited for company on his way home?"

"It is scarcely probable," answered Mrs. Bradford, "for few persons are to be found who will run the risk of travelling at so late an hour as this. In truth, I have endeavoured to console myself with the hope that my fears are groundless, but the more I reflect upon the subject the less reason do I see to believe that he has not met with some serious accident."

"Try to forget it for a little time," exclaimed Sally, "and I'll be bound he'll soon return home as well as he went out. As for highwaymen, I think there's not much chance of his having met with any of them, for we have not heard of one being in the neighbourhood for a long time past, and that is perhaps the reason why he has remained out a little longer than usual to-night."

"Nay," answered her mistress, "it is kind of you to try and comfort me as you do, but nothing will convince me of his safety, till I have ocular proof of it."

"Then you will not be very long without it," exclaimed Sally, "for I hear the sound of horses tramping up the hill; and if I'm not mistaken, master will presently be here."

"'Tis he, I have no doubt," answered Mrs. Bradford, in a tone of pleasure; "so return to the house, Sally, and make all things ready for his reception."

The faithful domestic instantly obeyed this command, and her mistress remained where she was in anxious expectation of her husband's appearance. Bradford, as we have already seen, went first of all to put up his horse, and having done this he was making his way towards the house, when he encountered his wife, whose alarm for his safety had been so unnecessarily excited. A few words of explanation were all that were required; and then taking from his pocket a small packet, he placed it in her hand, saying—

"I have played the truant from you longer than usual, my dear Ann, but the contents of that parcel will prove to you that I have not forgotten you during my absence. It is a pair of buckles—not of diamonds it is true, but such as are more fitting the station we occupy in society. Wear them, Ann, for my sake;—to-morrow is your birthday, and a happy day we'll make of it, come what may."

"Come what may!" exclaimed his wife, half reprovingly; "ah, Jonathan, say not so, for a thousand things may happen that we dream not of. In this world, nothing, you know, is certain."

"Ah," replied her husband, laughing, "it is thus that all you women look out for the coming storm. 'Tis your nature to do so; and yet, how much better it is to hope all things for the best."

"Forgive me, my dear husband," she replied, "for my thoughts have been sso gloomy, that I have not yet been able to dissipate them. The buckles you have bought me I will wear to-morrow, and with Heaven's good leave it shall be a merry holiday to all beneath our roof."

"Why that's well said, wife," exclaimed Jonathan, "for nothing ever affords me half so much happiness as when I see you happy and free from care. And now, Ann, I have news for you; and I have brought guests with me who will remain here to-night."

"Indeed, who are they?"

"One, Mr. Doxey, a lawyer; another, Mr. Redpole, the surveyor of Oxford; and the third, Mr. Adam Hayes, a wealthy gentleman, who is here to complete the purchase of the Manor House."

"Does he intend to reside there?"

"He will remove there without delay, I believe," answered her husband, "and we shall then change the present churlish possessor, for a man of whom everybody reports most favourably. That, at any rate, will be an advantage to our neighbourhood, which sadly needs a few spirited gentlemen such as Mr. Hayes."

"Has he any family?"

"A wife and daughter," answered Bradford; "but the former only will accompany him, for the young lady, I understand, is about to be married immediately, and will remain at Oxford."

"How long will Mr. Hayes be our guest?" asked Mrs. Bradford.

"Only till about the middle of the day to-morrow," answered her husband; "for he has only come to complete the purchase of the estate; and as soon as he has paid the remainder of the money he will return home to quiet the fears of his wife, who entertains a superstitious notion that he will be murdered for the sake of the money he has brought with him."

"Was it not inconsiderate of him to travel with money about him at so late an hour?'

"Why, it would have been so," answered Bradford, "but he had plenty of company on the road; and it was therefore hardly likely that robbers would venture to make an attack upon him. Besides, he took care not to divulge the secret of his being in possession of a large sum, so that he would have no reason for suspecting that he would be attacked on the road.'

"But when the purpose of his visit here is known, may it not be imagined that he is a prey worth attacking?"

"It would be too dangerous an experiment to make," answered Bradford, "for our house is nearly full of people, and an act such as you speak of would lead to the immediate capture of the evil doer. Besides, he will have it with him in his own bed chamber, and no one, I should think, would run the risk of being taken in the act of committing a robbery. Then to-morrow, at an early hour, the money will be paid away, and he will be at liberty to return home, and soothe the fears of his wife, who, it seems, has been frightened by a foolish dream.'

"Have you no faith in dreams, then?" she asked.

"Not the slightest."

"And yet," answered his wife, "we have heard of many instances in which dreams have been most strangely realized.'

"Mere chance, depend on it," exclaimed Bradford; "for what can dreams possibly have in connection with the events of our lives? They are the offspring of superstion and when indulged in, too frequently lead to unhappiness. Such has been the case with Mrs. Hayes, who, in spite of her present notion upon the subject, will by and by confess that she has been deluded by a mere chimera of the brain."

"Is her husband as sceptical upon the subject as you are?'

"Quite so," answered Bradford, "though I fancied that on our way here he sometimes gave way to the warning he had received previously to his leaving home. However, I believe he got rid of the notion as s on as he found himself near the end of his journey, and that he now sees the absolute folly of giving way to the impressions that were produced by nothing more substantial than a mere dream."

"Did you meet no one on the road?" asked Mrs. Bradford.

"Only two men."

"Where they strangers?"

"I believe so; but it was too dark for me to see who they were, and we passed them without interruption."

"Which might not have been the case, observed his wife, "had they suspected that one of your party was in possession of a large sum of money."

"If they were rogues, we were too many for them," answered Bradford; "but I rather think they were a couple of honest travellers, on there way to London."

"Then they are coming towards our house?"

Most assuredly they are," he replied; "and I think it quite probable that they will pay us a parting visit."

"But not to stay here I hope."

"I think it vere likely they may want a night's lodging," replied Bradford; "and it so, I don't see how we can refuse them, seeing that we have beds to spare, and if would be hard to turn them adrift, since they would not find another house of public accommodation without walking at least half a dozen miles farther. So we must be prepared to receive them, and I dare say they will leave us early in the morning.

Mr. Hayes and his two friends now made their appearance, and Mrs. Bradford instantly hurried away to make the necessary preparations for the accommodation of her guests.

"Now, landlord," exclaimed the first-named gentleman, "having first seen to the comfort of our horses, we will next pay some little consideration to our own. We shall need supper, of course; and after a few glasses of wine, we shall be glad to go to bed, to repose ourselves after our journey."

"Everything will be in readiness for you presently," answered the host, "for my directions have been already given, and I may venture to promise that all will turn out to your satisfaction. Luckily, all our best rooms are just now disengaged, so that you can have the choice of which ever you please."

"Have you seen anything of the two men we passed on the road?" asked Lawyer Dozey.

"They have not arrived yet," replied Bradford; "but I dare say they will presently call in as they pass."

"I only wish I could fancy that they intended to pass," exclaimed Redpole, "for though I have not much about me to lose, I have a queer notion about those two fellows that I cannot get rid of."

"Why have you a queer notion," asked Mr. Hayes, "when they offered us no incivility?"

"They don't interrupt us I grant," answered the surveyor; "but for all that I can't help thinking that they are not the best of characters. I may be mistaken, and yet somehow or other, I didn't like the look of them."

"Psha!" exclaimed Mr. Hayes, "why it was too dark to see what they were like."

"So it was, but I can't think what business they could have to be out so late at night."

"They might think the same of us."

"That's all very true," answered Redpole; "but if called upon we could all give a good account of ourselves, which I have a notion is more than they could do."

"Upon my life," observed Mr. Hayes, "I think you are a little too hard upon those men, who I dare say are every bit as honest as ourselves. They seem to be a couple o travellers who, I suppose, are making their way towards London."

"And why," asked the other, "shouldn't we believe them to be a brace of highwaymen?"

"Because they offered us no molistation."

"For a very good reason;—they saw we were too many for them, and it was ever natural to suppose that we were armed."

"Well," said Mr. Hayes, "you are bigotted in your opinion of them, I see, so I shall argue no further upon the subject. All that I hope is that I may not lose my money, and if things go on smoothly, to-morrow night may see me snugly seated at my own fireside."

"What time," asked Mr. Dozey, "will you see the lawyer who is to transfer this new property to you?"

"As soon as possible after breakfast," replied the old gentleman, "for I suppose the business will occupy three or four hours, and I am anxious to return to Oxford before night sets in. It is true, I shall not then have much money about me, but sometimes that is so much the worse, for under the circumstances travellers are in more danger of being murdered by the disappointed villains who attempt to rob them."

"Pray don't talk about being murdered," exclaimed Redpole, "for it will make me so nervous I shall not be able to get a wink of sleep to-night."

"Excuse me, sir," interposed Jonathan Bradford; "but you may make yourself quite easy, for in my house no danger is likely to happen to you."

"It's not for myself that I'm speaking," returned Mr. Redpole, "but my friend Hayes has a large sum of money in his possession, and I am thinking that if it were known to any body it might prove too great a temptation."

"Phsa!" retorted the old gentleman, "how can it possibly be known?"

"It may very naturally be surmised that you have not come to make a purchase of an estate, without having the necessary sum about you to complete the bargain."

"Then don't alarm me when there is no occasion for it," exclaimed Mr. Hayes. "For my own part I have got over the foolish notion that just now possessed me; and if I am only left alone, I shall go to sleep as full of confidence as ever I did in my life.

"I am glad hear you say so, sir," observed Bradford; "for, in my own mind, I am confident you have nothing to fear. It's some time now since we had any highwaymen in these parts, and I think it's hardly likely we shall ever be troubled with any more, for five or six of them were hung about a year ago, and ever since we have been quite clear of their company."

"And don't you think some of their comrades may return when the affair is a little blown over?" asked Rodpole.

"There's no saying how that may be," replied the host; "but it's no use looking at the worst side of the question; and, for my own part, I have a notion that this neighbourhood is too hot for that kind of gentry. The people hereabouts have armed themselves, and we take it by turns to patrol the roads for the protection of each other."

"Then you feel quite confident in your own mind that there is no ground for apprehension?"

"I do, sir; and would almost venture to stake my existence that nothing will occur to injure or alarm those who have favoured me with this visit. But supper is now ready, gentlemen; and if you will follow me I will conduct you into the house."

This invitation was a very agreeable one; and accompanying the host, they entered th snug parlour of the George Inn.

CHAPTER III.

THE TWO MYSTERIOUS TRAVELLERS.—A LITTLE INSIGHT IS AFFORDED INTO THE MOTIVE OF THEIR VISIT.—JACK RACKBOTTLE IS RATHER PUZZLED BY THE QUESTIONS THAT ARE PUT TO HIM.—HE CONFERS WITH SALLY UPON THE SUBJECT, BUT GETS NO NEARER TO THE TRUTH.

SCARCELY had Bradford left the court-yard with his guests, than two other persons—the mysterious travellers who had been passed on the road—occupied nearly the same spot. They looked round them cautiously, and upon ascertaining that they were not being watched, the elder of the two—an adventurer named Dan Macraisy—whispered something to his companion, who immediately left him to make an examination of the other part of the premises. Being thus left alone, the one who remained slowly walked round to make his own observation, muttering as he did so the various thoughts that were passing through his mind.

"So!" he exclaimed inwardly, "this is the 'George Inn,' kept by Jonathan Bradford, who, luckily for my designs, will not know me when we meet together, so that all may be done quietly and without the least shadow of suspicion falling upon us. Ay, and the prize is worth trying after too, for the old gentleman carries money about him that may be counted by hundreds, and if the affair that brings us here is but cleverly managed, it may all be ours, and we shall be the last persons suspected of being concerned in the robbery. But where's that comrade of mine gone to, I should like to know? Confound the fellow, he's always absent when most needed; and if anything happens to mar this project, it will be through some thoughtless folly of his own."

Then seeing that no one was near, he ventured to pronounce the name of Caleb Scrimmidge in an audible whisper.

"Well, Dan; what's the matter with you now, Dan?" asked the other hastily approaching him.

"Go to the devil with your, Dan!" exclaimed this companion, angrily. "What do you mean by calling me Dan, when I don't want any of the people here to know my real name?"

"Let's see, what is it I'm to call you then?"

"I've told you that for the present I'm to be Squire O'Connor, and that you are to be my cousin."

"And where's our house supposed to be?"

"Where should it be but at my beautiful estate in Kilkenny."

"Which you never saw and never will."

"Never mind that," replied the other, "but remember all I've told you, and above everything else don't forget that you are my cousin."

"Yes," replied Caleb; "and very nicely you've cozened me all along with your gammoning and bamboozling. First you prevailed upon me to rob my master, Mr. Timothy Tick, the clock and watch maker of Seven Dials, and then to run away with you that we might both set up for gentlemen. And pretty gentlemen we are, going tick, tick, tick to the gallows as fast as a repeater that has just broke its main spring."

"Psha! you're always grumbling."

"And isn't there enough to make me, I should like to know?"

"Well then, mark me fellow," exclaimed Macraisy, sullenly; "another word like those you have uttered, and I'll send a bullet in that fool's sconce of yours."

"Well, then, I'm dumb," answered Caleb; "so now tell me, if you please, what dodge we are to be up to next."

"I've told you that already," replied his companion. "Haven't I a scheme that will make your fortune? Haven't we ascertained that Mr. Hayes sleeps here at the George Inn to night with a heavy purse of money in his pocket? And don't I know the house—before the present landlord lived here—and every room in it, as well as if I had been born and bred under the roof; and won't I transmogrify that purse of money of his into my own pocket so cleverly that no one shall guess who did it?"

"Ah!" exclaimed Caleb, "that's the very part of the affair where I expect you'll be disappointed."

"You are a coward then?"

"Not a bit of it," he replied, "but I feel for all the world as if there was a halter already round my throat."

"Courage man!" exclaimed Dan Macraisy. "Go on boldly with the work, and you shall stand recorded——"

"In the Newgate Calendar, I suppose, alongside of Highwayman Billy, and Hot-pepper Jack—a wheel within a wheel, as we used to say at Seven Dials."

"I say," exclaimed his companion, "I can sniff a good supper on the the table for the guests at any rate. There's roast beef, horse-raddish, wine, brandy, and I don't know how many good things besides, mingling their delicious odours, and tempting the appetite of a man who is already sufficiently hungry."

"A good supper, wine and brandy!" repeated Caleb. "That reminds me that we have had a long ride and nothing to eat or drink. Suppose we venture to go in and ask the landlord if we may not sit down and enjoy ourselves with his other guests."

"Ask?" retorted the other. "Nonsense, man! that's not the way to get what we want."

"How would you act, then?"

"Why, I'd follow my own mother's wise maxim, to be sure," he replied. " 'Dan,' said she, in her dying injunction to me, the big tears rolling down her old cheeks like green gooseberries, 'Dan,' said she, 'my only child—my pretty innocent boy, remember your poor mother's last advice: beg, borrow, and steal, if you wish to be respectable; but if once you give way to those modest notions of yours, you'll be kicked out of doors directly by those hard-hearted people that can never see merit in any one except themselves.' "

"And you have followed the old lady's advice?"

"Shouldn't I have been a most undutiful son if I had not?" he asked. "The truth is, I know right from wrong, Caleb, and remembering the poor old creature's maxim, I have always tried to follow the excellent injunctions she gave in her dying moments. Now, if you want to make a favourable impression upon the host here, this is the way to do it:—Ho! landlord!—fellow! Boots! ho! hem!"

And putting his hands into his pockets, Dan Macraisy strutted up and down with all the airs of a fine gentleman.

"Well!" exclaimed his astonished companion, "if ever I saw such cool impudence in all my life! Your mother must have been a most religious old lady, Dan, and the good counsel she gave don't seem to have been thrown away upon you."

"Didn't your mother ever give you any good advice, Caleb?" asked the other.

"No," he replied, shaking his head, "she always shut me up on Sundays, though, to prevent me from playing at marbles on the tombstones, instead of going to church, and said that the halfpenny a-week she allowed me for superfluities, was better than a guinea a day not honestly come by."

"Poor woman—I pity her ignorance."

"Ah, she was an ignorant poor creature, I know," answered Caleb; "but she had the good word of everybody, for all that.—But I say, Dan, just see how the landlord is bowing and scraping to you from the window. That's all owing to your pompous way of calling out just now, I suppose; so here's for a try if I can't act the gentleman as well as you did.—What ho! landlord! fellow!—Boots! ho! hem!"

And he imitated the strut and swagger so awkwardly, that Macraisy could not help bursting out into a laugh.

"Capital!" he exclaimed. "Why, Caleb, if I have you under my tuition a little while longer, I shall make you as proficient as myself in all the polished manners of the best society."

"To confess the truth," he replied, "I feel as if I was born to be a gentleman as much as yourself; and now that you have taught me the way, I shall know in future how to make myself looked upon as no common individual.—What oh!—landlord!—Boots!—ho!—hem!"

"Did anybody call for Boots?" exclaimed Jack Rackbottle, suddenly presenting himself before them.

"I flatter myself, somebody did," answered Caleb. "We want to know what your master has got to eat and drink?"

"There's every kind of drinkables you can name," returned Jack, "but for the eatables I can't say so much, unless there's any cold remains of our dinner to-day."

"Cold remains!" exclaimed Dan Macraisy; "and why can't we have a hot supper, as well as those gentlemen that I see enjoying themselves in yonder room?"

"Why, they've been here this hour and more," answered Jack, "and first come first served, is a maxim all over the world, you know."

"Nonsense! we are quite as respectable as the other customers."

"Perhaps you are," he replied, "but I take it you won't pretend to be more so."

"By-the-bye," exclaimed Dan Macraisy, who had walked up to the window to have a good look in, "who is that elderly gentleman, that is seated at the head of the table?"

"Pray why do you wan't to know?"

"Oh, mere idle curiosity," he replied with affected indifference. "I only fancied I had met him before somewhere."

"Very likely you may," answered Jack, "for he's well known, and much respected. It's a Mr. Hayes, sir, of Oxford, who having made a large fortune in business, is going to retire to the Manor House in this neighbourhood to spend the rest of his days comfortably."

"Oh," exclaimed Macraisy, still pursuing his pumping system, "he is the old gentleman that I was told has lately purchased the Oakdale estate, somewhere near here?"

"You are partly right, and partly wrong," answered Jack, "for the purchase won't be completed till to-morrow."

"Well, its almost the same thing," returned Macraisy, "for I suppose he's got the money with him; and as soon as that is paid the property will be his."

"Exactly so," replied the boots, "and glad enough he'll be to get rid of the money, for I've been told that he's in a terrible fright lest any one should be tempted to rob him of it."

"Ridiculous!" exclaimed Macraisy; "as if he was not as safe at the George Inn as he would be in his own house. But it's always the way with people when they grow old; they suspect everybody, and look upon all they meet as so many thieves. By-the-by, you haven't had any rogues lurking about these parts for a long time, have you?"

"No, luckily, we haven't," replied Jack; "but there's no saying how soon we may have some of 'em again."

"Then I, for one, shall not stay long in the neighbourhood," exclaimed Dan Macraisy, "for I have, myself, some little property about me that I should not like to loose. It's frightful to think that there's so much crime going on, and that honest men, like myself and my friend, can't travel with a bit of money without running the risk of being robbed and, very probably, murdered."

No. 3.

"Have you much farther to travel?" asked Jack; unable to fathom the mysterious trangers.

"We wanted to have reached London to-night," answered the other; "but finding that impossible, we must put up somewhere on the road. Your master has a couple of spare beds, I suppose?"

"You had better ask him," replied Jack; "for I don't know what arrangements he can make now that these three travellers have arrived before you."

"Perhaps they may all occupy the same bedchamber."

"That I'm sure they'll not," answered the boots, "for I heard Mr. Hayes say that he wished to have a room to himself."

Here a significant look was exchanged between Dan Macraisy and Caleb; but the former, afraid of giving rise to any suspicions, immediately resumed the conversation.

"It seems then," he said, "that you are not able to tell us whether we can sleep here to-night?"

"I know nothing about it," he replied; "but you can soon get all the information you want by asking master or missis."

"Have you any other visitors in the house?"

"Only two, and as they've gone out pleasuring, it's not certain whether they'll return here to-night. But what makes you ask me so many questions about my master's affairs?"

"Not out of any idle curiosity, I assure you," answered Macraisy; "but I wished to ascertain what chance there is of our being accommodated with a bed here till the morning."

"Well then, between ourselves," answered Jack, "I think my master is as likely to refuse you as not."

"Refuse us! and why should he do that?"

"Because you have arrived very late; and I know when that's the case he never likes to take strangers into his house."

"But we have a right to demand accommodation; and especially when there is no other inn within a reasonable distance. However, he will not prove quite so churlish as you would make him appear, I dare say; and when he sees how travel-worn we are, he'll give us shelter for the short time we need it."

"It's not for me to say he won't," replied the boots, "but I know Mr. Hayes was very particular in asking what other guests were in the house, and I suppose by that the old gentleman was thinking of the chance of being robbed."

"But do we look like robbers?" demanded Macraisy, with well-feigned anger at the insinuation.

"I don't mean to say you do," answered Jack; "but every man considers that he has a right to do as he pleases in his own house; and as these gentlemen will pay well for their accommodation, my master may not choose to run the risk of offending them by receiving more visitors than the house will conveniently hold. Besides, if you want company to the next inn on the road, I don't mind going with you myself, rather than there should be any bother about it."

"I tell you, fellow, I have valuable property about me, and I don't feel inclined to chance being stopped on the road. One customer is as good as another, for aught I know and we have as much right to be accommodated as those that came before us."

"You must tell my master that," replied Jack; "and if you can prove your respectability, I daresay he'll put himself out of the way rather than send you further in search of a lodging."

"Prove our respectability!" exclaimed Caleb Scrimmidge. "Let him just send up to London, and he'll soon find out who and what we are."

"I'm afraid it would take up too much time to do that," laughed Macraisy, "so he must be content with the account we are able to give of ourselves. Not but what you are right, old fellow, in saying that our character could soon be ascertained there, for I flatter myself that few men are better known——"

"At the police-office!" thought Caleb within himself.

"Well, if you were to talk to me for a month I could give no other answer than I have," exclaimed Jack Rackbottle. "The proper person to speak to is master, and he'll soon tell you whether you can remain here till the morning."

"Then go and tell him a couple of gentlemen wish to speak to him."

"I can't do that," answered the boots, "for the other guests have invited him to sit down with them, and he would not be best pleased to be called away from his company."

"But I want to know whether we may not be allowed to join their society?"

"Then I think I can answer for it that they don't wish to be intruded on by strangers."

"You are insolent, fellow."

"I'm sorry you think so," answered Jack, "but I always fancy it's as well to speak one's mind plainly."

"And so you won't take my message to your master?"

"No," he replied; "but if you wish it, I'll take you into another room, where you can wait till my master leaves the company, which he'll do presently, when more wine is wanted."

"So, we are to wait his leisure like a couple of lacquies?"

"You can see misses directly, if you like."

"We want to see your master, fellow, and no one else," replied Macraisy. "Women are apt to be superstitious of strangers; and situated as we are to-night, we want a straight-forward answer as to whether we are to be accommodated here."

"Then you can't do better than follow my advice," answered Jack. "There's a nice snug little parlour, with a good fire in it; and as soon as master leaves the company, I'll send him to you and your friend."

"Do as the chap says," whispered Caleb to his companion, "for I'm tired of waiting here, and I daresay we shall make it all right as soon as we see the governor."

Finding that no other alternative remained, Dan Macraisy thought proper to accede to this suggestion; and grumbling at the immovability of the boots, he accompanied Caleb into the house, determined, at all events, not to be disappointed of the prey he had set his mind on. As for Jack Rackbottle, he knew not what to make of the two persons who had just left him, though it must be confessed his opinion of them had been changed for the better by the boasted respectability of the references they could give in London. He determined, however, to reveal all that had passed to Sally, and therefore proceeded forthwith to the kitchen, in fulfilment of the promise he had made at an earlier hour in the evening,

"We've got some more visitors in the house, Sally," he exclaimed, "and rum 'uns they are, I can tell you; for though I've been talking to 'em for the last half hour, hang me if I can make head or tail of 'em for the life of me."

"Have they ever been here before?" she asked.

"I've never seen 'em here," he replied; "and yet I should think they know the house pretty well, for the elder of the two found his way to the little parlour as easily as if he had been one of our oldest customers."

"And are they going to sleep here?"

"That's more than I can tell," replied Jack, "but they don't seem very likely to take No for an answer, and I rather think master will not find it easy to get rid of 'em."

"What if they should be robbers in disguise!" exclaimed Sally, looking round her with alarm.

"Well, to tell you the truth, I had a notion of that sort myself," replied the boots "but then they talked so loudly of the respectability of their London acquaintances, that I gave up the idea, and now I am as much in the dark about them as ever."

"Don't you know what brought them this way?"

"No," he replied; "they were uncommomly close in everything about themselves; but one of 'em let it out by chance, that he had a good deal of property about him.

"Perhaps that was nothing but an empty boast."

"Very likely it was," answered Jack; "but I suppose they'll persuade master into letting them sleep here to-night; and all I hope is that they'll take their leave of us as early as possible in the morning."

"But suppose they should be robbers, and have heard that Mr. Hayes has a good deal of money about him?"

"They know all about it," replied Jack; "but I don't think they are robbers, because they seemed afraid of being robbed themselves, and that's one reason why they want to stay here. But you seem to be terribly afraid of those gentry all of a sudden, Sally, and that reminds me of something else that I was going to say to you. Don't you think the best cure for all this alarm would be to take a husband without waiting till the six months you talked of are up?"

"Ah! now you want to be coaxing me. I see, Mr. Rackbottle," she exclaimed; "but I know very well that the world would cry shame on me if I was to forget my firs husband so soon; and it was only a few days ago that misses spoke to me upon the subject, and said she hoped I should not go and make myself the common talk of the neighbourhood."

"Does she know that I have a sneaking kindness for you?"

"She knows nothing from me," answered Sally; "but I dare say she guesses something of the kind, as anybody else would, seeing that we are so much together."

"Well, I don't know that it much matters," returned Jack, "for it will soon be made public enough, and there's no occasion to be ashamed of good honest love like yours and mine. Besides, the marriage will not be an imprudent one, for both you and I have a little bit of money; and by its assistance we shall be able to start in some business, that may keep us in comfort all our lives."

"Don't you think we had better talk of that when it is nearer the time of our marriage?" she asked.

"Why not do so while we are courting?" returned Jack Rackbottle. "It's necessary to make arrangements for the future, you know; and half the pleasure of life is in looking forward to the future."

"Then you don't think there's such a thing as disappointment?"

"In the present case I hope there won't be," he replied, "for you have not thrown any cold water on my love, and I certainly do look forward to the time when you and I shall be as happy together as the days are long. I'll never be jealous of you as your last husband was, but will try to convince you more and more how grateful I am to you for choosing me in preference to all other men."

"Ah!" exclaimed Sally, "that's just what all your sex say before they get married; but afterwards they change their note and are jealous on the slightest cause."

"Do you think that will be the case with me?"

"I hope not," she replied; "but how can one answer such a question as that till the times comes for proving it? However, to confess the truth, I think better of you, and if I should find myself afterwards mistaken, it will be the more shame to you; that's all I know about it. But why are we talking so much upon this subject, when you came to tell me about the two strangers that have just arrived?"

"Bother the strangers!" exclaimed Jack; "what need we care about them, when love is so much more pleasant a subject?"

"Well, I'm sure you are very polite, Mr. Rackbottle," retorted Sally. "Bother the strangers, indeed! and what may not happen to you and I, if they should turn out to be bad characters?"

"We have no reason to believe that they are anything of the kind," he replied, "for they have come to the house like other travellers, and I suppose will leave us in the same quiet way that they arrived."

"And yet I thought just now you seemed to fancy that they are no better than they should be?"

"What signifies one's fancies unless there's some foundation for 'em?" asked Jack. "All I can say is that they won't let anybody know what their business is, and when that's the case we are apt—right or wrong—to think people can be up to no good. However, master will be the best judge of who and what they are; and if he don't object to let them have a night's lodging in his house, we may suppose that he is quite satisfied with their being respectable chaps."

" You may think of them as you please," answered Sally, " but for my own part I shall not feel comfortable till they are clear away from the neighbourhood."

" But you haven't seen e'm yet."

"And what's more, I don't want to see 'em," she replied tartly. "I have a notion that they are down in these parts for no good ; and as for their being Londoners, so much the worse, says I, for we know well enough what bad people come from there."

" I suppose there's good as well as bad there," answered Jack; "so it would be hard to think ill of these two men merely because they happen to come from London. Besides, our master will see them presently; and if he don't like the look of 'em, it will be easy for him to say that they must find a lodging somewhere else."

"I would rather they slept in the house than he should do that."

" Why ?"

" Because we shall have the mischief, if there is any, more under our eye," she replied.

" What do you mean?"

" That if they are forced to leave the house, they may linger about the place and do some of us an injury before they go away."

" Oh, as for that," answered Jack, " I don't think the fellows mean any harm, for they seem to be travellers, and are very likely as honest as ourselves. At any rate, we have nothing to fear from 'em, so you may rest very comfortable to-night as far as you are concerned."

" Do you think I could rest comfortable in my bed, if I thought they intended to rob our master's house?"

" I don't suppose you could do that, Sally," he replied ; ' but I can't see what reason you have for such a notion as that."

" As for my reason," answered the other, "I don t know why you should expect me to give any, when I'm only doing my duty in keeping a sharp eye to the interest of my master and mistress. They may be deceived in their people, and I'm determined to know who and what they are, if my ingenuity don't fail me."

" Take my advice," exclaimed Jack, " and don't interfere in the matter, for if any body could have found out who and what they are, I should have done so in the conversation I just now had with 'em. But they are determined to keep everything snug to themselves, and all the trying in the world will not get a word from either of 'em."

" Have they any luggage?"

"None that I saw."

" Then they must be pretty travellers to come out without so much as a change of linen."

" There may be something in that," replied Jack ; " and yet it would be hard to set 'em down for rogues merely because they happen to have no luggage with 'em. Who knows but they may have sent it up to London by one of the waggons?"

"Ah!" she exclaimed, " I see you are determined to keep to your own opinion, and so will I to mine in that matter. The more I think of it the worse everything looks ; and all I hope is, that my notion may turn out to be wrong. But I'm not very often deceived in people, Mr. Rackbottle; and if I'm not otherwise engaged to-night, I shall keep watch upon these two men till they are fairly away from the place."

" Well, there can be no harm in that," he replied ; "but I would advise you not to let 'em know what you are about."

" Leave me alone for that," answered Sally, " for if I have but the opportunity, I'll keep my eye upon them, and they shall not be aware of what is going on."

She then bustled away to answer the parlour bell; but the opportunity she desired was not afforded, for Mrs. Bradford required her services early in the morning, and she was desired to go to bed as soon as she had conducted all the guests to their various chambers.

CHAPTER IV.

AN EVENING'S CAROUSE.—A FREE AND EASY MODE OF INTRODUCING ONESELF.—DAN MACRAISY ENDEAVOURS TO MAKE HIMSELF AGREEABLE.—BREAK-UP OF THE PARTY VND PREPARATIONS FOR BED.

THE supper-cloth having been removed, Mr. Hayes and his friends determined to pass an agreeable evening, and the host was equally resolved that nothing on his part should be wanted to increase the hilarity of his guests. Everything indeed seemed to promise that the expectations which had thus been raised should not be disappointed; and the future Lord of the Manor had by this time quite forgotten the superstitious fears which his wife's solemn warning had at first made upon his mind. Wine in abundance had been placed upon the table, and the glasses had circulated several times, when Mr. Hayes, addressing his friends, begged that they would not spare the bottle, as it was his intention to defray all the expenses of the evening's entertainment.

"A noble proposition, and vastly condescending," whispered Mr. Dozey in the ear of the surveyor, who was sitting next.

"Ay," returned the other, "and correct too, as I can prove by the rule of three."

"If I may be premitted to say a word," said Jonathan Bradford, addressing himself to the chairman, "I would request to observe that you must not expect to surpass us all in generosity. I have some rare old wine in my cellar which cannot be better broached than in a bumper to the health of the new Lord of the Manor. I mean, of course, to our guest Mr. Hayes; what say you, gentlemen, to my proposition?"

"For my own part, I pronounce it excellent," answered the lawyer; "and as for the matter of the speech, it was delivered like an orator."

"Capital—capital!" chimed in Mr. Rodpole.

"Nay," exclaimed the chairman, rising from his seat; "on an occasion like this I cannot permit——"

"Pardon me for interrupting you, sir," said Bradford, "but in some instances I am a self-willed man, and in this I must enforce compliance in spite of any opposition that may be opposed. Pardon my absence for a few minutes, and I will presently return with some of the wine I have been vain enough to boast of."

With this he left the table, and hurried away from the room to execute his errand.

"Our host," observed Mr. Hayes, as soon as he was gone, "seems to be of the true metal, and shall not loose by his civility after I become his near neighbour."

"Ay, ay," added lawyer Dozey, "he has a kind and grateful heart, and deserves all the encouragement we can give him. His manner seems correct, too, in every sense of the law."

"I am sure of it," returned Mr. Hayes. "Good humour sparkles in his eyes like the bead in his own wine, and with as warm a glow. By the way, gentlemen, I know not that we can do better than drink the health of our worthy host during his absence."

This proposition was willingly assented to by his friends, but unluckily for the honour that was intended, Bradford made his appearance in the room before the toast could be drunk.

"Gentlemen," he exclaimed, "I have to announce to you that two strangers have arrived. The one, who is an Irishman, tells me he is of honourable rank and condition, and he has sent me with a request that he may be permitted to join your company. Shall I return to him with an excuse that this is strictly a private party of a few friends?"

"By all means tell him so, landlord," said both Dozey and Rodpole in a breath.

"Nay," interposed Mr Hayes good humouredly; "at a road-side inn such a message would appear ungracious. Surely one weary traveller should not be refused the good fellowship of a brother-traveller; and therefore I for one propose that both these strangers be admitted to our society."

"Oh, if you say that, there cannot be the slightest objection," exclaimed Lawyer Dozey.

"Certainly, not the slightest in the world," again chimed in the equally plain surveyor.

"Be pleased to fill your glasses gentlemen," said Bradford, who by this time had drawn the cork from one of the bottles. "Here is to the health of the new Lord of the Manor."

"Stay, gentlemen, pray stay a moment," exclaimed Dan Macraisy bursting into the room, without waiting for the ceremony of an invitation. "With your permission, I'll join in that toast myself—James O'Connor Esquire, on a pedestrian tour from my estate in Kilkenny, at the service of this good company. Fill, landlord, and do honour to the toast."

"A very extraordinary fellow this," again whispered the lawyer to the person next to him."

"Very," was the concise reply.

"Have the kindness to fill a bumper for me also," exclaimed Caleb Scrimmidge, entering the room in an equally abrupt manner, as his companion. "I'll drain her glass to the very bottom if it was as deep as the well at Aldgate. A bumper—a bumper!"

"Keep your distance, fellow!" muttered Dan Macraisy with a fierce expression of countenance. "Stand behind me, or you shall suffer for this intrusion."

Whilst uttering these words, he threw aside one flap of his coat, and pointed menacinglyto a pistol which was concealed there.

"What's the matter with you all of a sudden, Mr O'Connor?" asked the lawyer "Something seems to have disturbed you my good sir."

"Excuse my being out of temper, gentleman," he replied, "but this rascal of mine is enough to ruffle the temper of a saint. The truth is, he's a little bit of a greenhorn; but for the sake of his honest parents I keep him in the hope that he'll learn better manners in time, by the example I set him."

"Oh, oh," thought Caleb Scrimmidge to himself, "I am to be nothing more than his servant, aint I? He said he'd make a gentleman of me, and I suppose he means me to commence as a gentleman's gentleman. Imitations of my master I suppose are to be the first rudiments of my education. He threatens if I don,t mind what I'm about, to blow out my brains with that ugly-looking pistol of his, and I begin to wish I was safe back at Seven Dials again.

During this little self-communion, the health of Mr. Hayes was drunk, and the old gentleman rose from his seat to express his acknowledgments.

"Thanks, thanks, my kind friends," he exclaimed, "for the honour you have been pleased to confer upon me; but you forget that I am not quite Lord of the Manor yet, for the estate is not paid for."

"But it's all the same thing," observed Lawyer Dozey, "for the transfer of the pro perty will be made in the morning."

"When I have examined the title-deeds," he replied, "which shall be at as early an hour in the morning as possible."

"Let it be immediately after breakfast, then?"

"The sooner the better, then;" continued the old gentleman; "for to confess the truth, I shall be glad to be disencumbered of the money, for it is of considerable weight; andthere is besides the danger of being robbed, if there was a suspicion abroad that I have so much about me."

"Why you don't mean to say," exclaimed Dan Macraisy, with well-feigned surprise, "that you carry a large amount of money about you?"

"Do you think there is any danger, then?"

"Why," he replied, "perhaps I ought to be the last person in the world to say anything upon such a subject, for the fact is, I have a large bag of money my own pocket, which I wish was anywhere else."

"Had you no thought of being robbed?" asked Mr. Dozey.

"Well," answered the other, "I must needs confess that ever since I have been travelling I have done nothing else than look forward to the chance of being eased of the property."

"And yet," observed Mr. Hayes, "our host here assures me that the road is just now clear of highwaymen."

"It might have been all very well to say so a few days ago," replied Macraisy, "but now the road swarms again with the blackguard pick-purses."

"Is that assertion made upon any foundation?"

"The very best, I fancy," answered the other, "for it was only the other day I heard of a gentleman of my acquaintance whose pocket some of the villains had lightened of its contents and substituted pebbles in their stead, so that when he was going to pay for an estate, as you may be going to do perhaps, sir, he found nothing in his money-bags but a parcel of worthless stones."

"Luckily, that's not my case," exclaimed Mr. Hayes, "for I travelled hither in the company of friends, and was thus protected against any such misfortune as the one you have been speaking of."

"Are you sure your money is quite safe?" asked the surveyor.

"Oh, yes, it's all right enough," replied Mr. Hayes, taking out his money bags, and showing their contents. "The gold is all shining and correct to a farthing, you see. Here is the exact sum that I have got to pay away to-morrow, and my purse contains sufficient to defray the few xpenses I shall be at previous to my return home."

"Humph!" exclaimed Caleb Scrimmidge to himself, "he has got his eye upon those money-bags, and he'll never be satisfied till he has made them his own He'll put a clapper upon the whole lot before he has done with it; but how the job is to be managed is more than my poor simple brains can find out. But never mind, I suppose that's a discovery that will be made all in good time."

"Host," said Mr. Hayes, rising from his seat, "I am a man of regular and early habits, and with your leave I'll retire for the night.—By-the-by, though, which is the chamber I am to occupy?"

"Your's is the one over the bar," answered Jonathan Bradford. "My wife, I believe, has seen that all things are made quite comfortable; and when you are ready, Sally will light you up stairs."

"Oh, there's hardly any occassion for that," returned the old gentleman, "for during the last fifteen years that I have travelled between Oxford and London, I have invariably slept in that chamber."

"No doubt, then, you feel quite at home there," observed Dan Macraisy, in his usual free and familiar manner.

"I have always been very comfortable there, except on the last occasion," he replied, "and then I had a strange dream that I was lying there on the point of death."

"Heaven forbid that such a dream should be realized in my house!" exclaimed the host, shuddering.

"Well," returned the other with a laugh, "to speak my mind candidly, I am in no hurry to leave the pleasures of life that I have worked so hard to enjoy in my latter years. However, we must all die somewhere, you know; and so that it be in charity with mankind, why should it not be in that bed as well as any other?—So, good-night to all till we meet again at breakfast-time, soon after which, I hope my business will be so far arranged, as to allow of my immediate return home. Now, good host, a candle—and then to bed."

"I'll attend you, sir," exclaimed Jonathan, taking up a chamber candlestick, and conducting the old gentleman from the room.

"So," thought Dan Macraisy, "I know the chamber he's to sleep in, at any rate, and it shall be hard but I turn my knowledge to a profitable account. I shall sleep in the double-bedded room next to him, and by means of the parapit, shall be all to effect an entrance with little or no difficulty.—Caleb!" he added aloud, and in a tone of command; "why havn't you brought me the boot-jack, sirrah?"

"How should I know you wanted to go to bed before we've had our supper?" asked the other, in no very good humour, at finding that his companion was in such a hurry.

"You ought to be aware of my early habit of going to bed," replied Dan Macraisy, "and surely it was easy to see that I have my old vertigo coming on, and that I aught to retire to rest immediately."

"But I am expected to go as early as you do?" asked Caleb, half-inclined to show a mutinous spirit.

" To be sure you must," answered the other, winking at him, "for ill as I am, isn't it your duty, as a faithful friend and companion, to sit up and watch by me all night?"

" What ! without having my supper ?"

" Don't think of supper on such an occasion as this," exclaimed Macraisy, "but make up at breakfast-time for the loss of this one meal. I must to bed, I tell you, for I don't feel well enough to enjoy the company of these gentleman any longer. Now, young man," he added to Jack Rackbottle, who at the moment entered the room, "is the double-bedded front chamber disengaged for to-night ?"

" I believe it is," he replied ; "but how does your honour happen to know that room so well ?"

" Because my companion and I slept in it some years ago," answered Dan Macraisy, not in the slightest degree abashed by the suddenness with which this question was put. "I knew this house well enough at one time, and that was always my favourite room, for I chose it in preference to all the rest, though there are many better ones in the place."

" Is your friend going at the same time ?" asked Jack.

" Yes," he replied, "for I feel myself very ill to-night, and it would be hardly safe for me to go to bed without somebody to sit up. If I find myself better by-and-by, he shall lie down, for I like to be kind and considerate to my friends, though this one hardly deserves it either, for being such a cormorant as to prefer his supper to the performance of such a duty as this is."

" You forget," exclaimed Caleb, "that we have travelled far to-day, and have scarcely had anything to eat."

" So much the better," retorted the other, "for how can we ever expect to reach the end of our journey, if we consider our appetites in preference to everything else. So go and tell your mistress, my good fellow, that I particularly wish to be accommodated with the room I have mentioned, even though she may charge somewhat more for it."

" I'll tell her what you say, sir," answered Jack Rackbottle; "but for all I know, it may be already engaged."

" Then, in case it is not," exclaimed Macraisy, " run and secure it for me directly. Make haste, my good fellow, and you may depend upon my remembering you in the morning."

" I see how it is," whispered Caleb Scrimmidge to his companion, having first satisfied himself that the other persons in the room were busily engaged in conversing with each other'; " you are going to do something desperate to-night, and we shall be caught at it as sure as possible."

" So we sna'l if you are going to turn coward," answered Macraisy in the same low tone ; " but everything will go smoothly enough if you will only conduct yourself coolly as I do. If you are afraid, say so at once, and I'll manage the whole affair by myself, whilst you are fast asleep and snoring."

" But only consider the danger of being found out when there are so many people in the house."

" I consider nothing, but that a large sum of money is to be made, if you are not afraid to make a bold attempt for it," answered Dan. " We have no time to pick and chose how it is to be done, but must go to work determined to finish the affair in an off-hand manner."

" I rather think it will be in an off-hand manner altogether, if we don't mind what we are about."

" Psha ! you are afraid of your own shadow."

" Ain't it enough to frighten a fellow when he sees you determined to go helter skelter to work ?" demanded the other. " The people here have queer notions of us already, and depend upon it if the old gentleman loses his money, we shall be the first people suspected of the robbery."

" Let them suspect what they like," returned Dan Macraisy, " but as the money is all in gold, they'll not be able to swear to it, even if it should be found upon us. Besides, hadn't I the forethought to say just now that I myself have a large sum about me ?"

"Ay," replied Caleb, "but you were not able to show it though, as the old gentleman did his."

"More fool he for his pains," returned the other; "for the sight of it made my fingers itch."

"Then just take my advice and think this matter over before you go rashly to work," said Caleb Scrimmidge. "It's easy to get into a scrape, you know, but being once in it we may perhaps be sent on our travels at the country's expense."

"Whether it happens now or at some other time, you and I have nothing else to expect," answered Dan. "Every day brings us nearer to that or some worse fate; and as desperate men like us have nothing better in view, we must not stand very particular when a fine opportunity like the present offers itself."

"But how are you going to work?"

"Never mind how I do it," he replied; "but be ready for anything that may happen to turn up. The money is to be come at easily enough, I know; and as for what may take place afterwards, we must be prepared to brazen it out as well as we can."

"What will be the use of that if they drag us both before a magistrate on suspicion of being the robbers?"

"I might answer by asking you what's the use of meeting troubles half way," retorted Macraisy. "Here's one of the best chances that could have been thrown in our way, and yet would spoil everything by showing the white feather."

"Tell me what you are going to do, then?"

"That I may do, perhaps, when we get into our own chamber," answereed the other "You may, however, make your mind easy that there is no danger, for I see my way clear enough; and even if anything should happen that I don't expect, nothing will be more easy then for us to leave this place without being suspected for the persons that have made free with the old gentleman's money."

"If that should be the case," observed Caleb Scrimmidge, "the people here are greater fools than I take 'em for."

"Psha! why should they suspect us more than any one else?"

"Because we are strangers."

"And therefore must needs be a couple of robbers!"

"Ah! it's all very well to sneer at my opinions," answered Caleb, "but I've a notion they'll turn out to be right enough after all, and then it will be too late to be sorry for what has been done."

"Do you think, then, the people here are likely to keep a watch on us to-night?" asked Macraisy.

"They are likely enough to do it," he replied, "for it must be confessed we are a couple of rather suspicious-looking fellows."

"What is there about me to lead to suspicion?"

"Why you have swaggered so much that the old man with the money bags looked at you two or three times as if he fancied things were not quite as you would make 'em appear."

"There you are quite wrong," answered Dan Macraisy; "for if he had any such notion it's not very likely he would have shown all that gold he had in his pocket. We are right enough so far, I tell you, Caleb, and everything will go as smoothly as possible if you have only courage enough to keep your own counsel."

"I can do that easy enough," answered the other; "but you must not be too rash or I shall give up all notion of having anything further to do with this awkward business."

"Say no more about it, sirrah, but come with me," returned Dan; "my indulgence ruined you entirely, and now I am to be left to carry on this affair by myself. So follow me, for we are observed here."

"Stay a minute then, and let me have my supper before we go?"

"Here it is!" muttered the other, showing him a pistol which he slightly drew from his vest.

"I see it," returned the other with alarm, "but I am not particular fond of cold suppers."

"Then be cautious how you anger me, for there's no saying what a desperate man may do when he's driven to it. Keep the promise you made before we come to this place, and I can promise you that we shall leave it with a good round sum of money to devide between us."

"I must do so, I suppose answered Caleb, "though I feel already as if there were a halter round my neck. But, I say, those two old gentlemen have finished their conversation, and they seem to be looking towards us, as if they suspected we were up to no good.'"

"Then I must speak to them, and put them off their guard again," returned Dan Macraisy; and then bowing towards Lawyer Dozey and the surveyor, he added, " I hope you'll excuse us gentlemen for leaving the table, but we thought you might have business matters to talk over together, so we placed ourselves beyond ear-shot."

"Oh, there was no occasion for that," answered Rodpole, " for my friend and I were only speaking of the excellent bargain Mr. Hayes is just about to complete, and which will make him a person of some consequence in the neighbourhood."

"Ay," observed Dan Macraisy, "that is when he has paid down the remainder of the purchase money."

"Which will be deferred no longer than to-morrow morning."

"And then I suppose he means to pass the remainder of his days in the Manor House of Oakdale?"

"Yes," replied Lawyer Dozey, " and I hope he may live to enjoy himself there for many years to come, for he has worked hard enough in his time, and it will be no small gratification to see himself surrounded by the comforts that his own industry has created."

"Is he very rich?" asked Caleb.

"Sufficiently so for the ambition of a man who has only one daughter to provide for," answered the man of law. " His private affairs we have, however, nothing to do with further than any interest we may feel in the welfare of a man, who has so conducted himself as to gain, and that so deservedly, the respect of his fellow beings."

"I should like to be at his house warming when he comes to settle himself here," observed Scrimmidge.

"No doubt you would," exclaimed his comrade, "for I'm ashamed to say you are always looking after the chance of good eating and drinking."

"Perhaps," observed Mr. Rodpole, "your friend only means that he would like to witness the scene of happiness that must be anticipated on so auspicion an occasion."

"Yes, yes," exclaimed Caleb, eagerly catching at the suggestion, " that's exactly what I meant you to understand. However, its not likely that either of us can be at the Manor House, for we are both going to leave this place early in the morning."

"Is your destination far off?" asked Mr. Dozey.

"We hardly know at present where it may be," answered Scrimmidge, "for its as likely as not that we may soon find it very necessary to cross the ocean."

"Follow me, Caleb," exclaimed Macraisy, who began to be afraid that more might be said than could be easily mended. And then, taking his companion by the arm, he hurried him from the room after an abrupt " good-night" to those who were left behind.

"That's an odd couple as ever I saw in my life," observed Rodpole, as soon as they were gone, " and hang me if I can make out yet who or what they are."

"Does it matter to us who or what they are?" demanded the lawyer. " As far as we are able to judge, they are a couple of travellers on their way to London; and they may perhaps be wondering about us as we do about them."

"But I was thinking about Mr. Hayes and his money."

"And that they may want to commit a robbery?"

"Exactly so."

"Then take care not to speak your mind too openly," replied the lawyer; " for there may be an action for slander, and thumping damages may be given again you."

At this moment Jack Rackbottle, who had just before entered the room, approached them with a bow.

"Oh, if you please, gentlemen," he said, "missis bid me make up a good fire in the little back-parlour, where our gentlemen customers smoke their pipes and drink their grog."

"Well, my good fellow," said the surveyor, "and pray what other message have you to give us?"

"Why," he replied, "she also desired me to say that, if you would not mind sitting there, the room is much snugger than this one."

"Does she particularly wish us to leave this room?" asked Mr. Dozey.

"If quite convenient to yourselves, she does," answered Jack, "for the truth is, we expect a small body of soldiers here and a baggage-waggon."

"To remain the night, I suppose?"

"Yes, sir—they'll stop here till the morning."

"And this room is required for their use?"

"Exactly so," grinned Jack; "they generally come into this room to eat, drink, and smoke a little before they go to bed. Shall I show you into the little back-parlour, gentlemen?—'tis a nice snug place, and you'll meet with no interruption there."

"Yes, yes—you may as well lead the way there, young man," replied Mr. Dozey; and then, taking the arm of the surveyor, he added—"I don't know but this change is a very agreeable one, for we shall be by ourselves there; and I am anxious that you and I should look over those deeds again before we go to bed, in order that we may be sure of everything right for the morning."

"Ay," exclaimed the surveyor, "we'll settle the matter over a bowl of punch, for it's dry work we have to go through, and we shall need something to keep us awake till we have got through the job."

"I've made the room as warm and comfortable as I can for you, gentlemen,' exclaimed Jack Rackbottle; "for it's a raw, cold night out of doors, I can tell you; and I thought your honours wouldn't forget to leave something for the boots at the 'George,' if he put himself out of the way to make it all right for you."

Laughing heartily at this broad hint, the two gentlemen followed their conductor through the passage to the little back-parlour of which he had spoken, and where they were soon seated before a good fire, and with a bowl of punch before them.

CHAPTER V.

THE FARMER AND HIS WIFE.—TROUBLES AND ANXIETIES.—ARRIVAL OF SOLDIERS, AND THEIR DEPARTURE FOR THE GEORGE INN.

WHILST the events narrated in the preceding chapter were going on, Farmer Nelson and his wife—the parents of Mrs. Bradford—were bewailing themselves at home, on the cloud of misfortune, which had unexpectedly risen to obscure the prosperity they had hitherto enjoyed. A bad harvest had destroyed the hopes of a whole year of anxiety, and now, in the evening of life, they saw themselves in danger of being pressed with poverty, if not with absolute ruin. The old man had as long as possible concealed the worst features of their case from the aged partner of his bosom; but at length the fears which she had for some time entertained became painfully confirmed, and on the evening to which this part of our narrative belongs, she had acquainted him with the fears for which she saw so much foundation.

"It is in vain that you would conceal from me that which I can but too plainly foresee," she exclaimed, in reply to something which he had said in answer to her, "for though this is the first time I have ventured to speak to you upon the subject, I am nevertheless convinced that our ruin is near at hand."

"And can you resign yourself to such a misfortune in our old age?" asked her husband tenderly.

"It is our duty to do so," she replied, "and there is less difficulty in facing the worst, since neither of us have to reproach ourselves with having brought this misfortune on ourselves. We have been frugal and industrious through our lives, and that which is now about to befal us, could neither have been foreseen nor prevented, since all has been produced by an agency over which we had no control."

"So far there is some little consolation in your words," answered the farmer, "but it will be hard, too, if our latter days must be passed in poverty, after the efforts we have made to lay by sufficient to comfort us in our old age."

"Can we complain of being without comfort," she asked, "when we have the consolation of knowing our daughter has found a good husband in Jonathan Bradford?"

"Ay, there is happiness in that I own," replied the old man, "and I am not ungrateful to Providence for the great kindness he has vouchsafed to us in that respect. Bradford is, indeed, all that I could have desired to see in the husband of our daughter but with an increasing family he has difficulties enough to contend against; and rather than be an encumbrance upon him, I would seek assistance from the parish, much as I have always dreaded being driven to such an alternative."

"Nay," cried Mrs. Nelson, throwing her arms round the neck of her husband, "surely you do not think it possible that we shall ever be compelled to live upon the charity of our neighbours?"

"Let us hope things will never come to such a pass as that," answered the old man; "but if they should, we must bear up against our misfortunes with firmness and resignation. You and I have paid our poor-rates for years past with cheerfulness, and though nothing could be more painful to us than to receive parochial relief, there will be no shame in doing so, when we have the pleasing consciousness of knowing that the necessity has not arisen from any fault of our own."

"But our daughter and her husband would be disgraced were we to acknowledge ourselves to be paupers."

"Don't let us afflict ourselves with that thought now," exclaimed Farmer Nelson, "for things may not turn out quite so badly as our fears leads us to imagine. The few persons to whom we are indebted, know that we have the principle of honesty within us, and if we have but time afforded us to recover from the blow with which we have been so suddenly struck, we may yet recover the position it has always been our pride to hold. Have patience, therefore, and the clouds which at present appear to be so threatening, may clear away and encourage us to anticipate better hopes for the future."

"True," sighed the old lady, "it is our duty not to despair; but I cannot forget that we are both advanced in years, and are therefore ill able to contend against the difficulties that are rising around us."

"Difficulties shall not frighten me, old as I am," replied the farmer, "for I have yet some strength left, and it shall be exerted to the utmost rather than see you and myself dragging on a miserable existence by the charity of others. I will labour cheerfully for our mutual support, and instead of repining at the necessity for doing so, I shall feel an honest pride in the consciousness that we are indebted for our subsistence solely to my own industry."

"Have you spoken to any one yet upon this subject?"

"No," he replied, "I have not yet said anything, even to our son-in-law, whose advice will I know be most valuable. I am, however, about to step down to his house presently, and will then state to him fairly and openly the misfortunes with which we are threatened."

"And he may perhaps see some means or other by which we may avoid the ruin we so much dread."

"He will do more," answered Farmer Nelson, "for I know the goodness of his heart, and feel certain that he will offer to make any sacrifice in order to relieve us from these difficulties."

"Which you will not allow him to do, I hope."

"You may be sure of that," answered her husband, "for rather would I wear my fingers to the bone than do aught that might destroy the prospects of those who are endeavouring to support themselves by honest industry. Fortunately for Bradford he has a good house of business, and seems likely to make his way in the world; but he must have no hangers-on to clog his exertions, or we shall soon see him reduced to a condition as bad as our own."

"And that," observed the old woman. "would be far worse for us to bear than any sufferings of our own. We have but a short time to live, but our children have years to look forward to; and amidst all our misfortunes, I know of no greater consolation that we could feel than in the consciousness that those we love are protected against the troubles and misfortunes that have fallen on ourselves. Besides, we may still be allowed to remain in this farm, and if so, a prosperous season next year would restore us to what we were."

"That is exactly what I am looking forward to," replied Farmer Nelson; "and I should hardly think we shall be required to move away, because we have always borne a good character for honesty and industry. At all events, I will get our son-in-law to put in a good word for us, and if all turns out as I wish, the gloom that at present hangs over our prospects may soon clear away. Some of our neighbours, too, have offered to lend a helping hand to save us the expense of labour, till our means are better, and should that time ever come, those who befriend me now, shall see that I do not forget their kindness to me in my adversity."

"You think, then, our affairs are not quite so bad as you just now led me to believe?"

"There, it must be confessed, I am rather puzzled what answer to give," returned the farmer; "for all will depend upon whether those we owe money to will wait till I have an opportunity of selling my stock to more advantage than it would be disposed of at present. I am not asking for any very long time, but merely to be allowed to do that which will be for the benefit of others as well as myself."

"And surely they will not stand in their own lights."

"That is just the difficulty that I cannot clearly see my way through," answered the farmer; "for when once a man acknowledges he's going down in the world. there are always plenty ready to sink him still lower in his ruin."

"Have you any enemies?"

"None that I am aware of," he replied, "but till now, Fortune has always smiled upon us, and that is just the time when we are least likely to distinguish between our friends and our enemies. It is the hour of misfortune that tries our acquaintances, for when that comes the chances are that those who were loudest in their expressions of friendship, will be the very first to turn coldly away from us. However, we must not despair, for I believe there are many who will gladly lend their assistance, when it is known that I require nothing more than a short time to recover myself from the effects of the last unfortunate harvest."

"You think, then, time will not be refused?"

"Nay, I dare not venture so far as to say that," answered Farmer Nelson; "but I hope all things for the best, and with the assistance of our son-in-law, Jonathan Bradford, I fancy the few we owe money to, will not be so hard-hearted as to refuse the short grace that I am going to ask for."

"And when will our suspense be at an end?" asked the old lady.

"Before this time to-morrow night, I hope," replied her husband; "for there's nothing like striking whilst the iron is hot, and as the favour must be asked, the sooner the disagreeable task is performed the better."

Mrs. Nelson was about to make a reply to this, but before she could do so, a loud knocking was heard at the door, and the farmer hastening to the spot from whence the sound came, exclaimed—

"Who's there?—If ye are highwaymen this is not the house for you to come to. Move on then; content is the only wealth under these rafters; and that you cannot rob us of."

"Psha!" returned a voice outside, "we are friends; so open to us without delay."

The farmer obeyed unwillingly; and as he did so a sergeant and three or four other soldiers entered the room.

"What could you have been dreaming about, old gentleman?" exclaimed Sergeant Sam. "Highwaymen, indeed!—aint you convinced, now you see us, that we are soldiers of the king?"

"And what, pray, may be your business here?"

"Not for our own pleasure, you may be sure," answered the sergeant; "we have lost our way this dark night, and took the liberty of knocking at the door to ask if you can put us on our road."

"Most willingly," returned Farmer Nelson; "and I crave your pardon for the mistake I just now made."

"Humph!" exclaimed the other, "there's no great deal of offence given, old gentleman, though I must say it's vexatious enough that these rascally highwaymen should be allowed to cast such reflections upon respectable gentlemen of our cloth."

"It's a great shame," chimed in Corporal Sabre; "and if I had my will, they should all be hung up in chains to whiten, like our belts on a pipe-clay day. But we have no time to waste here, so perhaps old gentleman you will have the goodness to put us on our right way to Oxford."

"Are you going to Oxford?"

"Yes," answered the serjeant; "but owing to the confounded darkness, we have managed to lose our way. If you go a little from your own door you'll see our baggage waggon sticking fast in the lane, where I suppose it must remain till we can manage to get it out in the morning."

"Do you happen to know where you are?" asked the farmer.

"That's just what we want to discover," answered Sergeant Sam; "but I should suppose we are not in the high road?"

"No," returned Farmer Nelson, "you have got a little out of your way; but, if it is to Oxford that you are marching, I may be of some service, for in the morning early, I have business that will take me to the very place."

"But we must go part of the way to night."

"Very well, my friends," answered the farmer, "those that serve the king must be attended to, so I'll e'en set out to night, and guide you as far as you wish to go, for hese lanes of ours are dark and dangerous, and as full of windings as a labyrinth. So now, to light my lantern, and then I shall be at your service as soon as you please."

"There's a good soul!" exclaimed Sergeant Sam. "I like your readiness to serve us, and you shall be rewarded for your civility with what refreshments you please, when we reach the George Inn."

"The George Inn?"

"Ay, you know it, I suppose?"

"Perfectly well."

"It lies on the road to Oxford, don't it?"

"It does," answered the farmer, "and, strange to say, is the very place that I am going to."

"You know something of the people, then?"

"To be sure I do," answered the old gentleman, "for the landlord, Jonathan Bradford, is my son-in-law, and to-morrow is to be a happy day with them, for 'tis the anniversary of my daughter's birth, and friends will meet there to rejoice upon the occasion."

"I have seen them on former visits," exclaimed the sergeant, "and they appear likely to do well there."

"Ay, thank Heaven," returned the old man, "they are a happy, thriving, honest couple, and deserve all the encouragement they have met with. If you remember my daughter, sergeant, she is the very image of her mother, who you see sitting in yonder corner, near the fire."

"'Tis a pleasure to you, I dare say, old gentleman, to see your child so comfortably circumstanced?"

"I know not of any pleasure that could be equal to it," replied Farmer Nelson, "and, to speak the truth, it more than makes amends for the troubles that have fallen upon myself in my old age."

"Why, you don't mean to say that you have any troubles?"

"So anybody might suppose on merely looking round," answered the old man, "and yet enough has taken place within the last few days to have turned my brain, but that I knew my daughter was beyond the reach of the misfortune that has overtaken me. I and my partner can resign ourselves to our evil destiny now; but had poor Ann been at home and depending upon us, the thought of her ruin, as well as our own, would have been death to us."

"Things have been going cross with you, then?"

"So much so," he replied, "that I know not whether I shall be able to bear up against them. Luckily, however, I stand pretty well in the world's favour, and I believe there is not one person in the world that would injure me from any malicious feeling."

"You are fortunate then, my good sir, for I believe there are few persons in the world that can say as much."

"Ay," answered the farmer, "but then I was always careful never to refuse assistance to a friend or neighbour, when it was in my power to afford assistance. You may think I am boasting of myself rather too much, and yet I do it in the fulness of my heart, for 'tis a great consolation for me to reflect that, fallen as I am, there is no one to exult at it, or to say that I deserve it all for my want of feeling, when I had it in my power to serve others."

"At any rate," exclaimed the sergeant, "you have the satisfaction of knowing that you have a daughter to support you now that you are no longer able to stand your own ground."

"There you are wrong, sergeant," he replied, "for I have a pride above allowing myself to be dependant for support on my child."

"Psha! its nothing more than one's duty to take care of our parents when they need assistance."

"The duty I do not deny," replied farmer Nelson, "but whilst my hands are able to earn a living for myself and my wife, I will not be a clog on the exertions of those who have got their own way to make in the world. My son-in-law and his wife are industrious, and if Heaven will but reward their exertions with success, I can endure any troubles that may fall upon myself, and feel grateful for the blessings bestowed upon those I love."

"You are not likely to leave your farm, I hope?"

"I should be glad to think so," replied the old man; "but just at present, I know nothing more of what is to become of me and my poor old wife, than you do. As I said before, however, I have no enemies to be afraid of, and if it can be shown that the debts I owe are likely to be paid, there is every reason to believe, that I shall be allowed reasonable time to dispose of so much of my property, as will pay all demands upon me. But this is a subject that cannot be very interesting to you, gentlemen, so, whenever you please to give the order, I shall be ready to guide you on your way."

"But how about the roads hereabouts," interposed Corporal Sabre; "are they much infested with highwaymen?"

"They were at one time," answered Mr. Nelson, "but for the last few months we have not heard of one."

"I suppose that's because they hung a few of 'em as an example to the others?"

"Some three or four were sent to the gallows," answered the farmer, "and the effect was quite marvellous, for, from that day, we have been able to travel this part of the country without the least fear of being robbed and murdered."

"There's no chance of our meeting with any of them, I suppose?" observed Corporal Sabre.

"Not the slightest," he replied, "for people of that sort look out for those that are likely to carry money about them, and a highwayman would not expect to find any either upon soldiers, or a poor bankrupt farmer like myself."

"You've got your answer, at any rate, corporal," laughed his comrade, "so I think the less we say about these highwaymen the better it will be for all of us. Let's only think of getting on to the George Inn, for when once we find ourselves in comfortable quarters there, we are sure to meet with pleasant company in Jonathan Bradford."

"You know my son-in-law, then?"

"Merely through calling there sometimes, in passing from London to Oxford," answered the sergeant. "We generally stay there a night, and a merry one we make it, too, I promise you; and if you are going to stay there, farmer, you'll say that this was one of the pleasantest evenings you ever spent."

"But what says the old woman to such an arrangement?" exclaimed Corporal Sabre,

laughing. "She, I'll be bound, will not think it a very good joke, if he keeps it up all night, with a parcel of racketty soldiers like us."

"My good dame never interferes unless there's occasion for it," answered the farmer. "Besides, it's our own daughter's house that I am going to, and it would be hard indeed if any mischief could be made out of that."

"Has she been married to Jonathan Bradford long?" asked the sergeant.

"About five years."

"And they are happy, I suppose?"

"As the days are long."

"Well, I'm glad to hear it," exclaimed the sergeant, "for marriage is such a lottery that the chances are against rather than in favour of those who venture into the noose."

"Ay," observed the corporal; "and it don't follow that a whole life is to be happy, merely ecause the first five or six years happen to have been so. There's no accounting for troubles, you know, for they come on us unawares, and very often just at a time when it seems impossible for anything to disturb us."

"You speak as if you had experienced something of the kind yourself," exclaimed Farmer Nelson.

"No," he replied; "we soldiers lead a merry, devil-may-care sort of life; and if any troubles fall upon us, we have generally only ourslves to thank for them. Our pay is always going on, you know, old gentleman; and as for the girls—who have the smiles of half so many of them as we lads of the scarlet coats ?"

"And some of you are sad wild dogs, I'm afraid," laughed Farmer Nelson.

"Why, there's no denying that," exclaimed the corporal; "but then how can that be wondered at, when we have such an example set us by our officers? They are the fellows for bewitching the girls ; and that's the reason, my good fellow, why the men folks always look so glum upon us when a regiment of us is marched into town. Why the first rub-a-dub-dub of our drums is quite enough to spread alarm and consternation wherever we go."

"Which I suppose will be the case at Oxford when you get there ?" again laughed Farmer Nelson.

"Why, I'm not quite so sure of that," answered the corporal, "for the young Collegians beat us out of the field there; and the prim old Doctors of Divinity keep such a sharp eye upon us, that we are obliged to mind our P's and Q's. However, we shall lead a jolly life enough there, I dare say, for there's always some fun going on in a place like that, if we choose to go the right way to work. But we are forgetting the time all this while, farmer ; so, if my comrades are ready, I think you had better guide us at once to the house of your son-in-law.'

"Won't you take anything before you start ?" asked the old man.

"No," replied Sergeant Sam; "we shall not want anyth ng till we reach the George Inn, for we had refreshments at the last place we stopped at, which was only about four miles off. All we want is to reach the place where we are billetted for the night ; and when once there we can enjoy ourselves as much as we like."

"But you'll find that the landlord keeps early hours, and by eleven o'clock he expects everybody in his house to be in bed."

"He'll be mistaken, then, for once, I'm thinking," answered the sergeant ; "for we have had a long march to-day ; and it's only fair that we should have our enjoyment for an hour or two in the evening. However, we shall see what sort of a humour Master Bradford is in—and, if I am not much mistaken, he will join us in a social glass, while we tell him some of the campaigns we have been engaged in."

"And how about the morning, if you have got to march at an early hour ?" asked Farmer Nelson.

"Ah, we soldiers can do with very little rest," answered Corporal Sabre ; "for sometimes when we are on hard service, we don't know what it is to get a wink of sleep for two or three nights together. That we are obliged to do, you know, and it's strange if we can't now and then do with a couple of hours' rest when it's for the sake of enjoying ourselves with a friend or two. But what is the use of talking when we don't know but Bradford will be as glad as any of us to pass a night in conviviality."

"I know he will not, though," exclaimed the farmer; "for he has his own business to attend to in the morning, and he never neglects that for anything or anybody."

"Perhaps his wife won't let him keep the company of his guests ?" observed Corporal Sabre.

"Nay," answered the old man, "though she is my own daughter, I will say that a more kind and indulgent wife is not to be found anywhere. But Jonathan Bradford sees a family of young children increasing around him, and like a prudent father, he is determined to discharge his duty faithfully."

"Then this son in-law of yours seems to be one of the right sort," exclaimed the sergeant; "and I suppose he is likely to make a fortune in the house he keeps?"

"These are not times when fortunes are to be easily made," replied Farmer Nelson; "but he will not throw away any chance for want of trying, and at all events he will do his best towards leaving his children tolerably well-established in the world."

" I say," exclaimed Corporal Sabre, " had'nt we better be making our way towards the George Inn, for time is passing on, and if we don't make haste we shall hardly arrive there before the house closes for the night ?"

" Why that's well thought of," answered his comrade, "and I should myself have been for starting earlier but that the honest farmer here will be both a guide and a companion on our way."

"Or if you like to stop till the morning," said tho old man, "we will manage to accommodate you in the best way we can."

" No, no, that would be acting against our orders," returned the sergeant, "and we have no excuse for staying away from the house we are billetted on, on a fine night like this. Besides, the distance is not very great, and cheerful conversation as we go along will make it appear like nothing.

"And when you get to Oxford," observed Farmer Nelson, "you will find yourselves in snug quarters, for all the soldiers that I have happened to meet with have declared that it's the best place in the world for ease and enjoyment."

"You can't say much about it from your own experience, then?" asked Sergeant Sam.

"To tell you the truth," he replied, "I only go there on market days when I happen to have anything to sell. The place is too gay and flaunty for a plain fellow like me, and I always prefer my own snug little home to any other place in the world that ever I saw !"

"Humph !" ejaculated the soldier, "if everybody was like you, we should have no towns or cities to live in."

"Different people have different tastes," answered Farmer Nelson. " and for my own part I don't care what others do, so long as they leave me to the enjoyment of my own opinion. Whether fortune smiles or frowns upon me, I always try to be as much the same as possible, and with my faithful old partner yonder, I have perhaps been one of the happiest fellows under the sun. And how could I very well be otherwise, when my only child is well-married, and die whenever I may, I shall have the consolation of knowing that she and her children are well provided for. But, come gentlemen, since you are determined to go, I am now quite ready to guide you as far as the inn of Jonathan Bradford."

This suggestion was immediately complied with, and after having, in the first place, extricated the baggage-waggon from the rut into which it had fallen, they again set forward to reach the place where they were to rest for the night.

CHAPTER VI.

THE GUEST AND THE LANDLORD.—MR. HAYES RECEIVES ANOTHER ADMONITION OF DANGER BUT DISREGARDS IT.—THE BED-CHAMBER.—AN INTRUDER.—AN EXCUSE EASILY FOUND AND AS EASILY BELIEVED.—THE LAST SLEEP.

HAVING paid another visit to the stable, as was ever his custom when putting up at an inn, Mr. Hayes left his horse to the care of the groom, and was crossing the courtyard to return to the house, when he was met by Jonathan Bradford, who had felt some little alarm at the disappearance of his guest. The old gentleman saw that his absence had created some consternation in the mind of his host, and thanking him for the trouble he had taken, explained the object for which he had left the house.

"You must not think, my good friend," he added, "that I doubt your care and attention to the faithful dumb animal that has borne me safe on so many journeys, for this is an old custom of mine, and I always make it a rule to see after the comforts of my horse before I go to my own bed."

"The rule is so excellent a one," answered the landlord, "that I should be glad to see it adopted by every gentleman who is fortunate enough to be the owner of so faithful an animal. Some travellers, however, are, I am sorry to say, too apt to forget in their own selfish enjoyment, the duty that belongs to others, even of their own specie.

For my own part, I could not rest comfortably unless I knew that my horse was as well attended to as myself."

" Were you coming out to look for me?" asked the old gentleman.

" To tell you the truth I was," answered Bradford, " for the night is rather dark, and I was fearful lest you might hurt yourself by falling into some of the holes that have been dug hereabouts for the purpose of carrying off the waste water. Besides, 'tis getting rather late, sir, and I thought you might perhaps want to be shown to your bed-chamber."

" Very considerate of you, indeed, my good sir," exclaimed Mr. Hayes, " for I must be stirring in the morning early, and it is now high time that I should be taking my rest. By the bye, do you happen to know what it is o'clock, Bradford?"

" The dial in my bar has just struck eleven."

" Humph! 'tis later than I intended to have sat up, but still there is plenty of time for as much rest as I shall require. Unfortunately, the main-spring of my watch is broken, so that for a time it is rendered completely useless to me, just when I so much need its service. What shall I do for one to-morrow when so much will depend upon bringing this business of mine to a close before the expiration of a certain specified time?"

" We have a watchmaker not more than half a mile from hence," answered Bradford, " and with your permission, I'll send it off to him early in the morning, so that you will be sure to receive it back by the time you have paid the remainder of the purchase money for the Manor Farm."

" As there will be no other alternative, I suppose that must do," exclaimed Mr. Hayes; " so take charge of it, my friend, and see that I have it again, before I set out on my return home. Ha, ha, ha! what a pleasant surprise it will be for my wife, when she sees me safe and sound, notwithstanding the strange notions that were put into her head by that foolish dream."

" I dare say, sir," answered the landlord, " if the truth were known, she forgot her terrors almost as soon as you were out of her sight. The impressions caused by dreams seldom last very long, for they are never founded in reason, and will generally give way to even the slightest consideration of the subject."

" You are right, Bradford," exclaimed the old gentleman, " and I was foolish to imagine that my wife would suffer herself to be made uneasy by any such nonsense. She seemed to think a great deal of it at first, it's true, but then there are plenty of excuses to be found for her, when I come to consider, that all the alarm she expressed was felt for the safety of her husband."

" Is she generally superstitious?"

" As little so as any woman that I know," answered Mr. Hayes, " and I can only account for it now by the seeming reality of the dream that haunted her last night. Woman's fears are easily excited, and it would be unjust to be angry with them for what, after all, is nothing more than a weakness natural to their sex. So I will not even indulge in a laugh at her when I return home, lest she should happen to take it unkindly of me."

" And you think, sir, there is no danger of your being detained in this neighbourhood longer than to-morrow?"

" Heaven forbid that I should," answered the old gentleman, " for were I to fail to show myself at home by the time mentioned, the alarm would be great indeed. The worst fears of my wife would appear to be confirmed, and I know not what might be the consequence."

" 'Tis pleasant to hear of such instances of attachment between husband and wife," observed Jonathan Bradford.

" The instances might be greatly increased," answered the old gentleman, " if marriages were more frequently contracted between persons of nearly similar dispositions. With respect to Mrs. Hayes and myself, we have been married now somewhat better than a quarter of a century, and I may venture to assert that during the whole of that long period, there has never been a misunderstanding between us, that has not been forgotten in less than an hour."

" And I, for my own part," returned Bradford, " can fortunately boast of being equally happily situated. Our circumstances, indeed, are more humble than your own, but we are both of us willing to obtain an honest living by industry ; and I may say it with some pride, that we have contrived to gain the good opinion of all our friends and neighbours. But I am forgetting, sir, that you are exposing yourself to the night-air all this while and that you are anxious to go to bed."

"I shall not lie down, I believe, Bradford," answered the old gentleman, "for, as it will be necessary for me to rise very early in the morning, I shall content myself with a snooze in the chair by my bedside. So you may bring me half a pint of sherry and some spring water, in case I should happen to be thirsty in the night."

By this time they had entered the house, and whilst the landlord went to fetch the wine, his guest, candle-in-hand, made his way towards the room in which he usually slept, when occasionally visiting at the George Inn. Having reached the foot of the stairs, he was about to ascend, when the door of the little back parlour opened and Lawyer Dozy made his appearance, rather flushed with the liquor he had been imbibing with his friend the surveyor.

"What, Mr. Hayes!" he exclaimed, "why I thought you had gone to bed a long time ago."

"And I certainly intended to have done so," answered the other, "but two or three trifling matters have detained me, and it is only now that I am going to take some rest."

"Then you have quite forgotten the alarm occasioned by the dream of your wife?"

"Like all other foolish things of the kind, it has given way before a little calm reflection," answered the old gentleman. "It was but a dream, and I dare say if the truth were known, Mrs. Hayes has by this time brought herself to place no more reliance in it than I do myself."

"Ay—ay, that may be all very well," exclaimed Lawyer Dozy, "but I have been thinking this matter over in my own mind, and I begin to have a great notion that you ought not to treat the warnings of your wife with disrespect."

"Excuse me, my good friend," laughed Mr. Hayes, "but I have a notion that you are now talking under the influence of the wine and the punch you have been taking."

"Upon my word I was never more serious in my life."

"Perhaps so," answered the other, " but I can venture to say that to-morrow morning you will wonder how you could ever have given way to this strange notion."

"To-morrow morning!" exclaimed the lawyer ; "Heaven grant that we may all of us be alive by that time !"

"Psha ! you surely cannot be serious?"

"It's no subject to jest upon," returned the other, "nor should I venture to make a jest when I believe some great danger is at hand."

"What would you persuade me to do ?"

"I would advise you not to go to bed to-night."

"Believe me, I have no intention of doing so, my dear friend."

"Then sit up with Rodpole and me, and we'll make a glorious night of it instead of going to bed."

"And a very pretty state we should be in for business in the morning," observed Mr. Hayes,

"That may be," returned the lawyer, "but in my opinion, anything is preferable to running the risk of being murdered for the sake of the money you have about you."

"Psha!" retorted the old gentleman, " we are in a respectable house, and surely that ought to be sufficient to assure one of perfect safety."

"Ay—ay," answered Dozey, "I grant you the house is as respectable a one as any that is to be found on the road. The landlord, too, seems to be a very decent sort of fellow, but what has that to do with it, when it is impossible for him to know all the customers that apply here for shelter ?"

"I see how it is," observed the old gentleman, "your thoughts are still running upon the two men we passed on the road, and who have since requested to be accommodated here for the night."

"They are strangers, and therefore we may be allowed to look upon them with some little suspicion."

"And havn't they as much right to do the same with us?" demanded Mr. Hayes.

"One of them said he had a good deal of money in his possession, and yet he didn't seem to suspect that we were going to rob him of it."

"For a very good reason," returned the lawyer; "we are well known throughout this neighbourhood to be respectable men, and therefore they would not be justified in supposing that we are likely to entertain any dishonest views against them. In short, if they were to utter a word that might be construed into slander, I should take the liberty of commencing an action against them without loss of time."

"And yet you have not hesitated to give expression to an opinion anything but favourable to these two men."

"But I have only said it to you," answered Mr. Dozey, "and of course I may rely upon your not saying a word that would put me into the power of these two chaps. All I mean to say is that we ought to be very careful not to give them an opportunity of doing us any harm; and my advice therefore is, that you sit up this night, and pass away the time in talking and drinking."

"Preposterous!" exclaimed the old gentleman; "what danger can there possibly be I should like to know, in a house that bears so excellent a character as this? Besides, I have engaged my bed-room, and how could I invent an excuse for sitting up with you all night, when it is well known that I have very important business to transact in the morning? Why, I should be laughed at for my pains, and richly would it serve me right for being such an old fool."

"Have you, then, entirely forgotten the warning that was given by your wife before leaving home?"

"Ay," he replied, "but her warning—though kindly meant—was founded upon nothing more substantial than a dream that had troubled her during a somewhat disturbed sleep."

"But it made a great impression upon her, though."

"That cannot be denied," answered Mr. Hayes; "yet I would not mind wagering a trifle that, by this time, she has seen the folly of giving way to a superstitious feeling that I never knew her to yield to on any previous occasion. The truth is, she knew I was about to leave home with a large sum of money in my possession, and the thought of that so preyed upon her mind, that she could not forget it even in her sleep. However, a little serious reflection has, I dare say, by this time convinced her of the error she has fallen into."

"Don't you think it is the duty of everybody to take proper precaution after a warning has been given?"

"Where there is any sufficient ground for the warning, it is, no doubt, proper to listen to it," replied Mr. Hayes, "but in this instance, I can see no occasion for apprehending even the smallest danger. As for the two men your suspicions are directed against, they are perfect strangers to us, and for aught we know, may be quite as respectable and honest as ourselves."

"And on the other hand," answered Lawyer Dozey, "they may bear characters of a very different description."

"Then all we have to do is to keep so watchful an eye that no opportunity for doing us a mischief shall be given them. Surely, even in case of the worst, we ought to be a match for these two men, who have given rise to so much suspicion in your mind."

"How do you know but they may be armed?"

"Well, even granting they are, are not we armed also, in case any attack should have been made on us as we came hither?"

"We have pistols, it must be confessed," replied Dozey, "but the question is, should we be able to use them, if there should be any necessity for defending ourselves from sudden danger? For my own part, I can handle a quill as well as here and there one, but when you come to pistols, and other ugly things of that sort, I should rather be excused from taking an active part in any affray that might happen."

"One would suppose, to hear you talk, that it was a highly meretorious thing to speak of your own cowardice."

"I beg your pardon there, Mr. Hayes," returned the lawyer, "for you appear to be confounding prudence and cowardice as being one and the same thing. Now, I acknowledge being a careful, far-seeing man, but as for cowardice, I flatter myself there are few persons besides yourself who would venture to say as much to my face."

"Well then," exclaimed the old gentleman, "think less about danger and more of the business we have got to transact in the morning, for I wish everything to run smooth and straightforward, which is hardly to be expected, if we are not thoroughly prepared for any quibbles that the lawyer, on the other side, may raise up against us."

"Never fear, my dear friend," answered Dozey, "that we shall be able to overthrow any obstacles that may be put in our way, if we are only fortunate enough to escape the danger that Mrs. Hayes spoke of before you left home."

"Pray don't bring up that subject again," exclaimed the old gentleman, "for I am sick of hearing of the peril you are imagining, without any foundation for it. If these men are rogues, we must take care to defeat any project they may have formed; but if they are honest, we shall enjoy a hearty laugh together at the absolute folly that made us so suspicious of them."

"We shall see how that will turn out," answered Lawyer Dozey, "but at all events, I should be very glad if you would only promise to sit up and enjoy yourselves with Rodpole and myself, for the one night. What say you to my proposition, sir?"

"That I would not do anything of the sort upon any consideration," exclaimed the old gentleman.

"Very well," returned Dozey; "there's no persuading you I see; but if anything unfortunate should occur, I will not take any of the blame upon myself."

"My dear sir," replied Mr. Hayes, "pray make yourself quite easy upon that matter, for I can assure you I feel not the slightest fear as far as I am myself concerned. Indeed the respectability of the house, and the well known honesty and integrity of the landlord, should of themselves be quite sufficient to remove all injurious suspicions from our minds. So, now, Mr. Dozey, I shall wish you a good night, and at a very early hour in the morning you may expect me to rouse you for the purpose of completing the business we came here to transact."

The lawyer saw that it would be in vain to offer any more advice or remonstrance, and Mr. Hayes ascended the stairs to the bed-chamber which he had always occupied, on occasions of similar visits. Seating himself on a chair by the bedside, he remained for some few minutes absorbed in thought, and then taking from his portmanteau the bags of gold he had brought with him, he arranged them on the table before him that they might be ready against they were wanted in the morning. This done, Bradford entered with the sherry and water which had been ordered; and almost immediately afterwards took his departure, having first ascertained that nothing more would be wanted during the night. Pursuing his train of thoughts, and occasionally sipping small quantities of the cooling beverage, the old gentleman felt quite an almost imperceptible drowsiness creeping over him, which he could not resist; and he was just on the point of falling into a sound slumber whilst sitting in his chair, when a slight noise startled him, and opening his heavy eyelids he perceived Dan Macraisy standing within the distance of a few feet from him.

"Who's there?" exclaimed the old gentleman, sharply. "Tell me your business here, sirrah, or I shall make no scruple of sending a brace of bullets through your body."

"Stay till you have heard a little reason," answered Dan Macraisy, without appearing to be at all disconcerted, "and then form your own conclusion as to the motive that has brought me here. I suppose, sir, if a man commits a mistake, and apologises for it, there may be some excuse for his having entered another gentleman's apartment, even though he may have gone there without having been invited?"

"That," answered Mr. Hayes, "must depend very greatly upon the circumstances that lead to the intrusion. You were aware, sir, I suppose, that this was the bed-chamber which I had engaged for my own special use?"

"Indeed, my good sir, I was not aware of anything of the kind," exclaimed Macraisy, "and the mistake arose entirely through my own room being the one next to your's. The door was not locked, and upon entering, you may judge what my surprise was at perceiving what appeared to be an intruder seated fast asleep in a chair in the apartment, that I naturally believed was my own."

"Your explanation may be perfectly correct, sir," answered Mr. Hayes, involuntarily glancing round towards his money bags; "but the accident was a most unfortunate one, for at the moment before waking up I was dreaming that a robber had suddenly pounced upon me, and demanded all I had about me."

"It was very strange, certainly," returned Dan Macraisy, "but I hope you don't suspect I had any evil purpose for coming here ?"

"I daresay not," replied the old gentleman, "but having heard your explanation, I shall be very glad to be left alone again, for I feel weary and inclined to sleep."

"Ain't you going to get into bed first ?" asked the other.

"No," he replied, "it will be no great hardship to sleep one night in this easy chair, and I shall then be ready in the morning early to finish the business that brought me away from home."

"Humph!" exclaimed the other, "you are about, I believe, to pay the remaining portion of the money for a snug property that you have purchased somewhere in this neighbourhood ?"

"That is what I am here for," answered Mr. Hayes, "and most heartily glad shall I be when the money is safely placed in the hands of this person from whom I am about to make the purchase."

"You are not afraid of being robbed in a respectable house like this, I should think ?"

"To tell the truth," replied the old gentleman, "I suspect almost everybody, so long as the money remains in my own keeping. Such is not usually my disposition, and sometimes I feel half inclined to be angry with myself for entertaining a suspicion of the kind, whilst under so respectable a roof."

"And I feel rather sorry," exclaimed Macraisy, "for I can't help thinking that your suspicions may have lighted upon me and my travelling companion."

"I would not injure any man by an unjust suspicion," returned Mr. Hayes; "but it must be confessed I have heard some of my friends throw out hints that it would be as well to keep a sharp watch upon all persons who are not known to the landlord. You must not, however, take any offence at it, because the suspicion may rest upon one person as well as another."

"Have they any reason to believe there are dishonest persons in the neighbourhood ?"

"On the contrary," replied Mr. Hayes, "I have been told that the place is remarkably free from highwaymen, and it is even said that they are not likely to come here for some time to come, because three or four of them were hanged a short time back, and ever since then so sharp a look-out has been kept up, that it would be dangerous to, show themselves till the affair has blown over."

"So much the better," said Dan Macraisy, "for, to tell you the truth, I, like yourself, am travelling with a large sum of money about me, and it would be my ruin if any of the villains were to rob me of it. However, I don't think there's much danger of it, for we are in a respectable inn, and to-morrow I shall reach London, long before night sets in."

"Have you travelled far ?"

"No, only from Oxford, where I had some heavy accounts to receive from some of our customers."

"And your companion ?"

"Is an honest simple-hearted fellow, who has the honour of calling himself a distant relative of mine. We met together by a mere chance, and I allowed him to accompany me on my way up to town, because the foolish fellow had a notion that he would be robbed on the road if he went alone."

"Has he much money with him to lose ?"

"He won't trust me with that secret," answered Dan Macraisy; "but I rather think he has a pretty good sum, because I know he has always been honest and industrious, and I believe hoarding up money has been one of his chief delights."

"Did you see us on our road from Oxford to this place ?"

"Yes, sir," he replied, "and to tell you the truth we took you all for so many highwaymen."

"At any rate, the compliment was returned," smiled Mr. Hayes, "for we set you and

your companion, down in our own minds for gentry of the same description. Indeed' even now one or two of my friends are far from feeling satisfied that you are merely travellers journeying onwards to the metropolis."

"At all events the landlord can't have as bad an opinion of us," exclaimed Dan Macraisy, "or he would not have allowed us to stay in his house to-night. By-the-bye, considering all these suspicions, it seems rather singular that I should, by a mere accident, have made my way into your sleeping apartment."

"And it is still more singular," added Mr. Hayes, drily, "that in the surprise of the moment, I did not discharge one of my pistols at your head, under the supposition that you had intruded upon me for some bad purpose."

"That would have been very awkward, I confess," returned the other; "but then it would have been no less so to yourself seeing that you would have had to pay dearly for your haste."

No. 6.

"Nay, I should have been justified when all the circumstances were made known," replied the old gentleman; "for having a large sum of money in my possession, I should have been pardoned for supposing that your purpose in coming into my room was for the purpose of committing a robbery."

"I hope you do not suspect me of such a design now?" exclaimed Dan Macraisy with alarm.

"Why no," replied the other; "I think, upon comparing circumstances; the excuse you have given is very likely to be founded in truth. Indeed, had I not been of that opinion, I should before now have rung the bell for the landlord, and complained to him of the alarm that has been occasioned me."

"And yet, after all," he replied; "it appears to me that you are more to blame than any other person."

"How so?"

"Because, considering the large sum of money that is in your possession, it would only have been an act of prudence to fasten your own room door before you dropped off asleep."

"Your hint shall not be thrown away upon me," exclaimed the old gentleman; "for as soon as you have taken your departure, I shall take care to prevent a repetition of the alarm I have unnecessarily been put to."

"Ay, fasten yourself in," replied Macraisy; "and then there can be no fear of receiving another visit such as mine has been. So, now, sir, I wish you a good night, and may your sleep be a long as well as a sound one."

The fellow then swaggered out of the room with all the airs of a fine gentleman; and Mr. Hayes, having first locked and bolted the door, returned once more to his easy chair, and after offering up a prayer to Heaven, resigned himself to a slumber from which he was never to wake again.

———

CHAPTER VII.

DAN MACRAISY RETURNS TO HIS COMPANION IN INIQUITY.—CERTAIN PLANS ARE PROPOSED AND DISCUSSED.—THE SLEEPING-DRAUGHT.—CALEB SCRIMMIDGE MEETS WITH A BIT OF PLEASANT NEWSPAPER INFORMATION.—THE MIDNIGHT ASSASSINATION.—THE ESCAPE OF THE TWO STRANGERS.

"Now, Caleb," whispered Macraisy to his comrade, as soon as he had entered his own bed-chamber, "tell me if anything have happened since I have been absent, to lead to the notion that our purpose here is suspected by any one?"

"How should I know what people's thoughts may be?" answered the other, rousing himself up. "I watched and listened as long as I could, and at last went off to sleep, because I had nobody to talk to."

"Hush!" returned his comrade; "if you speak so loud we shall be overheard by the old gentleman in the next room."

"What, the one you are going to——"

"Silence, scoundrel, or I'll stop that infernal tongue of your's for ever!" muttered Dan, interrupting him. "All seems to be going on well enough, if you don't spoil it; and if my plans should be defeated through your means, I will take your life, even if my own should be sacrificed through it afterwards."

"I'll tell you what it is, old fellow," exclaimed Caleb, "you look so precious wild about the eyes, and grab me so tightly by the shoulders, that hang me if I don't begin to feel sorry that you and I ever happened to meet together."

"Nonsense! there's nothing whatever to fear, if you will only act like a man of courage and discretion."

"But I don't happen to have either of them."

"Then go to the devil for a fool, as you are!"

"Thank you all the same for your civility, Mister Dan," answered the other, "but as

I shall do that quite soon enough, I dare say, I would much rather wait till my time comes naturally."

"Didn't you promise to assist me?"

"I did; but I thought it was to be only a simple robbery, and now it seems likely that there is blood to be spilt."

"That will depend upon whether any resistance be offered."

"Which is sure to be the case when the old gentleman finds he is going to lose all his money."

"Hadn't he better lose his money than his life?" asked Macraisy.

"Yes, to be sure he had," answered the other; "but he may not have time to argufy the point; and if he utter only one cry of alarm, I pretty well guess what the end of it will be."

"Of course, if my own life be risked, there will be only one way to get out of the scrape," answered Dan Macraisy. "Not, mind you, that I will shed the old man's blood if there's any way to help it; or, if matters should come to such an extremity as that, you must promise me not to let fall so much as a hint that you could throw any light upon the subject."

"Is it likely I should do that?" asked the other, "when I should be taken up and hanged for being your accomplice?"

"Why, you would be a fool if you did," answered the other, "so always keep that in your remembrance, and we shall keep clear of all danger, let what may happen to-night."

"Ugh!" shuddered Caleb, "how can I ever forget it, when I know myself to be guilty of shielding a murderer from justice?"

"Psha!" retorted his comrade; "you are not asked to take any part in it, for I would not trust anybody but myself, unless he had as much courage and determination as I have. This is no child's play, Caleb, that we should go rashly to work; but when all is over, both of us must talk and act with as much coolness and unconcern as if we knew nothing at all about the affair."

"But you seem to forget that I have such a thing belonging to me as a conscience Mr. Macraisy.'

"Then by all means get rid of your conscience as soon as you can," answered the other, "for, between ourselves, it is a very bad thing to be troubled with, when we know we have been guilty of that which may some day or other put a rope round our necks. Now, for my own part, I very seldom venture to look back to the past actions of my life, for, between ourselves, there are so many ugly things that will rise up in view, that I have determined never again to look either before or behind the present moment."

"Did you ever happen to be in as bad an affair as this?"

"Ask me no questions as to what I have done," answered Dan Macraisy, "for I always wish to avoid recalling unpleasant recollections to my mind. All we have to do is to make sure what we have undertaken; and if the affair be managed to my satisfaction, you shall have no reason to complain of the reward that it is my intention to give you."

"So you have told me before," exclaimed Caleb; "but I should like to know at once what I am to have."

"That will depend upon how you behave yourself," replied Dan. "All you have to do is to try and please me; and, if that be done, you may expect to be employed again the next time I require your assistance. So keep that in your mind, my boy, and by-and-by I shall make something of you."

"Ay, you'll make me your dupe, perhaps.'

"Upon my life you are the most provoking fellow I ever had to deal with!" exclaimed Dan Macraisy. "Why not place your confidence in me, as I do in you? for that's the only way that we are likely to manage our little affairs cleverly."

"Why, the truth of it is, I am heartily sorry we ever met each other," replied Caleb, 'for you have filled my head with all sorts of bad notions, and I am always expecting to fall into the hands of the people that want to discover us, for the sake of the reward that has been offered for our apprehension."

"Psha! haven't these disguises of ours proved a safeguard to us so far? and are we more likely to be found out now than when the search after us was so hot that we scarcely knew which way we could turn for safety? But you are a terrible coward, Caleb; and if either one of us has more cause of complaint than the other, it is myself at finding that I am connected with a fellow that has no more courage in him than a mouse. So don't let me hear any more of this nonsense, Master Scrimmidge, or you and I shall have a word or two of a sort."

" Let me ask one more question and I'll have done. Do you think it likely the old gentleman will lose his life ?"

" That will depend upon circumstances," answered Dan Macraisy; "but for your satisfaction, I'll tell you that I have no wish to shed his blood if there be any way to avoid it."

" Humph! I suppose if he resist, or attempt to raise an alarm, there'll be no chance for him ?"

" Not much, indeed," replied the other; "for in that case, either his life or mine must be sacrificed, and it's not in reason to suppose that I should hesitate about which it should be. Besides, we are both of us out of money just now, Caleb, and that of the old gentleman will just serve to supply our wants till the next good chance turns up."

" I don't know what you may intend to do," exclaimed Caleb, "but, as far as I am concerned, I mean to retire from this kind of business, if we are only fortunate enough to get over this affair."

" Psha! what have you got to be afraid of?"

" The gallows."

" Ah!" replied Macraisy, carelessly, "if you have that always before your eyes, I would much rather have your room than your company. The gallows, indeed! What do you think would have become of me if I had always been afraid of a shadow like that ?"

" A shadow, do you call it? Now, I have always thought there was a deal too much substance about the thing."

" Ay," replied the other; "but its only weak-minded people like yourself that are afraid of it. Did you ever hear of its preventing crime? whilst, on the contrary, a victim never swings upon one of those instruments of punishment, but two or three hundreds of pockets are sure to be picked within sight of it. Why, a public execution is one of the finest things in the world to draw together a number of gaping fools, that are sure to return home with less than they came."

" But for all that, it ain't a pleasant affair to think of; and, for my own part, I never go to sleep but I'm sure to dream of a gibbet and somebody swinging on it."

" Then I suppose if anything particular, as you understand me, Caleb, were to happen to the old gentleman in the next room, you would be so agitated as to betray my secret by your cowardice ?"

" I can't answer for how that might be," he replied, "but I think its more likely, than not that I should feel particularly uncomfortable if anybody looked hard at me."

" In that case," exclaimed the other, "my wisest plan will be to keep you out of this affair."

" It may be all very well to say that," returned Caleb, " but if a murder were to be committed in this house, it would not give me much trouble to guess who it was that did it."

" And you would betray the secret ?"

" Well, I'll not go so far as to say that," answered the other; "but there's no telling what one might say, or how one might look, if sharp questions were put upon the subject. As for yourself, Dan Macraisy, you have nothing to be afraid of, so long as I see you are not going to cheat me out of my share of what's to be made; but if I find any false play going on against me, you must not expect me to keep the secret a moment longer."

This was quite sufficient to convince Dan Macraisy that he had but a poor dependance to rely upon, and quick as thought, he determined to trust the secret no further with a man who was so easily to be frightened into a confession. He therefore determined to give him a potion that should send him to sleep till after the robbery was accomplished ; and still speaking to his companion in a tone of pretended kindness, he said—

"Well, my boy, I dare say you mean well enough, and that everything will be right so make up your mind for what is going to be done, and in the meantime, just open the window very gently and see what sort of a night it is out o' doors."

"Why a very queer one, I can tell you, Dan," he replied, after having obeyed this order. "It lightens tremendously all round, and presently I expect we shall have a rattling storm."

Whilst he was saying this, Dan Macraisy, without being perceived, contrived to pour a small portion of laudanum into the glass of brandy and water, which he stirred up, and then deposited the phial in his pocket, without having drawn upon himself the observation of his unsuspecting companion.

"Now," he said, "drink that up, my good fellow, and I'll answer for it you will not care for anything that may take place to-night."

"After you," replied the other ; "take a hearty swig at the glass, and then I'll follow your example."

"I'd rather not take any more at present," answered Dan Macraisy, throwing himself upon a sofa, "for I feel a sudden illness come over me, and I'm afraid the job we've been speaking of can't come on after all, unless I should get a little better presently. Throw over me everything that's warm, Caleb, for its one of my old ague fits coming on, and I don't expect to be able to crawl out of bed again for at least three or four days to come."

"Won't you take any of this hot brandy and water?" asked Caleb, offering him the glass.

"No, no," he replied, as if in great pain, "drink it all yourself my good fellow, and don't disturb me, but let me sleep on, let it be for ever so long a time."

"I'll not disturb you, Dan Macraisy, you may depend upon it," said the other, seating himself in a chair as his companion appeared to fall into a deep slumber. "It's very kind and generous of him, though, to give me all this brandy and water after paying for it out of his own pocket. He seems to sleep soundly enough ; and when he begins to snore I'll gently creep down to the kitchen and make love to the cook, just to find out whether she has not something nice in the cupboard that will do for my supper. Dan, there, don't seem to care about eating anything, but for my own part I feel confoundedly hungry, and whilst he is dreaming of something else, I'll go and fortify the inward man with whatever the house may happen to afford. By the by, I wanted something to pass away the time, and as good luck would have it, here is a London newspaper, which, of course, will let me into the secret of some of the things that have been going on since I left my old master, without so much as giving him a hint that I was tired of his company."

He opened the paper, and occasionally sipping out of the glass, read and made his remarks as follows—

"Let me see—first of all, I must look out for my friends ' Old Bailey,' that's not one of 'em at any rate. ' The parliament will assemble on the twenty-first, to take into consideration a young woman out of place.' Plague take it, I'm getting so sleepy that I have lost the line where I left off. Yaw ! what's this next paragraph in the name of wonder ? ' If the young man that ran away from his apprenticeship in Seven Dials'—why that's me to a dead certainly—' If the young man that ran away from his apprenticeship in Seven Dials, will return to his unhappy parents'—his unhappy parents—ha, ha, ha ! that's capital !—' he will be received with open arms, and his past misconduct will be overlooked by his master, the watch-maker, who has wound up the affair to the satisfaction of the young man's unhappiest of mothers. He will be allowed to sugar his own tea, and butter his toast on both sides.'

"Here's glorious news !" exclaimed Caleb Scrimmidge, throwing down the newspaper in a paroxysm of delight. "I'm forgiven, and won't I be off in the twinkling of a bedpost ! Won't I cut away from this confounded place, and try to do that that won't make people angry with me again. But hush ! I must not let that Dan Macraisy hear me, or his pistol will be going off as well as myself, and then I'm afraid there would be an end of all my good intentions. That chap's as fast asleep as a watch that has not been wound up for a week ; but I've a notion his pistol would not be asleep too, if I were to attempt to make my escape without going through the ceremony of bidding him good-by. Confound it, I'm going to sleep for the want of somebody to talk to, so here goes to wake up my companion, and if he be angry about it, he must be pleased, again, that's all I know about the matter. Here Dan—Dan, I say, rouse yourself up, for I have some glorious news to tell you."

"Is the house on fire?" demanded Macraisy, pretending to rouse from a deep slumber.

"No, that's not it," answered Caleb, "but I've just found out that I've been forgiven by mother and old master."

"How have you made that wonderful discovery?" exclaimed Dan Macraisy in no very good humour at finding that the sleeping draught had not taken effect.

"Why it's all here," he replied, "in this newspaper that I found by chance lying upon the table."

"And what does it say?"

"That I'm forgiven by everybody, and may return to Seven Dials as soon as ever I please to go."

"Humph! and you would be fool enough to be a slave once more to that tyrant of a master of yours?"

"I beg your pardon there, Mister Dan, for though he was a rum-tempered fellow enough, there's plenty worse than he to be found in the world, I can tell you. And as a proof of it, he has advertised me in the newspaper, and affectionately requests that I'll go back and make him happy once more."

"So then, I am to be deserted just when I most want your services?"

"That's a matter that requires some explanation," replied Caleb, yawning; "but somehow or another I feel so sleepy that I hardly know how to keep my eyes open."

"What can have made you so sleepy all of a sudden?"

"Why, that's more than I can tell you," he replied; "but I suppose my journey here has made me tired."

"Then go to sleep for a little while, and I'll wake you as soon as it's time to do what is to be done."

"I don't know that it will be of much use to do that," answered Caleb Scrimmidge, "for ever since I looked into the newspaper I've changed my mind a good deal upon the subject we have been talking about. Avoid evil company, was an old copy that I used to write when at school, and I'm thinking that it will be better to turn my mind once more to watchmaking than to run the risk of being hanged or transported."

"Have you forgotten, then, what a large sum of money is to be made with a very little risk?"

"I own the money is rather tempting," answered Caleb ; "but I'm not quite sure that the risk is so trifling as you would make it appear. This house is full of people just at present; and if the old gentleman were to raise only one cry, we should have every one upon us directly."

"And do you think there's no way of quieting him?"

"A pistol might do it perhaps—but that would soon disturb every person in the place; and then, what sort of a chance of escaping should we have, I should like to know?"

"Psha! there's no occasion for a pistol to be discharged, for the sight of one would be quite enough to keep the old man silent."

"Very likely; but he would be sure to raise an alarm the moment we left his room."

"I tell you, Caleb, you are a coward!" exclaimed Dan Macraisy; "and I'm heartily sorry that I was fool enough to have trusted you with a secret that you may turn against me."

"Is it likely that I would betray you?"

"Of course it is, if you thought to save yourself by getting me into a scrape. But I warn you to be careful how you act, for I shall keep my eye upon you—and if I see any chance of treachery, I'll find means to have my revenge for it, even though it should be certain to bring on my own destruction."

"Nonsense!" returned Caleb Scrimmidge; "you needn't make yourself uneasy about that, for I'm not so bad as you fancy; and if I can only once get clear out of this precious scrape, you shall never hear of me again, I promise you. Watchmaking is a safe and honest pursuit; but when one turns one's mind to looking after other peoples' property, there's no knowing what mischief may com of it. So 1 think the best thing we can do will be to dissolve the partnership between us, and then we shall see which of us will afterwards get on best in the world."

"Do as you like about it," exclaimed Macraisy, who now saw that the sleeping-draught would soon have its intended effect; "and as you have thought proper to leave me in the lurch, I rather think I shall give up the affair for a bad job. And yet it's a great pity, too, for the sum of money that we might have made so easily would have been a famous one to have been divided between us. It would have set you up in business, Caleb; and as for myself, I should have gone abroad till the affair was for-gotten and blown over."

"Ay," again yawned Caleb; "but another copy of mine, said that *honesty's* the best policy, and I've a notion that there's a great deal of truth in it."

"And so you have made up your mind to return to your master, in consequence of the advertisement you have seen in the paper?"

"Yes, I rather think I shall."

"And you'll not lend me a helping hand towards easing this old gentleman of his money?"

"Well, to tell you a little bit of my mind, I don't think I shall."

This answer rather perplexed Dan Macraisy, for he began to fear that he had let his companion too far into the secret of the plan he had in operation. Taking an oppor-tunity, however, he, unperceived, poured a few more drops of laudanum into the remains of the brandy and water, and then affecting an air of indifference, he said—

"I don't know but what you are perfectly in the right, Caleb, to keep yourself out of the reach of danger; and after turning the affair over in my own mind, I rather think I shall give up all notion of having anything further to do with the business."

"Then, why not go to bed at once, lest you should afterwards be foolish enough to change your mind?"

"Because I prefer lying on the sofa," he replied. "We are to start early in the morning, you know, and there's nothing like being ready dressed, when there is anything to do, in case of over-sleeping oneself."

"Why you don't mean to leave the house till after we have had our breakfast, I hope?" exclaimed the other.

"It's a very poor chance you'll have of getting breakfast here, I am thinking my man!" answered Macraisy, "for we have better than fifty miles to travel before we get to the end of our journey, and we must be off betimes, or we shall be two days doing it instead of one. However, you can stay behind if you like, for it seems likely we shall not do any more business together."

"That may be," returned the other; "but surely you are not going to leave me in that shabby manner?"

"I don't want to do so," he replied; "but I find you such a slow coach that the sooner we part company the better."

"Humph! you've got some fresh scheme in your head, I suppose?"

'There you are mistaken, my good fellow, for just now I'm quite at a loss what to be up to."

"Then you have quite given up all notion of helping yourself to the old gentleman's money, I suppose?"

"Quite."

"Well I'm glad to hear you say so, for I could not help thinking all along that mischief would come of it."

"And why did you think so?"

"Because there's too many people in the house to do anything of the kind without being found out."

"Mightn't the suspicion fall upon some body else as well as us ?"

" I rather think we should be the first persons suspected."

" Do you think we are known, then ?"

"I dont know how that may be," replied Caleb Scrimmidge, " but I thought they looked very hard at us both when we made free to force our company on them ; and its as likely as not that they may take into their heads to keep watch at our chamber door till the morning."

" Let 'em do so if they please," exclaimed his companion, " and by-and-by they'll have the satisfaction of finding that all this trouble has been thrown away. But I see you are getting sleepy, Caleb ; so go to bed, and I'll rouse you up as soon as it's time to start."

" Well," returned the other, yawning and rubbing his eyes ; " it must be confessed I have grown rather drowsy all of a sudden. However, it's not worth while going to bed if we are going to leave our quarters so early, so I shall take a snooze in this easy chair, and when I'm wanted, you can just give me a call."

" And remember," exclaimed Dan Macraisy, " if there should be any stir in the place by-and-by, you can swear that you and I retired to our beds early, and that we never left the room afterwards."

" To be sure I can."

"And you are satisfied, of course, that I have given up all idea of taking the money from Mr. Hayes ?"

"Oh, yes ; that's all right, my boy. Y-a-w!"

" Well," continued Dan, " as you are very sleepy, I shall not keep you awake any longer ; only remember what I've said, for such curious things sometimes happen that it's always wise to be on the safe side. So good-night, and pleasant dreams to you."

The compliment, however, was not heard by Caleb Scrimmidge, who was completely overpowered by the strong narcotic he had been imbibing ; and sinking back in his chair, he gave audible manifestations of the soundness with which he had gone off to sleep. For some time, Macraisy ventured not to stir ; but at length, being tolerably certain that the sleep of his companion was not feigned, he rose noiselessly from the sofa on which he had thrown himself, and having passed a light to and fro over his eyes three or four times, to ascertain the genuiness of his slumber, he next proceeded to open the window, preparatory to attempting the act he contemplated. As he did so, a broad flash of vivid lightning showed him clearly the parapet by which he might make his way towards the chamber that was occupied by the person he designed to rob ; and springing out at a single bound, he crawled along on his hands and knees till he had reached the place of destination. Here he paused for a minute, and perceiving by the light which was burning that the old gentleman was asleep in his chair, he gently opened the window, and with noiseless steps approached the portmanteau which contained the gold which had offered so irresistible a temptation. In an instant the lid was opened, the well-filled bags secured, and Dan Macraisy was about to escape with his prize, when the old gentleman suddenly awoke, and with a loud cry, rushed forward to seize upon the robber. In an instant a knife, which was upon the table, was in the hand of Macraisy, and ere those who had been alarmed by the outcry could reach the top of the stairs, Mr. Hayes fell beneath a mortal blow, and his assassin escaped to his own room, where he found Caleb Scrimmidge still as fast asleep as he had left him. To leave the house just then was impossible ; and throwing himself once more upon the sofa, he listened with no little uneasiness to the confusion and uproar which the discovery of the murder had occasioned.

CHAPPER VIII.

CIRCUMSTANTIAL EVIDENCE.—AN INNOCENT MAN ACCUSED WHILST THE GUILTY ONE IS NOT SUSPECTED.—JONATHAN BRADFORD IS ARRESTED AND CONVEYED TO THE STRONG ROOM OF THE VILLAGE.—THE MURDERER MAKES THE BEST EXCUSE HE CAN TO HIS COMPANION, AND SUCCEEDS IN LULLING HIS SUSPICION.

ALARMED by the outcry, the host and hostess rushed from the bar, and making their way up stairs, entered the room just at the moment when the assassin had succeeded in making his escape. The first thing that met their view was Mr. Hayes seated, or rather reclining in his chair, whilst from a wound in his bosom the life-blood was quickly gushing forth. On the floor were strewed the money bags which the murderer had been compelled to drop whilst making his precipitate retreat, and on the table lay the knife reeking with the blood of the unfortunate old man.

"Great Heaven! our guest has been murdered!" exclaimed Bradford, taking up the knife, and gazing upon it with a look of horror. "This blood-stained weapon was doubtless the instrument with which the crime was committed, but where shall we seek for the villain who perpetrated so foul, so black a deed?"

At this moment the dying man raised his arm, and pointing towards Jonathan Bradford, muttered a few words that were scarcely audible.

"Speak, sir, I implore you!" exclaimed the host, distractedly, "denounce the villain who has done this deed, for never will I rest till he has suffered the penalty of this night's bloody work."

"He has already denounced you, villain!" cried Mr. Dozey, who with the surveyor and several other persons, had just before entered the room. "Was not his hands pointed towards you, and did not his words plainly denote that you were his murderer?"

"Merciful Heaven! what does all this mean?" exclaimed Jonathan, horror-struck at hearing these words. "Who dares accuse me of this crime, and upon what ground?"

"It is I who accuse you," answered the lawyer, "and I ground my charge upon the last words of the dying man."

"Oh, indeed, indeed sir, you accuse my husband wrongfully," cried Mrs. Bradford in an agony of horror which had hitherto rendered her incapable of uttering a word. "He is as innocent as yourself of the foul deed that has been done, and we have witnesses enough in the house to prove that both he and I were in the bar at the very moment when the cry of murder was raised."

"It is all very easy to say so, Mrs. Bradford," replied the lawyer, "but the declaration of the dying man must be allowed to have some weight, and I, myself, saw Mr. Hayes in his dying moments, point towards Jonathan Bradford as if he would denounce him as the man who had committed this fearful crime. His words, too, add heavy testimony to the same fact, and it is therefore my duty to order the accused into custody until the charge is either substantiated or satisfactorily disproved."

"Oh, sir," exclaimed Bradford, wildly, "do not, I implore you, drive an innocent madness by accusing him of a deed from which his soul shrinks with horror."

"If you be innocent, as you say," asked the other, "how was it that I found you with the blood-stained knife in your hand?"

"I took it from the table upon which I suppose it had been thrown by the murderer, who, in his hurry to escape, had left behind him the gold that tempted him to do this act."

"And pray how do you account for being in possession of the murdered man's watch?" demanded Mr. Dozey, as he recognised the chain which was hanging from Bradford's waistcoat pocket.

"He put it into my hands scarcely an hour since, to get it repaired for him by the time he was to return home in the morning."

"The excuse is so lame a one," exclaimed the lawyer, "that I think you will find very few people willing to believe it. In short, there is so strong a case against you, supported by circumstantial evidence, that no one in his senses can doubt that yours was the hand which committed the murder."

"My husband a murderer!" cried Mrs. Bradford, wildly, "and who is it that dares accuse him of so dark a deed?"

"It matters very little who it is," answered the lawyer, with professional coldness, "for the fact is pretty evident, and he will find it a more difficult matter than you imagine, to convince a jury to the contrary. No one knew better than your husband that Mr. Hayes had a large sum of money with him to pay for the estate which he was about to purchase, and which has unfortunately led to this most disastrous occurrence."

"But surely, sir, the asseverations of an innocent man are worthy of some credit," exclaimed Jonathan.

"You must wait till you have an opportunity of making your defence before those who are competent to receive it," answered Mr. Dozey. "For my own part, I have but one duty to perform, and that is to make a charge against you of having murdered and attempted to rob the man who, as your guest, you were bound to have protected, even at the hazard of your own life."

"And Heaven knows I would have done so," replied the accused, "but that the crime was committed before I had time to hasten hither to his assistance. The knife you found in my hand had only been snatched up from the table the moment before you entered the room, and the money which still lies scattered upon the floor is just as it was left by the assassin when he was compelled to make his escape through the alarm which had been raised."

"You speak of the murderer having escaped," observed Lawyer Dozey, "and yet I see no way by which he could have done so, except through the door by which you entered the room, and which it was, therefore, impossible he could have done."

"Is there not the window?"

"That is closed; and even if it had not been so, it is too high from the ground to render such a supposition reasonable."

"You avail yourself of everything that is against me, but will listen to nothing that is in my favour," exclaimed Jonathan Bradford. "I see that I am marked out for destruction by those who will not listen to reason, but Heaven will not desert me in the hour of need, and I do not yet despair of being able to prove that I am as innocent of this crime as are those who have charged me with the commission of a crime that my soul abhors."

"You seem to mistake my motives," answered the lawyer, "but whatever you may think of them, I most solemnly assure you that I am actuated in this matter only by what I conceive to be the performance of an imperative duty. Prove your innocence to the satisfaction of a jury, and if they acquit you, no one will rejoice at it more than I shall."

"And can you think of no one else besides my husband," asked Mrs. Bradford, "who may have done that of which you have accused him?"

"Who else can I accuse?" he asked, "but the man who I found in the room under circumstances that everybody must confess are extremely suspicious? I have no animosity of my own to serve, and therefore cannot be actuated by any unworthy motive."

"But you may be led away by an unfortunate prejudice."

"Indeed, I assure you I am not."

"Then why persist in an accusation when there is every reason to believe that my husband would not be guilty of such an act, as the one he has been charged with?"

"The course I have pursued," answered Mr. Dozey, "has been forced upon me by the fact, that the dying man pointed towards him, with the evident intention of denouncing him as his murderer. The weapon too that was found in your hand, goes very far towards confirming the suspicion, and there are even further reasons for believing that the accusation has not been falsely made out."

"Heaven above knows that they are false," she exclaimed, "and yet you would tear him away from his home, and those who are dearer to him than all else that this world contains."

"I am sorry to occasion so much pain," replied the lawyer, "but the duty, however disagreeable it may be, must be performed."

"It is no part of your duty, sir," exclaimed Jonathan Bradford, "to brand me with this infamous crime upon so weak a foundation as this. There are those about the place who know that I was in a different part of the house when the cry of murder was raised, and yet, because I happened to be the first that hastened into the room to render my assistance, I am to be accused of the crime."

"I don't intend to pass any judgment upon the matter," answered the lawyer, "but it is only natural for a man to deny such an assertion as I have made, and you have only done as others would under similiar circumstances. Be that as it may, however, there is sufficient ground for the course I have adopted, and at present I see no reason for changing the opinion I have formed."

"Then you believe me to be guilty?"

"At present I can see no reason to think otherwise."

"And rather than put a more favourable construction upon the affair, you will blast my character for ever, and perhaps send an innocent man to meet death on the scaffold."

"I have not heard anything yet to lead me to suppose that the opinion I first formed is an erroneous one. The dying man was unfortunately deprived of the power of speech, but I have little doubt he would have accused you, had he been able to do so."

"Heaven pardon you the thought," exclaimed Bradford, "for I know in my own mind, that had Mr. Hayes been able to speak he would have cleared me from all blame and accused those who did that of which I have been wrongfully accused."

"Who is it that says my son-in-law is a murderer?" demanded Farmer Nelson, who at that moment entered the room, followed by three or four of the soldiers whom he had guided from his own house to the inn.

"I say so," answered Mr. Dozey, "and as a magistrate of this county, I bid you, soldiers, to do your duty. Let neither this man nor his wife escape."

"What are they accused of?" asked the farmer.

"Of the heinous crime of murder," replied Mr. Dozey. "My friend, Mr. Hayes, who slept last night in this room, and whose body now lies before your eyes, has been robbed and murdered. We detected this man and woman in his chamber; the blood-stained knife with which the deed was perpetrated was in his hand, the money that had tempted him was lying scattered upon the floor as you see it, and this watch which I took from Bradford's pocket, I am ready to swear, is the one that I saw in the possession of Mr. Hayes, only a short time before he left us to go to bed."

"All this," exclaimed the farmer, "may serve to cast suspicion upon my son-in-law, but if you knew him as I do, you would not believe him capable of committing so heinous an offence."

"But what doubt can you throw upon my assertion, that the dying man himself affirmed Bradford to be the murderer?"

"Who dare say that?" cried the heart-broken wife, "when no one could distinguish a word that was said?"

"There could be but little doubt though, of what he meant," answered Mr. Dozey, "for he pointed towards your husband, and the expression of his countenance was quite sufficient to convince any one that he accused your husband of the dreadful crime, which has hurried him to a premature grave."

"Is there no one else who may have done this?" asked farmer Nelson.

"No one that I can think of."

"Are there no strangers lodging here?"

"Yes," exclaimed Mrs. Bradford, as a sudden thought flashed across her mind, "there are two men who came here last night. They were strangers, too, and from their manner I was most unwilling to give them the accommodation they asked for."

"Ha!" cried the farmer, "then why should they not be suspected as well as anybody else?"

"Because they are in their own room," answered Mr. Dozey, "and had they been in this it would have been impossible for them to have escaped in the short interval that elapsed between the alarm that was given and our presence here. Besides, I have told you that Mr. Hayes, as distinctly as he was able, charged Jonathan Bradford with having been his assassin."

"Surely you must allow that you have very slender grounds for making so serious an accusation?"

"It is in vain to say so," exclaimed the host, "for his prejudice is immovable, and nothing will ever convince him that I am not the monstrous villain he would make me appear."

"There is no prejudice in the matter, I assure you," answered Mr. Dozey; "for I firmly believe in all I have said, and nothing but an imperative duty has urged me to adopt the course I have. Let it but be proved that I have been too hasty in my conclusions, and I will not only acknowledge my error, but make every reparation that may be demanded from me."

"Which will be but a poor satisfaction," exclaimed Bradford, "when my character has been destroyed."

"Nay; only show to the world that you have been wrongfully accused, and the world will esteem you no less than they have done before."

"But," replied Farmer Nelson, "you are about to tear him from his family and home, and consign him to a prison, which will at once seem to confirm all you have alleged against him."

"Only with the unthinking part of the community though," answered Mr. Dozey; "and their opinion will be hardly worth troubling one's self about. If your son-in-law be innocent, a little inquiry will serve to prove it, and then he will not have much to complain of for having suffered a few hours of unmerited incarceration."

"And you would consign him to a prison upon no better ground than your own mistaken opinion?" sighed Mrs. Bradford.

"How else can I honestly perform my duty?" asked the lawyer. "The wife of the murdered man will expect that every exertion is made to discover the perpetrator of this foul act, and no alternative is left me but to pursue that course which I conceive to be the best to secure the ends of justice. By a singular coincidence, she anticipated this catastrophe; and heavily will the blow fall upon her when she hears how fearfully her words have been verified."

"Yet she, perhaps," sighed Mrs. Bradford, "will not be so rash in forming an opinion against an innocent man."

"Mrs. Hayes would be the last person to be guilty of an act of injustice," answered the lawyer; "but she will not blame me for having taken the only steps that were open to me under these peculiar circumstances. Unfortunately, there is too much reason for suspicion in this affair, and whatever may come of it, I shall not blame myself for having taken active measures towards bringing to a just punishment the perpetrator of this most execrable deed. I therefore repeat my accusation, and the prisoner must not be suffered to escape till it has been proved that he is innocent."

"Oh, wife—wife!" exclaimed Jonathan, as he pressed her to his throbbing heart, "what a terrible doom is this that overwhelms us in the midst of the happiness we had so fondly anticipated."

"Alas!" she sobbed, "what will become of our poor children?"

"Heaven will shield both you and them," answered her husband; "for I am innocent of this dreadful crime, and surely he who is unjustly persecuted will not fall through the evil machinations of his enemies. But I must now leave you, dear Ann, for 'tis our sad fate to sever for awhile, and all that remains for us is to bear up against our misfortunes, till the moment comes when we shall once more meet together in happiness and peace."

To part from her husband under such circumstances was more than the hapless wife could endure; and falling into the arms of her father, she remained for an hour or two afterwards in a state of unconsciousness of all that was passing around her. In the meantime, Jonathan Bradford, under the charge of three or four soldiers, was led from the room and conveyed to the village cage, there to await the period when he was to undergo an examination upon the charge which had been brought against him.

In the meantime Dan Macraisy and his companion, Caleb Scrimmidge, who had been roused from his heavy sleep by the noise and confusion that were going on in the house, sat in their own chamber listening to all that was going on. The latter-named personage, indeed, was quite at a loss to make out what it could all mean, for Dan had taken care not to inform him of anything that had passed, and the laudanum which had been mixed with his drink had so far stupified his brain, that he was unable to collect his scattered thoughts together.

"I say, Dan," he whispered, "what the devil is the meaning of all this row in the house? There seems to be a number of people in Mr. Hayes' room, and just now I thought I heard the word *murder* pronounced, as plainly as ever I did in my life."

"How should I know any more about it than you do yourself?" demanded the other. "There's something the matter, I suppose, but we needn't trouble our heads about the affair; for even if a murder has been committed, neither you nor I can know anything about it, that's quite certain."

"But it would be awkward if we were suspected."

"Not at all," answered Dan Macraisy, "for here we are, both in our own room, and there ain't a soul in the house that can say we have left it since we came to bed."

"Have you been asleep ever since I went off so suddenly?"

"To be sure I have. Do you suppose I'd keep awake, when I know what a long journey we've got before us?"

"I didn't suppose that, Dan; but——"

"Psha! what strange notions have you got in your head now?" interrupted the other. "I suppose, if a murder had been committed, you would think it could have been done by no one but me?"

"I should be sorry to think that of you, Dan."

"And why?"

"Because if you were to get into trouble, they would be sure to suspect me of being an accomplice."

"Then don't alarm yourself at all about it," exclaimed Dan Macraisy, "for there's not the least danger, unless you are fool enough to appear afraid of being suspected of having a hand in this murder."

"Ah! you know a murder has been committed, then?"

"I know just as much about it as you do yourself," answered the other, checking himself. "I have certainly heard a strange noise in the bedroom of the old gentleman, and it seemed to me as if some one were accused of having killed another; but it's no business of mine, and I shall leave 'em to settle it among themselves."

"Wouldn't it have been as well if we had gone to ask what's the matter?" exclaimed Caleb Scrimmidge.

"You can do so if you choose," replied Dan; "but for my own part, I have no inclination for fishing in troubled waters. If I were to go and make myself busy in the matter, who knows but what you and I might be suspected of having had a hand in robbing and murdering the old gentleman?"

"How do you know he has been robbed and murdered?"

"By making good use of my ears to be sure," answered Macraisy. "The first thing that woke me from my sleep, was a cry of murder; and directly afterwards I could hear that the bed-room of Mr. Hayes was filled with a number of people. Then I heard old lawyer Dozey say that the old gentleman had been killed, and who do you think, Caleb, he accused of doing it?"

"I can't guess."

"Why, the host, Jonathan Bradford."

"Jonathan Bradford! impossible!"

"Impossible or not, he'll have to answer for it; and I shouldn't wonder if they afterwards bring the charge home to him."

"But *you* know he didn't do it?"

"How should I know anything of the kind, when I was fast asleep in this room till they roused me up with a cry of murder? No—no, I'm comfortably clear of all suspicion; and what's better, I hope they'll not ask me any questions upon the subject."

"Because you'd find it rather difficult to answer 'em, I suppose?"

"What do you mean by throwing out that insinuation?"

"I was only thinking how curious it was that you had a notion of robbing the old gentleman a little while before I fell asleep."

"Psha! I was only joking."

"But there's many a true word said in jest."

"That may be," exclaimed Dan Macraisy; "but if you remember one thing I suppose you do another, so you must do me the justice to acknowledge that I afterwards said I would have nothing to do with it, as you refused to lend me a helping hand?"

"Yes, you said so, but that might only be as a blind."

"Come, come," exclaimed the other, "you are carrying this too far, old fellow, and I'm not going to have my character taken away by every fool that chooses to utter his unmeaning nonsense. You must be careful what you say, and if any questions should be asked, all you have to do, is to say that you and I were both fast asleep till we were woke up by the noise and confusion in the house."

"Then they'll wonder why we didn't go and see what was the matter."

"Let 'em wonder and be hanged!" exclaimed Dan. "We are not to be supposed to have known that a murder had been committed, so it's easy to say that we fell asleep again, and didn't wake again till all the uproar and confusion was over. But hark! I ear them clattering down stairs, so I suppose by this time they have determined to take the accused man to a place of safety."

"But suppose he should be innocent, Dan?"

"What have we to do with that? If he's innocent he must make it appear so to those that will have to try him; and if they won't believe it they'll find him guilty, and then the gallows will soon put him out of his misery. So let that be a consolation to you, Caleb, and now don't utter another word till you hear me speak, or we may both get into a scrape sooner than you expect."

Caleb Scrimmidge knew his companion too well to disobey this last injunction, and throwing himself back in his chair, once more he pondered over the events of the night in no little terror. In short, though he would not venture to say so much, he had a strong suspicion that the murderer and he were in pretty close neighbourhood to each other.

CHAPTER IX.

THE ADVERSITY OF THE MASTER BRINGS OUT THE GOOD QUALITIES OF HIS DOMESTICS. —FARMER NELSON'S DESPAIR AT THE UNFORESEEN CHANGES THAT HAVE TAKEN PLACE IN A ONCE HAPPY FAMILY.—"FRIENDS IN NEED," PROVE THEMSELVES TO BE "FRIENDS INDEED."

OF all those who pitied the misfortunes of Jonathan Bradford, never perhaps were more sincere in the expressions of their grief than Jack Rackbottle, and Sally, both of whom were sincerely attached to their master, who had so suddenly fallen into trouble. The former accompanied Bradford as far as the place where he was to be confined, till the period arrived for his examination before a magistrate, and being refused admittance to see him, he remained watching about as if he found some little consolation in being near one whom he loved all the more for the heavy affliction into which he had been plunged. As for Sally, she wandered about the house, refusing to listen to any consolation, and thinking only how she could best minister to the relief of her mistress, whom excessive grief had almost driven to despair.

"Heigho!" she sighed, as she left the house to look for Jack Rackbottle, whose long absence had somewhat troubled her. "I wasn't miserable enough before, but all them shocking things must happen to render my life a burden to me. My poor master and mistress, both accused of the murder of Mr. Hayes, as if it were possible that either of them would be guilty of such a cruel act. But I for one will never believe they are culpable, for its impossible, and so say thousands of people as well as myself. He, so civil, so kind, so good-natured to evey one! She, who I don't believe would hurt a fly, and who was always the first to lend a helping hand to any poor neighbour that was in want of her assistance! The poor old father, too, at his time of life, to be driven crazy by the troubles of his children, when he knows they don't deserve the hardships they have met with! Then there's the poor dear children—my heart is ready to break when I look at them, and remember the sad fate that is theirs through no fault of their own.

"Then there's that Jack Rackbottle; I wonder where he can possibly be stopping so long when I wan't to see him and hear how matters are going on. He ought to be ashamed of himself for leaving me all alone, for I'm almost frightened out of my life, and fancy every moment that I see the ghost of poor Mr. Hayes standing bolt upright before me. Ugh! what's that?" she exclaimed starting and turning round as Jack Rackbottle approached and laid his hand upon her shoulder.

"Oh, don't be so frightened, Sally," he said, "for its only I, and you know I would not harm you for the world."

"I'm glad to see you come back at last, sir," exclaimed Sally, "but it was not very kind of you, I think, to go away and leave a lone woman like me when you know how terrified I have been ever since poor Mr, Hayes was so barbarously murdered. However, as I said before, I'm glad you come back at last."

"It's something to be glad at anything, as this wicked world of ours goes, Sally," he replied. "For my own part, I'm too melancholy to find consolation in anything, and I shall n:ver be happy again till matters turn out better than they are at present."

"Well don't talk about that now," exclaimed Sally; "but tell me, sir, how you left poor master and missus."

"Why they wouldn't let me see 'em after they were taken into the cage," he replied; "though I begged any prayed just to be allowed to go in for a moment, and offered 'em all the money I've saved up, and that I meant to start us in life when we got married. But the hard-hearted wretches were as deaf as a post, and I was obliged to come back without seeing the unfortunate prisoners. And now having told you all I know, just tell me how farmer Nelson bears the troubles that have fallen so heavily on him in his old age."

"Ah, poor old gentleman," she replied; "I verily believe he is going stark-staring mad, for he looks so horribly wild that I never saw anything like it. And enough to make him too, for who could ever have dreamt of such a misfortune as this a little while ago."

"Have you seen him lately?"

"Yes," she replied, "he came here about an hour ago, and almost frightened me out of my life, for he put his fingers about little Jane's throat, and stared so wildly that I made sure he was going to strangle the poor child."

"Didn't you do anything to prevent them?"

"Yes," answered Sally; "but when I screamed out, he called me Ann, as if he mistook me for his daughter, and burst out crying for all the world as if he had been a child."

"Where is he now?"

"In the garden; I saw him there just now, talking to the trees, as if they were so many rational creatures that understood what he was saying to them."

"Poor old man!" exclaimed Jack Rackbottle, in a tone of commiseration, "he must certainly be going out of his mind."

"That I am quite sure of," she replied; "for only look at him now, as he walks up and down—his white hair streaming in the wind, and his arms swinging to and fro, just as if he were preparing to make a leap over the quickset-hedge."

"Ah, Sally," exclaimed the other, "how will he ever be able to bear it, if he should ever be calm enough again to hear the sad tidings of the ruin that has fallen upon those he so loves?"

"Why," she asked, "have you any news to tell him that you have not told me yet?"

"No," replied Jack; "but what I do know is quite enough to break any one's heart if it were as hard as a stone. Our poor master and missis taken to the strong room in the cage, and both of them charged with a crime they would never have thought of committing."

"How did they seem to bear it as they were being dragged to that horrible place?" asked the female.

"Ill and badly enough, I can tell you, Sally."

"Did'nt poor Mrs. Bradford almost cry her eyes out?" she asked.

"She wept bitterly, indeed," answered Jack Rackbottle, "and both of them looked so sadly and pale, that I shall never forget it the longest day I have to live."

"And couldn't you get to speak to them?"

"Only once, and that was as they were going along."

"What did they say?"

"They told me to come back and fetch Farmer Nelson and the children to see them, because they are about to be taken to another prison a long way off, where they may perhaps never be able to see their friends again."

"And still they of course say, they are innocent of the dreadful crime they have been charged with?"

"Yes, both of 'em do that."

"And everybody, of course, must believe 'em."

No. 8.

"I'm sorry to say," answered Jack Rackbottle, "that a great many people fancy they are guilty."

"Why, how can they do that?"

"You and I may well say that, Sally," he replied, "but the truth is, there are some people that say, the knife and watch being found on our master, is a proof that he committed the deed he has been charged with. Then it so happened that you and I were both sent out of the way, and though we know well enough that nothing was meant by it, other folks will talk, and they chose to say that it was done on purpose that we might not be witnesses against them."

"And what do you think will be the upshot of all this?"

"Why, I'm afraid that what the lawyer calls the circumstantial evidence, is so strong against them, that they will be found guilty."

"Surely they wont hang them?" cried Sally.

"As sure as they have necks, they will though, if matters go the wrong way against them," answered the other. "They'll be hung in chains upon the heath, and I shall never dare pass that way after sunset, though upon second thought, I don't think master's ghost would follow me, after the good friends we have always been."

"And are you likely to be called upon to give evidence against them?" asked Sally.

"So they tell me."

"Will you do it, Jack Rackbottle?"

"I believe it would be of no use to resist," he replied; "but it shall be no fault of mine if the lawyers get anything out of me that will criminate either of them."

"Isn't it a horrible thing," asked Sally, "to be forced to give evidence against one's will?"

"You are right," he replied, "but the law is so strong that it would be useless to resist it."

"But why did you say just now, that you should be afraid to cross the heath after nightfall?"

"Because people already begin to talk of it as a certainty, that master—if not missus also, will be hung there in chains."

"On the heath?"

"Yes, on the little green hill that stands in the midst of it."

"Mercy on me!" exclaimed Sally, "why, Mr. Nelson can see that place from the window of his own farmhouse. I shall never dare tell him the report that people have been raising."

"It would be cruel of you to do so," answered Jack Rackbottle, "for things may not turn out quite so bad, and for my own part I never like to look at matters on their worst side. Let us hope for the best, Sally, and who knows but this murder will by-and-by be traced to the right person."

"Ah!" sighed the female, "but unfortunately there is no reason at present for suspecting any other person, though you and I know that some one else did it. But hush! here comes poor old Mr. Nelsoun, and I don't want him to know the worst if we can any how help it."

The broken-hearted man was indeed seen approaching them, leading by the hand the eldest child of the unfortunate Jonathan Bradford and his wife.

"I want no telling of what has happened," he said in a tone of harrowing despair, "for I know it all—all, and the news has fallen upon my heart like an ice-bolt. The winds seem to howl in mine ears as I pass along. Your son and your daughter a murderer—murderess! But then I also hear an angel sometimes with a sweet, soft, voice, whispering 'innocent! innocent! innocent!' That's consoling—that's comfort. And yet, for all that, my heart aches, and I feel that the only rest I can ever expect in this world is to be found in the cold, dark grave."

"What can we say to him," whispered Jack to his companion, "to drive this notion out of his mind?"

"Say nothing to him at present," she replied, "for it would perhaps be dangerous to rouse him just now."

"Ann—Ann!" resumed the old man in the same tone of deep melancholy. "Give me a draught of water, Ann. But no—I forgot—she is no longer here. My child!

my beloved daughter! they have torn her from me in mine old age, and left me to die a lonely, miserable old man. They have peeled off the green ivy from the decayed winter-tree, and left it in its snow, desolate and alone!"

"Mr. Nelson," whispered Sally, as he was preparing to leave the place with the child.

"Ha!" he exclaimed, starting wildly, "who is that that calls upon my name?"

"Dear, sir, don't you remember me?"

"No."

"Not Sally?"

"No, I tell you," he replied sternly, "not I—I know nothing—nobody. This world is all illusion—all deception—cruelty—craft—cunning—wickedness!"

"But we are friends, sir."

"Friends!" he exclaimed, "I know of none such, for they smile in your face, and the foolish man believes they are angels. Yet tear off the treacherous visor, and what are they then? Demons! demons thirsting for your heart's best blood, and thinking only how they may trample on and destroy you."

"Dear sir," cried Sally, "remember your children."

"Ay!" he exclaimed bitterly, "even your own children can be ungrateful like all the rest of the world! Oh, misery! why have I lived so long as to hate all mankind?"

"Grandfather," cried little Jane, running towards him, "I want my mother. Where is she?"

"Ugh!" he replied, shuddering and recoiling from her, "hence from me, accursed one, lest in my frenzy I dash out thy brains. Yet stay—stay," he added, checking himself as a sudden thought seemed to pass through his mind; "I will not harm thee darling. Come nearer—closer—closer to my heart, for you remind me of days when sorrow had not found its way to my bosom. Let me look in thy face, little one. Those meek blue eyes—such were thy mother's—sparkling, full of joy, and radiant with the happiness that childhood only knows! Just such a beauteous, rosy child was she at thy age. Oh, heavens, why does my mind wander back to the past! Alas! how well do I remember the summer morn, when, on the grass before my own cottage, in the flower garden, the first step she took was to catch a gaudily painted butterfly, that had dazzled her with its beauty. How my poor heart rejoiced! how proud my wife was! and ah! how much more did we seem to love each other from that happy moment! Alas!—alas! those were indeed days to think of, and yet how sad—how melancholy does the recollection of them make me."

"Dear sir," cried Sally, "take comfort, and remember there may yet be happiness in store for you."

"Hush!" he exclaimed; "say nothing—tell nobody, for I would have all a secret as the grave."

"Nay, hear me."

"Speak to me not," he murmured, as he wiped away a tear that was stealing down his furrowed cheek. "It's a shame, you'll say, for an old man like me to weep—but I am better now, and my heart beats less violently than it did." Then addressing himself to little Jane, he added:—"Come, child, come, follow me, and I'll take thee to thy mother. Come, come, come; be not afraid of me, for I love thee still, and am now almost the only friend thou hast left in the wide world."

Sally again endeavoured to prevail upon him not to go away, but her words were not heeded, and the broken-hearted old man, left the place, leading with him the child whose youth and innocence had at length roused him from the lethargy into which his soul seemed to have fallen.

"Well, if that ain't a shocking sight for any one to look upon, I don't know what is," exclaimed Jack Rackbottle, as the old gentleman disappeared from their view. "His wits seem to be clean gone, and I don't know but what it's better that it should be so, for heaven only knows what would have become of him, if he had learnt what people say of his daughter and her husband."

"Why he would have treated their croaking with the same contempt that I do," answered Sally. "Other people may believe in the guilt of our master and missus if they like; but for my own part I shall always look upon 'em as martyrs, and it shall go hard but I'll find out who it was that committed the murder that they have been so unjustly accused of."

"Do you suspect any one?"

"At present I suspect two or three persons."

"Who are they?"

"Why first and foremost there's those two strangers who came and slept here last night."

"Well, to tell you the truth," replied Jack, "I've had queerish notions about those two chaps myself."

"And don't you think they were as likely to have committed the act as anybody else?"

"I certainly did think so," replied Jack, "till I was told that the notion was too ridiculous a one to be entertained."

"Who told you so pray?"

"Lawyer Dozey."

"And what does he know about it any more than you or I do?" asked Sally.

"That's a very natural question of yours," exclaimed Jack, "and I asked the old gentleman the very same question."

"What answer did he give you?"

"Why, he said that the two men were in bed and fast asleep at the time when the alarm was given!"

"That's more than he can tell."

"Be that as it may, he sticks hard and fast to it, and moreover, says that the only persons he found in the room of the murdered man were our master and mistress."

"Well," answered Sally, "and they went there as anybody else would when they heard the cry of alarm."

"But then," he replied, "there's that awkward affair of the knife being found in the hand of our master."

"And who knows but he may be able to give a very satisfactory reason for it?" exclaimed the female.

"I only hope he may," answered Jack Rackbottle, "and whether other people choose to believe him or not, I for one shall never think otherwise than that he is innocent."

"So shall I," she replied; "but what will be the use of that, if he should be found guilty?"

"Nonsense! I don't believe you'll find twelve men in the county that would do such a thing."

"Ah! it's all very well to say so," answered Sally, "but the lawyers have such a way of making black appear to be white, that I wonders juries are not oftener led astray than they are. However, we'll have good counsel to defend our master and mistress when the time comes, and who knows but we may succeed in getting 'em clear off?"

"I hope we may," he replied; "but somehow I begin to be terribly afraid that things wont go so smoothly at the trial as you and I would have wished."

"Psha! why throw cold water upon one?"

"Because if matters should turn out better than we expect, the surprise will be all the more agreeable."

"Won't they let you and I see them?"

"I'm afraid not."

"And why should they keep us away?"

"I don't know why it is," answered Jack Rackbottle, "but I suppose they are afraid of our trying to prove that they are innocent of the murder."

"Then I can tell them that all their care will be thrown away," exclaimed Sally, "for as far as I am concerned I'll do all that is in my power to get them out of this terrible dilemma. By good luck, I've got a little money by me, and if justice is to be got anyhow, I'll part with every penny of it to save those that I know are innocent from being hanged."

"And I, also, have a little money hoarded up in an old stocking," returned the other "and I'll not grudge the last farthing of it, if I can only find out who the murder was committed by."

"Then let us club our money together," exclaimed Sally, "and we know not what good may be done."

"I only wish we were sure of getting our master and mistress clear out of their dilemma," said Jack Rackbottle, "for then I shouldn't mind having to work hard all the rest of my days."

"But first, and foremost Jack, I wish to get permission to see them both, for I think it would be a great comfort to them, if they were only certain that all people have not turned against them in the midst of their misfortunes."

"At all events," returned Jack Rackbottle, "I fancy they must feel pretty certain that you and I will not believe them to be guilty of the crimes they have been charged with. And as for lawyer Dozey, he ought to be ashamed of himself for accusing people that had no more to do with the murder than himself."

"Ah!" exclaimed Sally, "and take my word for it, he will too, for I don't mean to let the matter rest where it is, and if he have a bit of shame left, I'll bring it out of him, or my name's not what it is. Why he might have accused you and I, Jack, and have been quite as near the mark as he is now."

"To be sure he might, and I almost wish he had, for we are better able to bear the brunt of it than those that he has been the means of sending to prison on a charge like this."

"Ah!" sighed the kind-hearted female, "and then only think of the suffering those two poor dear children will have to go through? Who'll ever look upon 'em after the falsehoods that have been told of their father and mother?"

"Why Farmer Nelson and his wife, to be sure."

"You talk like a simpleton, Jack," she exclaimed, "when you saw with your own eyes just now what a dreadful state the old gentleman is in. He'll not live much longer, it's my opinion, and as for his wife, if this affliction don't kill her, it's a wonder to me."

"At any rate," exclaimed her lover, "the children will never want a couple of staunch friends, whilst you and I have health and strength to work to get 'em a piece of bread."

"That's something like, Jack," she replied, "and if I had never cared about you before, I should now begin to look upon you as deserving my good opinion and respect. However, let us hope matters won't turn out so badly as people fancy, for it's hardly to be supposed that innocent people will be made to suffer for the crimes of others."

"But who are the others that we are to lay the blame to?"

"Why, there's no saying to a certainty," answered Sally, "but I've a very queer notion about those two strangers that slept here."

"Notions won't do unless you have proofs."

"But proofs may be found if I mind what I'm about," she exclaimed, "and my suspicion against those chaps is so strong, that I shall keep my eye upon them, as long as they remain in this neighbourhood."

"Which I've an idea will not be very long," replied Jack, "for I heard one of 'em tell the other that they must be off to London directly, because he has some particular business that calls him there."

"Whether his business is particular or not he'll find that he can't do just as he likes," returned the female, "for I heard lawyer Dozey say that as they happened to be in the house at the time of the murder, they must stay and tell the magistrates all they know about the matter. So they'll not be able to get away till to-morrow anyhow, and in the meanwhile I'll lose no time in trying to fish out all I can about them."

"Have you any reason for suspecting them?" he asked.

"Why, there ain't much ground for it at present," answered Sally, "but I've noticed a good deal of mysterious whispering among them, and for the life of me I haven't been able to get the notion out of my head that they may be a couple of highwaymen."

"Highwaymen!" exclaimed Jack. "Do you think master would have let them sleep in this house, if he had fancied such a thing?"

"It's very certain he wouldn't," she replied, "but he was so much taken up with his other guests, when they came here, that I don't suppose he gave the matter a thought. I, however, didn't like the look of the fellows from the moment I first saw them, and the more I think of it the more I feel certain they are here for no good purpose."

" You must have some better foundation than that, though, before you persuade other people to be of the same opinion."

"Only give me a little time and a fair opportunity," answered Sally, " and I'll be bound I shall be able to make something of this before I have done. Perhaps I may have a couple of cunning fellows to deal with, but with all their artful ways I may by-and-by prove myself to be rather too much for them."

" Have you told Mr. Dozey what you think ?"

" Not yet," she replied, " because he has been too busy for me to get a word with him, and I'm waiting till he is more at leisure."

" Then take my advice, and keep your suspicions to yourself till another time. Depend on it, the old gentleman will only laugh at you for your pains; and as for the two strangers, they'll leave the place as soon as the examination is over, and it will be a chance if ever they show their faces in this part of the world again."

" And won't that show their guilt ?"

" It would look rather queer certainly," replied Jack, " but what difference can that make, if they are not to be found when they are wanted ?"

·" Then, I suppose you think I should only be wasting my time in keeping a sharp look out upon these two men ?"

" Why, I'll not go quite so far as to say that," answered Jack Rackbottle, " because I know you mean it all for the best. But I shall leave you to manage that part of the business in your own way, while I see what can be done towards getting our master and mistress out of the terrible dilemma they have fallen into."

" Only do that," she exclaimed, " and I promise——"

" What?"

" To marry you as soon as they are safe from all farther danger."

·" It's a bargain," cried the other, " and if I don't keep you to your promise, never believe a word I say again as long as I live. So, do you go and see what has become of Farmer Nelson and his children, and I'll go and try to find Mr. Dozey, who is a good-natured old man enough at bottom ; and I've a notion he'll not be very spiteful to Master Bradford and his wife, if I can only see him and reason upon the improbability of the murder having been committed by the persons he has given into custody."

He ran off as he said this, and Sally, after watching him as long as he remained in sight, went to seek for Farmer Nelson, to console him with the hope that a favourable change would take place."

CHAPTER X.

THE EXAMINATION AND COMMITTAL.—DAN MACRAISY AND HIS COMPANION IN A BIT OF A QUANDARY.—THE TRIAL OF THE PRISONERS, AND THE RESULT.

NOTWITHSTANDING the dreadful nature of the charge that had been brought against him, and the difficulty he would have in satisfactorily proving his innocence, Jonathan Bradford maintained a greater degree of firmness than might have been expected. This was partly owing to his anxiety to keep up the spirits of his wife, who had been charged with him, and for whose sake he would willingly have died, could such a sacrifice but have saved her from the fearful death which stared her in the face. One thing, however, grieved him exceedingly ; no friend was permitted to see them till after the examination had taken place, and they were thus left to uncertainty as to their children, and the few persons from whom they might have derived consolation and advice, under the present difficulty. Thus shut out from the world and those they best loved, they were left to the free indulgence of those terrible thoughts, which were forced upon them by the one harrowing idea, that they were already doomed to perish ignominiously for the crime of another. At first, the heart of Mrs. Bradford seemed to be crushed beneath the weight of misfortunes which had thus fallen upon them, at a period when their prospects were fair and brilliant in the extreme ; but the example of firmness manifested by her husband soon wrought a marvellous change in her, and looking up to heaven for support, she resolved—come what might—to endure all with firmness and courage. It is true, the thought of her children would sometimes drive her almost to madness, but she knew it was in vain. to repine, and calmly yielded to the sad destiny ; she even ventured to indulge a fainthope that the evidence against them would not be sufficient to support the charge.

At length came the time when they were to be conveyed before the magistrate, who was to hear the case and decide upon the probability which had been so strongly urged by their accuser. On arriving at the mansion where the examination was to take place, they found a great number of their friends and acquaintances, who had been drawn thither partly by curiosity, and partly through pity for the misfortune of those whose characters had been impeached. Mr. Dozey, who was the first witness examined, deposed all the circumstances from the moment when they had left Oxford, dwelling particularly on the fact of Mr. Hayes having brought with him several hundred pounds for the purpose of completing the purchase of an estate in the neighbourhood, and which money there could be no doubt had been the inducement which had led to the terrible catastrophe which was the subject of the present inquiry. He minutely described the circumstances under which he had found Jonathan Bradford and his wife, in the bed-chamber of the murdered man, the agitation they both exhibited at the moment when he first saw them, and swore positively to having found Mr. Hayes' watch and a blood-stained knife in the possession of the male prisoner. As for the female, he added, there could be no doubt that she was persent to aid and assist in perpetrating the foul crime.

Mr. Radpole confirmed all these statements with great precision, observing that, in his opinion, there was no other person in the place against whom the shadow of a suspicion could rest. Bradford, he stated, was perfectly well aware that his unfortunate guest had a large sum of money with him ; he had been told so even before they had left Oxford together, and no doubt, he said, the scheme of murdering the unsuspecting man had been projected on their journey to the George Inn.

Three other witnesses spoke to facts which were supposed to tend to implicate the two prisoners ; and then Dan Macraisy and Caleb Scrimmidge were called upon to give their testimony in addition to that which had been already heard. Luckily for the former named personage, Caleb was first questioned, for the interval gave his companion time to recover himself ; so that when his turn came to be examined, he was able to comport himself with as much firmness as if he were himself entirely innocent of the crime, which he was assisting to fix upon two persons whom he knew to be entirely blameless. He was, however, cunning enough to profess very little knowledge of what had taken place during the night, declaring that he and his companion had retired early to rest after a long day's journey, and that they had both slept so soundly that neither of them knew anything of the murder till informed of it the next morning. Macraisy further affirmed that he was himself travelling with a large sum of money in his possession, and expressed his thankfulness that he also had not been sacrificed for the sake of his money. This statement was made with an air of such unblushing effrontery, that no one could possibly suspect the falsehood with which he was endeavouring to conceal the crime which he had himself committed.

Each witness that had been examined seemed to add very materially to the chain of evidence which had been brought forward to prove the guilt of the unfortunate prisoners. Jonathan Bradford listened to every statement that was made with eager attention ; but though many were watching him with inquisitive eyes, no one could perceive any change in his countenance that might be supposed to be indicative of conscious guilt. On the contrary, he stood up with a firm erect mien, glancing round occasionally upon the spectators, as if anxious to gather from their looks whether they believed the charge which had thus been brought against him. Now and then, too, he whispered to his afflicted partner, as if to bid her be of good heart, and not to sink beneath the afflictions which threatened to over-whelm them in ruin. Altogether the manner of the accused may be said to have made rather a favourable impression upon those who had come to hear the ex-amination, for there was a strong feeling beginning to manifest itself against the two strangers, and many persons were there present who suspected that they were not so free of the crime as they would fain make it appear. Even the magistrate himself entertained a feeling of compassion towards the accused, for the evidence against them was wholly circumstantial, and there was still a possibility that they were as innocent of the crime as they solemnly asserted. He was, however, bound to adopt only one course, for the accusation had been formally made, and as far as the evidence had hitherto gone, the main features of it were corroberated by the evidence of each suc-cessive witness that had been called.

The case having been brought to a close, the magistrate consulted with his clerk for a few minutes, and then, as the prisoners declined making any statement at that stage of the proceedings, the commitment was made out, and they were ordered to be conveyed to the jail at Oxford, there to await their trial, which would take place within the next two or three days, as the assizes were appointed to commence there on the following morning. Dan Macraisy and his companion were, with the other witnesses, bound over to appear at the trial, and cautioned not to leave the neighbourhood till after a verdict had been returned in the case of the prisoners, whose examination had just taken place. The business having been thus brought to a close, the two prisoners were removed, and conveyed away to their destination, without being allowed an interview with their friends. Dan Macraisy and Caleb watched the melancholy group till they disappeared from view, and then returned towards the George Inn, resolving to remain there that night, and to set off in the morning to Oxford, where their presence would be required to give their testimony against Jonathan Bradford and his wife.

"Hang me if I like this affair at all," exclaimed Dan, "and I can't see what they can want with our evidence, when they've got quite enough without the little that we are able to give."

"What makes you so fidgetty about it?" asked the other. "I noticed all the time the examination was going on, how pale and frightened you looked; and if other people had seen it as well, you'd have stood a good chance of being suspected of being guilty of——"

"What?" demanded the other, impatiently interrupting him.

"Of being the murderer of the old gentleman."

"Psha! you talk like a fool," returned Dan. "I neither looked pale nor frightened; and why should I, when I have the consolation of knowing that I had nothing at all to do with it?"

"But suppose old Lawyer Dozey had taken it into his head to accuse us instead of Jonathan Bradford?"

"Oh, it's all very well to suppose this thing and suppose the other," exclaimed Macraisy, "but people must have some grounds for it before they can make a charge against respectable people."

"Respectable people!" laughed Caleb Scrimmidge. "One of us a gentleman adven-turer, that would be puzzled to explain what he is, and the other the run-away appren-tice of a watchmaker. Egad! respectability has come to something, if the like of you and I may venture to lay claim to it."

"At any rate, we must appear to be so," answered his companion, "or by-and-by we shall have the people hereabouts taking too much notice of us. Follow my example, my good fellow, and you'll always find that impudence will carry you safely through the world when nothing else would do it."

"If I follow your example too closely, I'm afraid it may some day bring my neck into a halter."

"Thank you for the compliment," exclaimed Dan Macraisy "but between ourselves, I don't see that there is a great deal of difference in us, for both are rogues, only that you haven't the courage to show so much of it as I do. There, however, you and I, perhaps, don't agree, so the less we say about it the better."

"But you seem to have a notion that suspicion may by-and-by be directed against us?" continued Dan.

"I didn't say a word about *us.*"

"Wel , against *me*," exclaimed Dan.   · What reason have you for supposing that I shall be suspected?"

"Because you boasted so much about having a large sum of money in your possession; and if they should happen to ask you to produce it, you'd be puzzled how to do it."

No. 9.

"Couldn't I say that I had sent it up to London this morning, for fear of being robbed and murdered like Mr. Hayes, for the sake of the money I had about me? If they come to those sort of questions Caleb, I shall always have an answer ready for them, for I've lived too long in the world to be caught out by people that are less cunning than myself."

"Do you expect to be always on the safe side?"

'I mean to be so as long as I can; and when good fortune forsakes me, I must fall, as many a better man has done before me."

"But you don't seem much to fancy being called upon as one of the witnesses against Jonathan Bradford."

"Is that to be wondered at when the man never did me any harm in his life?"

"Ain't he supposed to have committed a murder?"

"Yes, some people suspect him, but I have a right to have a different opinion if I like; and something seems to tell me that he had no more to do with it than you had."

"Or than yourself had."

"Ay, have it that way if you like," exclaimed Dan Macraisy; "but what the devil made you look so hard at me when you said so? Don't you know I was in the room with you all the night long, and ain't that enough to convince you that I had no hand in the affair?"

"How should I know you didn't leave the room when I went to sleep like a top, and half-a-dozen murders might have been committed before I woke up. C found that brandy and water! I've half a notion some sleeping stuff must have been put into it."

"Who the devil is likely to have served you such a trick as that?" demanded Dan Macraisy, with alarm.

"Why, to tell you the truth, I don't know of any one that was so likely to have done it as yourself."

"Come—come, old fellow, lets have no more of this!" said Dan, in a tone half-serious, half-coaxing. "A joke's all very well in its way, sometimes; but I was too tired last night to think of playin any tricks on you, and I rather think, if the truth were know, I was asleep some time before you."

"I'm sure you wasn't though."

"How can you be sure?"

"Because you were wide awake enough while I was reading that advertisement about my self in the newspaper; and I know I fell off as sound as a roach before I had got to the end of it. By-the-by, I must look over it again, for if I'm not mistaken, they promised me forgiveness if I would return; and I begin to see that it will be better to follow the honest occupation of a watchmaker, than to be strolling about the country like a vagabond, with the chance of being some day or other taken up on suspicion of having committed either a highway robbery or a murder."

"Keep my company, old fellow, and there will be very little fear of any harm befalling you."

"Now there you and I differ, for I've a notion that yours is just the company to get me into trouble."

"Humph!" muttered Dan, "do you want to quarrel with me?"

"Quite t'other way, my good fellow," he replied, "for I've a respect for my life; and I don't think it would be worth much if once you and I happen to fall out."

"Then see that you don't offend me, for the least thing will change me from a friend to an enemy."

"But we are not going to be together much longer," exclaimed Caleb; "and when we part, I hope it will be for ever."

"That will depend upon yourself," answered the other, "for if you ever dare say a word about what took place at the George Inn, whilst you and I happened to be in the house, I shall be down upon you before you expect me. So keep your tongue quiet, or you'll have reason enough to be sorry for chattering about matters that had better be forgotten as soon as possible."

"You needn't be afraid of my talking about what has happened here," replied Caleb Scrimmidge, "for I don't like to think about it; and I shall be afraid, as long as I live, lest people should take it into their heads that you and I had something to do with the mur——"

"Pshaw! what do you want to make use of that ugly word for?" interrupted Dan. "I don't like to hear it, and what's more, if you go on repeating the same thing, I shall do something that you will not be likely to forget in a hurry."

"Why any one would think that your conscience was rather troubled about this affair last night."

"If any person thinks so, he would be in the wrong," answered Macraisy, "for I deny having anything to do with it; and if people choose to say to the contrary, it will be at their own peril. But for all that, I should like to get away from this neighbourhood as soon as we can, because there's always ill-natured folks willing to do one an injury, and I feel rather uncomfortable at being obliged to stay in this country to give my evidence against a man that, for anything I know, may be innocent of the crime they have charged him with."

"I'm pretty sure he's innocent."

"What reason have you for saying so, Caleb?"

"A very good one, I think," answered the other, "for it's not very likely that a man like Jonathan Bradford would commit a murder, when he has a wife and family that he seems to be so fond of."

"Ay," exclaimed Dan Macraisy; "but you seem to forget that the money which was known to be in the possession of Mr. Hayes, was a temptation not easy to be resisted."

"I should hardly think it would be a temptation to a man that was well enough off in the world, without coveting the money that belonged to another," answered Caleb.

"Then you mean to tell me that Jonathan Bradford had nothing to do with this affair?"

"Ay, that's exactly what I do think of it."

"What made you give your evidence to-day, then?" asked the other.

"Ah, that's easily explained," he replied, "for I found that you were going to have a say upon the subject, and I knew very well that it would not do for you and I to give different accounts of the matter. So I told him I was fast asleep when the alarm was given, which was true enough; and therefore I couldn't be expected to throw much light upon the subject. In short, I could do no harm by what I said, and you have therefore nothing at all to grumble about."

"But you are so frightened, that I've a notion they'll by-and-by begin to suspect that you and I know something more of this affair than we are inclined to admit."

"Do you suppose then I haven't more gumption than to get ourselves into a scrape?" asked Caleb Scrimmidge.

"I fancied at one time that you had some little sense of your own," replied the other, "but the last few hours have proved you to be anything but a safe fellow to trust a secret with. However, you must not open your mind to any one that asks questions, and if we get safe out of this scrape, I may perhaps remember you the first time I happen to get hold of some money."

"Thank you all the same, Mr. Macraisy," exclaimed the other, "but between ourselves, I would rather not have anything more to do with you after a separation takes place between us. For my own part, I mean to try and do the respectable."

"By settling down as a watchmaker, I suppose?"

"Yes, I mean to wind up my follies, and henceforth honesty shall be the mainspring of all my actions."

"How long do you think your good resolution will last?"

"Till my evil star brings you and I together again," replied Caleb, "and it shall be no fault of mine if ever we meet, for I'm heartily tired of leading this vagabond life; and when once I get out of it, I'll keep out of harm's way."

"You don't speak your mind very plainly," exclaimed his companion, "but you throw out strange hints, and sometimes I fancy you suspect me of knowing something about this murder."

"Why should you think so if you are innocent?"

"Because one can't be easily deceived by people that haven't the sense to keep their thoughts to themselves. It's true, you have not ventured to speak plainly upon the subject, but half words often go for a good deal, and if you don't mind what you are about, we shall have a quarrel now before we part."

"Humph!" muttered Caleb Scrimmidge, "you are beginning to get tired of me, I suppose?"

"I'm tired of seeing you make such a fool of yourself," retorted his companion; "for if any mischief should come of this, I know well enough that there will be no one to blame for it but yourself."

"But what mischief can you be afraid of, if, as you say, you know nothing about this affair?"

"Psha!" exclaimed Dan Macraisy, "hasn't the notion yet entered your thick skull, that the fact of our having slept in the house on the night of the murder, may give a parcel of idle, gossipping people an opportunity of saying strange things about us? Not that I care much about it, only that it would be rather awkward if we were to be taken up for a matter that we know nothing of."

"Awkward?—it would be confoundedly unpleasant, I think."

"Well, unpleasant; if that word suits you better," continued the adventurer. "The charge would be a very dangerous one for both of us, Caleb, and I therefore advise you to be extremely careful in what you say to any one, and mind how you answer the questions that are put to you at the trial, for these lawyers are such precious cunning chaps, that they'll turn your words any way they please, if they can only see a chance of bothering a witness or making him commit himself."

"Do you suppose then I'm not a match for 'em?"

"If you are it's a great deal more than most people can say," replied Dan Macraisy, "so I wouldn't have you think too much of your own superior wit or acuteness. All you've got to do is to pretend to know as little as possible, and leave 'em to try to get the rest out of me, if they can. However, they won't have many questions to ask if you do as I have said, and swear point-blank that we were both fast asleep, and know nothing of the murder till we were told of it in the morning, some hours after it had taken place."

"I can swear to having been asleep myself," answered Caleb Scrimmidge, "but how can I say that for you when I know nothing about it?"

"Then tell 'em you saw me in the room with you up to the last thing of your being awake, and leave the rest to me."

"But I shall be all in a twitter."

"Nonsense!" exclaimed the other, "rouse yourself, Caleb, and act the part of a man, if you know how. Remember, life or death may be in the balance, and if you go and make a fool of yourself by saying too much, you and I may have to change places with Jonathan Bradford and his wife. You see, therefore, this is no child's play; so turn it over carefully in your own mind, and when you are called upon to give your evidence let it be done as coolly as if you and I were talking the affair over between ourselves."

"I'll try," answered Caleb after a pause, "but I can see a wonderful difference between talking the thing over with you, and being bullied and blustered at by one of those Old Bailey lawyers. I remember hearing one of 'em cross examine a poor devil of a witness till the chap didn't know what he was saying, and ever since that time I've been afraid of that sort of gentry."

"Then as they'll most likely call me first," replied Macraisy, "just notice the cool way that I shall answer their questions, and then all you'll have to do will be to follow my example."

"Thank you for the hint Mr. Macraisy," but perhaps the less I follow your example the better it will be for me."

"Well, then, take your own way, and see what a dilemma you'll get yourself into. It's not only for myself, Caleb, that I speak, for whatever may happen to me must be shared by yourself; so recollect that, and do as you like afterwards."

"You seem to take me for a fool, Dan," exclaimed the other, "but perhaps I may go through this matter better than you expect. When a fellow finds himself in a mess it serves to sharpen his wits for him, and so it may turn out in my case, if you'll only have patience to wait till the time comes. Besides, I've got your lesson pretty well by heart now, and if I can only pluck up a little courage, I may beat the lawyers in spite of all their brow-beating."

"Why, of course you can, if you choose to make up your mind to it," replied Dan. "But now let's change the conversation, for we are close to the George Inn, where we must sleep to-night, and it won't do for us to appear as if we were out of spirits, and afraid of looking other people in the face,"

Caleb Scrimmidge had no great fancy for sleeping in the house in which a murder had been 'so recently committed, but he knew it would be in vain to remonstrate with his more hardened companion, and they entered the inn together with an appearance of as much unconcern, as if they knew nothing of the terrible tragedy that had so very recently taken place within its walls.

Passing over a few subsequent events that are not of much importance, we will at once proceed to the morning on which Jonathan Bradford and his wife were to be tried for a crime of which they were as innocent as the judge by whom their case was to be heard. Conscious of their own rectitude, the two persons took their places at the bar with a firm bearing, which surprised the numerous spectators who had crowded the court to be witnesses of a case which had created so much excitement. Both of them appeared to be calm and dignified, and it was with a clear, unshaken voice that they pleaded "Not Guilty" to the charge which had been brought against them. To the opening address of the counsel for the prosecution, they listened with much apparent attentions; nor did they exhibit any marked emotion when Mr. Dozey, the first witness, took his place in the box to give his evidence against them. To all present, however, the clear straight-forward statement made by the old gentleman seemed to be very conclusive as to the guilt of the two prisoners; and from the moment that he had described the details which are already known to the reader, there seemed to be a general impression amongst the audience that the case was clearly established. The other witnesses spoke in corroboration of what had been already stated, and then came the turn of Dan Macraisy, who, without betraying the least emotion or alarm, answered all the questions that were put to him with an appearance of calm self-possession that would have disarmed all suspicion against him, if any such had existed in the minds of any of the present. It is true the interrogatories put to him were not of much importance; but he swore to having been fast asleep at the time when the murder had taken place, and added that he had himself heard Mr. Hayes mention the fact of his having a large sum of money in his possession, at a time when the male prisoner was in the room. As for Caleb Scrimmidge, he trembled excessively when his examination commenced; but a look from Macraisy was sufficient to remind him of the conversation that had passed between them, and from that moment he gave his replies with tolerable clearness and decision. His evidence, however, was not of much importance, as it only went to confirm the statements made by previous witnesses, without adding any new facts to those which had been already elicited. The case being concluded, the judge summed up, and the jury, after a few minutes deliberation, returned a verdict of "GUILTY" against both the prisoners.

The judge then, in an impressive address, dilated upon the heinous nature of the crime, and after imploring the convicts to make the best use of the time that remaided to them in this world, sentenced them to be hanged in chains on a gibbet, within view of their own house. They were then removed from the bar, and conveyed the same evening to the strong room, to which they had been sent on the night of the murder, as the most convenient place to the spot where the vengeance of the law was to be carried into effect.

CHAPTER XI.

THE TWO CONVICTS WAIT FOR THEIR DOOM.—A PARTING INTERVIEW AND A MOTHER'S DEEP DESPAIR.—A REPRIEVE ARRIVES FOR ONE OF THE PRISONERS.—A STRUGGLE BETWEEN DUTY AND AFFECTION.—THE FINAL RESOLUTION.

ACCORDING to the regulations observed upon all similar occasions, the two prisoners on being brought back to the cage were confined in different cells, and this perhaps was felt as the severest part of their sad destiny, as it debarred them from the only society which could have afforded consolation amidst the overwhelming misfortune which had fallen upon them. Most earnestly did Bradford implore for some relaxation in this one instance, and Sergeant Sam, whose heart was melted by their sufferings, readily undertook to try what was to be done towards obtaining for them the interview they so earnestly desired. Not daring to quit his post—that of watching over them—he entrusted one of his comrades with the task of seeing the judge, who was still at Oxford, in order to obtain from him permission that the two prisoners might be allowed the interview they so much desired. The promise was no sooner made than steps were taken to carry it into effect, and the convicts having been informed that the messenger had already taken his departure, waited with trembling anxiety to learn the result of the application in their behalf. To both of them, the period that must intervene ere the return of the messenger, seemed to be an age. Mrs. Bradford threw herself upon the straw mattrass with which her cell was provided, in the vain hope of finding a short oblivion in sleep, whilst her husband in his own narrow room, paced hurriedly up and down, muttering as he did so the bitter thoughts which passed through his almost maddened brain. In this manner nearly the whole day passed away without bringing the tidings they so anxiously looked for, but at length the door of Jonathan's cell was heard turning upon its hinges, and the next instant the kind hearted sergeant entered, leading with him the trembling and almost fainting wife. A low moan of mingled gratitude and grief escaped them, and Ann Bradford sinking into the arms of her husband, remained for a short period without the power of giving utterance to the feelings of her overburdened heart.

"My messenger has just succeeded in getting the favour you asked for," exclaimed the sergeant, in the interval of silence, "and I was so well pleased at receiving the permission that I could not delay your meeting, even for a moment. So I brought your wife here at once, Master Bradford, and now I'll leave you to talk over your grievances together, though before I go it may be as well to prepare you for some good news that I may have to bring you by and by."

"Good news!" sighed Jonathan, "alas! what have we to expect in our present hapless situation?"

"Why," returned the sergeant, "perhaps I ought to have told you before, the thing is quite certain, that a petition has been forwarded to the judge for the pardon of your wife, and his lordship was considering it at the time when my messenger came away."

"Ah!" exclaimed Bradford, "then she at least may be spared the dreadful doom that has been unjustly passed upon her."

"I would not have you make too sure of it," returned the other, "for the thing is not settled yet, and perhaps the judge may not pay any attention to the petition that has been sent to him. It was foolish of me, I know, to mention it to you just yet, but for the life of me I couldn't help letting it out, because I thought it might afford some little consolation in the midst of your misfortunes."

"'Twas kindly meant of you, my good friend," exclaimed Jonathan Bradford, "and believe me it has afforded me a ray of hope that till this moment I had not expected. Let but my poor suffering wife be pardoned, and I will meet my doom, horrible as it is to think of—without a murmur or reproach."

"Well, I shall now leave you for a little while," said the sergeant, " but if I may offer a bit of advice without giving offence, I should say, don't mention what I have told you to your wife, because the application for mercy, may not be of any use. Be it which way it may, however, I shall know about it before long, and the moment the news reaches me, I'll come and let you know what answer has been given to the petition for mercy. By the way, I may as well tell you, too, that permission has been given for any of your family to visit you to-day, so that I suppose you may expect to see some of 'em before long."

Upon this, the sergeant left them, and after the lapse of a few minutes, the sorrowing wife began to recover from the swoon into which she had fallen. But the recollection of their melancholy fate immediately recurred to her, and throwing her arms round the neck of her husband, she gave utterance to the overwhelming grief with which she was oppressed.

"Nay, dear wife, be comforted," exclaimed Jonathan, "for hope has not yet entirely abandoned us, and even if it had, this one embrace repays me for all my anguish—all I have suffered—all that I can suffer from this unjust persecution."

"And I," sighed his wife, "ought perhaps, to take shame to myself, for yielding to despair, when you so nobly stand up against the misfortunes that have overwhelmed us. Instead of repining at my destiny I will endeavour to be happy. To be near you, to press your hand—to hear your voice once more assures me that the worst of our sad trial is past. They shall not part us again, dear Jonathan, for to-morrow closes the short journey of our life, and then the same moment hurries us into eternity, where misery and persecution awaits us no more. But you are much changed, husband, in the brief interval that separated us."

"And you also, Ann," he replied, gazing mournfully upon her.

"Ay," she exclaimed, "both of us are changed—but 'tis with sorrow, not with conscious guilt."

"Tell me, are you not afraid to die?"

"I am prepared."

"And to suffer undeserved ignominy?"

"Ay, since 'tis the will of Heaven!"

"But the pang of bitter remembrance?"

"Why should we repine," she asked, solemnly, "when 'tis His will? We must forego all—forgive all! Even the real murderer, for whose crime we are about to suffer! Who he is, or what he is, alas! we know not, but his crime, though laid to us, we must forgive from our very hearts."

"My dearest wife," exclaimed Bradford, again pressing her to his bosom, "you have indeed, taught me my duty, and your pure virtuous fortitude has put my manhood to the blush. From this moment I will hold the world as nothing, and we will now talk of Heaven only, that land of promise in whose glorious haven you and I may hope speedily to repose. There the storm beats not, but the unclouded sky shines ever on a calmness like its own."

"The picture is a sweet one to contemplate," she sighed, "and the thought of our future happiness almost makes me wish that the last sad moment of our existence here had arrived."

"Are you so anxious to die, my love?"

"My spirit feels like the lark," she replied, "that vaults and vaults towards the blest abode that all desire to go to."

"But our children, do you not remember their helpless state, when we are taken from them?"

"They are never out of my mind!" she replied, "and they—they are the links that still bind me to this earth. Once I saw them ill and thought they were dying, and bitterly did I repine, for all hope seemed to have forsaken me. It was sinful of me perhaps, but I am bitterly punished for it now, Jonathan, and feel the magnitude of my guilt; for alas! how much better it would have been to have followed them to their graves, than to know that I am now about to leave them to the mercy of a cold, unfeeling world."

"Nay," said Jonathan, "have you then abandoned all hope of mercy on this earth?"

"I have; but why that question?"

"Because I thought it possible, that if my life be sacrificed, yours might yet be spared. In a word, Ann, I have endeavoured to console myself with the hope that you may be pardoned."

"And do you think I could accept life on such terms?" she asked. "Of what value do you imagine existence would be to me when deprived of you?"

"But our children require their mother's care."

Before she could make any reply to this, the door was thrown open, and Farmer Nelson, leading by the hand the two children of the unfortunate captives, entered the cell. The old man stood for a moment or two as if paralysed by the sight before him, and Jonathan advancing, endeavoured to change the current of his thoughts by an appearance of cheerfulness that was foreign to his heart. In the meantime the children had run into the open arms of their parent, exclaiming with childish wonder—

"Mother!—dear mother!—why don't you come home to us?"

"Home!" she replied, with faltering tongue, "I—I will come soon, dearest, very—very soon."

"Why not now?" continued the child.

"Oh, how shall I tell them the dreadful truth?" murmured the heart-broken mother. "How will they understand the fearful doom that soon will make them orphans! Home! where is their home? No mother's voice—no father's admonition. Henceforth they will be abject outcasts, branded with the name of infamy, through the crime for which we—innocently—are about to suffer the last dreadful penalty of the law. Oh my children! my poor orphan children!—what will become of them, when a heartless world shuns them as degraded beings?"

"Ann!" exclaimed Farmer Nelson, as for the first time he found the power of utterance, "as to you I have been a father, so will I be to them when deprived of your care. True, I am grown old and feeble, and my years are fast hurrying me to my grave. Ay, the grave will soon be my home, and there shall they rest with me as the early spring flowers that are strewn upon a corse. In the cold earth we'll hide ourselves buried as deep beneath the surface as shame and misery can dig!"

"Alas! alas!" cried Mrs. Bradford, noticing now the great change that grief had wrought in him; "how wild and bewildered he looks! Oh, father, speak to me, I implore you! It is your daughter, Ann, who thus pleads to you—your beloved—your only daughter. Do you not know me, father?—No reply!—Give me your blessing father—your blessing ere I die!"

"Blessing!" he replied, almost unconsciously; "would you crave a blessing of the mildew, whose office 'tis to blight the golden corn? Would you ask a blessing of one who could find it in his heart to utter the deepest curses against all the world?"

"Father!" she cried, throwing herself at his feet in a paroxysm of mental agony, "will you not hear one who till now never asked of you a favour in vain?"

"You are not guilty," he replied, gazing upon her with a vacant look; "but what of that, when the world—base and lying as it is—says you killed a man in cold blood?"

"But you have not these cruel reports?" she exclaimed, grasping his hand convulsively.

"Release me!" cried the old man, struggling to cast her off. "Touch me not, for I am leprous, contagious. All that I ever loved on earth have withered, one by one, children, kindred, friends!—And you, the last, are now about to be torn from me! Let me begone, I say, for my brain burns, and I may do some of you a mischief!"

The heart-broken old man buried his face in his hands, when he had given utterance to these words; but presently afterwards, once more raising his head, he saw the two terrified children gazing upon him with looks expressive of wonder and surprise.

"To think," he murmured, in hollow accents, "that I am never again to look upon those children! There are roses in their cheeks; but the canker of this brow shall never blight them."

"Will you not be a protector to them when we are gone?" asked the mother, with anguish.

"Who am I that I should promise to protect the orphans?" he demanded. "Do I not already stand upon the verge of the grave, to which a few short hours may hurry me? No, no, no; the sight of them would call up the remembrance of that which has driven me mad! Let me be one, then!—let me begone, I say!—I now remember all, and bitterly do curse the evil destiny that has brought us to this fearful pass."

Whilst giving utterance to these words, Sergeant Sam opened the door to ascertain what was going on; and the old man, seizing the opportunity, rushed out of the cell, and effected his escape before any effectual opposition could be offered to him.

"Alas!" groaned Mrs. Bradford, covering her face with her hands, "our misery can now go no further. The picture is too terrible."

"Take the children away without disturbing her again," whispered Jonathan Bradford. "Let some one lead them home, for the sight of them will only serve to increase their mother's misery."

"Mother! will you not say good-bye to us before we go?" exclaimed the elder child as the sergeant was preparing to lead them away.

"Ah! my children," she exclaimed, suddenly starting from the sort of lethargy into which she had fallen. "Nay, in mercy, do not attempt to separate us, for never will I part with them again till the last sad moment tears them away from these arms."

This exertion proved too much for her, and staggering backwards a few paces, she fell fainting into the arms of her husband. The sergeant, upon perceiving this, hurried from the cell to procure such restoratives as might be nearest at hand. In a few moments afterwards he returned with a paper, which he held up with an expression of honest exultation.

"Good news, Master Bradford," he exclaimed, "here is the reprieve for your wife that I told you of."

"A reprieve for her!" answered the prisoner, eagerly, "then now I am indeed content. My children will not have to mourn for the loss of their mother, and I shall die in the blessed consciousness that so far my prayers have not been offered up in vain. Ann—Ann!" he added, as the hapless woman opened her eyes languidly, "here is good news for you;—a reprieve, dearest—a reprieve!"

"For you?" she exclaimed.

"No, better far—'tis for you."

"I'll not accept it, then," she exclaimed, throwing her arms round the neck of her husband.

"Not accept it?"

"No," she replied, "if the life of one must be sacrificed, dear Jonathan, we will die together. I will not—cannot survive you. We will die, as the judge told us we should, together."

"But our neighbours have sent a petition to him in your behalf, and he has mercifully sent you a reprieve."

"Rather call his act one of cruelty," answered the wife, "for he could not have afflicted a greater torture upon me than by sparing my life when yours is to be sacrificed. But his pardon is offered to me in vain, for I would rather perish with you to-morrow than drag on a miserable existence with the harrowing thought that both were innocent of the crime charged against them, yet one must needs perish by an ignominious death."

"I beg pardon for interfering," exclaimed the sergeant, "but here is the pardon, signed by the judge, and it's more than the sheriff dare do to hang you after that."

"Then tear up the paper," she cried, scarcely knowing what she said; "tear it up, I say, for rather would I die ten thousand deaths than live to mourn the loss of a husband who, I know, to be the victim of a terrible error on the part of his accusers."

"But your dying would do your husband no good."

"It may do him no good," replied the unhappy wife, "but I shall at least be spared the agony of having to reproach myself in future for preferring to prolong my own existence after having vowed to perish with him on the scaffold. Let them grant the same indulgence to him that they to me, and I will change places with him, or become the veriest drudge the world e till death, in any shape, comes to release me from my misery."

"Nay, my dear Ann," exclaimed Bradford, "you ask that which there is no possibility of granting."

"Do you ask me to live, then?"

"If you would not add to my regret at leaving this world," he replied, "do not forget that you are a mother, and that our children will need all the care and attention you can bestow upon them. Go, then, dearest wife, go. Wipe the tears of grief and sadness from their young eyes, and if a heartless world would reproach them for the past, tell them how innocent their father was, and say that he perished unjustly by an ignominious doom."

"Would you break my heart, Jonathan," she asked, "by insisting upon that which I am so loath to do?"

"You must not forget," he replied, "that you have a solemn duty to perform to others as well as to myself. Our children are too young to be thrown upon the world, and should evil befal them hereafter, think how they will reproach their mother, who, but for her own wilfulness, might have been spared to shield and protect them from the evils which afterwards befel them."

"Alas," she sighed, "it is hard to choose when thus called upon by a double duty."

"It may be hard," answered Bradford; "but the reprieve has been granted, and no persuasion or entreaties of yours will prevail upon the judge to alter it."

"That is what I feared," she replied; "but nothing can prevent me dying of a broken heart, when you are taken from me."

"Nay, think better of it," exclaimed her husband, "and reconcile yourself to a destiny that nothing can avert. Will it not be some consolation to know that you are spared for the performance of one of the greatest duties that falls to the lot of a mother—that of rearing her children in the paths they ought to follow through life?"

"They will not be friendless,' she replied, "whilst my father lives to afford them his protection."

"But his days, I fear, will be but few; and even should he live, we may expect from what we saw of him just now, that he will linger on in a state of hopeless madness. All these things are to be remembered, Ann; and, upon cooler reflection, I am sure you will not disobey the almost last wish of your husband I look to you as the assertion of my innocence when I am gone; and there is a ray of satisfaction in that thought which, like a shooting star, o'erleaps the grave, and seems to lift me at once to the topmost pinnacle of hope and happiness!"

"Can you talk of happiness," she asked, "when about to leave the world with a foul brand of infamy upon your name?"

"When I know the brand is undeserved," answered Bradford, "I can submit to the temporary degradation without uttering even so much as a murmur. It is not so, however, with conscious guilt, for the heart then shrinks from the trrrible doom, and the culprit feels that his name will be handed down with well-merited obloquy and contempt. You, however, and other friends will still remain true to me; and I feel assured that my memory will not be suffered to remain under the stigma that is at present attached to it."

"Alas!" sighed the unhappy wife, "who will believe my assertions of your innocence, when it is not likely to be forgotten that I was tried as a participator in the crime?'

"You look upon the worst side of the question," exclaimed her husband, "without thinking there is something far more favourable likely to turn up in your favour. In the course of time, and that too I believe before long, circumstances may transpire to show who the real culprit was, and then at least you will have the satisfaction of knowing that justice has been done to the memory of your dead husband."

"And what satisfaction will that be," cried Mrs. Bradford, "when you will have been sacrificed to the cruel prejudice of those who brought against you the charge of murder?"

"Ay," exclaimed the prisoner, "that was indeed a most unfortunate prejudice, and yet I can attach no blame upon my accuser, seeing that everything concurred to throw upon me the suspicion of having committed the accursed deed. The still recking knife was in my hand, and the watch of the murdered man in my possession, and these two circumstances combined together, were sufficient to form a fair conclusion that I was the perpetrator of the act which had just been committed beneath my roof. Then I became the victim, and now that judgment of death has been passed upon me, I must pay the dreadful penalty, whilst the real criminal escapes the doom he so well merits."

"Can you form no notion of who was likely to have done it?" asked Sergeant Sam, who was still in attendance.

"No," he replied, "I have taxed my memory to the utmost, but the only persons I suspect are two strangers who slept at our house on the night of the murder."

"You mean the two chaps, I suppose, that were brought forward as evidence against you?"

"I do."

"And have you never mentioned your suspicions to any one?"

"I have," replied Bradford, "but both of them were witnesses on my trial, and notwithstanding the severe cross-examination they underwent, their testimony remained unshaken."

"Ah!" exclaimed the sergeant, "they swear to being asleep at the time when the murder must have taken place. And a very ingenious excuse it was too, for, of course, they could know nothing of the matter, and it was impossible for your counsel to make them contradict anything they had said before. I shall, however, make some inquiries about the fellows, for I'll be bound their character w n't bear much looking into, and if I can only find a loophole to begin with I'll set about my work in such good earnest that they shall be made to give a better account of themselves than they have hitherto thought proper to do."

"Your well-meant endeavours will come too late, my good fellow," answered Jonathan Bradford, "for the time which is left me in this world is drawn into a very narrow compass; so narrow, indeed, that with all your exertion you cannot hope to effect the kind object you have in view."

"Well, nothing is to be done without trying," exclaimed Sergeant Sam, "and I'm not a fellow to be damped because a few difficulties are in my way. I shall set-to presently in good earnest; and who knows after all what may be the upshot of it? Perhaps with a little exertion I may be able to fix this crime upon the right shoulders, and restore you to your wife and family."

"Ah!" cried Mrs. Bradford, "will you indeed exert yourself to save my husband from this dreadful doom?"

"If I didn't I should never deserve to have a good turn done to me if I should ever want it," replied the sergeant.

"Wife, wife!" exclaimed Bradford, "I am afraid you are indulging in a hope that will prove illusive. Accept, then, the liberty that has been offered you, and I feel assured that for years to come you will not forget me. Go, Ann, leave me, and may Heaven watch over and protect you and our children from future harm."

"Mother—dear mother, come home with us!" cried the children, in a tone of piteous entreaty.

"Do you not hear them, Ann?" asked her husband. "They call upon you to go home with them, and surely you will not suffer them to call upon you in vain."

"Nay, my duty bids me stay here with you."

"And why should you do so," asked her husband, "when even if it were permitted, to die with me were vain, whilst to live for those you should love and protect, were noble? Go, then, and remember 'tis my last command."

"And never till now did you see me unwilling to obey your commands," she replied. "But your commands shall be complied with, though my own heart should break in making the sacrifice."

"You will return home with the children, then?"

"I will," answered the sorrowing wife, with a deep-drawn sigh; "and yet what a melancholy home shall I find it when you are not there to cheer and console me!"

"The children will demand all your care and attention," returned Jonathan Bradford, "and for my sake you must not forget the duty you are imperatively called upon to perform It may not be easy, perhaps, to forget the many, many happy days we have lived together, but do not repine at my death, since you may rest assured that the time will come when my innocence will be made manifest, even to those who are now loudest in the assertions of my supposed guilt."

"And what greater affliction," she asked, "can befal me than to know that you have perished unjustly?"

"Ay," he replied, "it is indeed to be regretted by those I leave behind, but to myself there is some consolation in knowing that my name will not always be branded with infamy. Leave me, ████ dearest wife—leave me now, I implore you, for my hours in this world are few, and ████ spend them in preparing for that awful change that I am doomed to undergo."

The moment for parting having arrived, the heart-broken wife could no longer support herself, and with a groan of unutterable agony, she sank fainting in her husband's arms. Taking advantage of this opportunity, the prisoner resigned her to the care of Sergeant Sam, and in a few moments afterwards Jonathan Bradford was left alone in the solitude of his miserable cell.

CHAPTER XII.

JONATHAN BRADFORD RECEIVES AN EXTRAORDINARY VISIT.—A FRIEND IN NEED.—THE ESCAPE.—THE CRYPT BENEATH THE CHURCH.—ARRANGEMENTS ARE MADE FOR THE FUTURE.

ABSORBED in the intensity of his own thoughts, Bradford remained for more than half an hour unconscious of everything except the pitiable condition to which he had been reduced. It is true, death in any other form would have had no terrors that he was not prepared to encounter; but the recollections of his wife and children still preyed heavily upon his mind, and caused a heaviness of spirit, that he found it impossible to shake off. At length his attention was arrested by a noise in the thatched roof over head, and sometimes he even fancied that he could hear his own name pronounced in a cautious whisper, as if some person from without were endeavouring to draw his notice towards him. The notion, however, was so improbable, that Jonathan would not venture to indulge it; and, throwing himself upon the bench, which served for a seat, he was about to turn his thoughts to other subjects, when the sound became louder; and raising his eyes he perceived that a large hole had been made in the roof, through which a rope was put, which soon reached to within a foot or two of the ground. Amazed at this, the prisoner started from his seat, and, upon hearing his name again pronounced, demanded who it was that spoke to him.

"Tell me first whether you are quite alone?" said the same subdued voice that had spoken before.

"I am," he replied; "but who is it that speaks, and why has this ill-timed visit been paid me?"

"'Tis I—Jack Rackbottle."

"Then fly ere it be too late," exclaimed the prisoner; "for, if you should be discovered, a severe punishment will follow."

"What do I care for the punishment if I can only contrive to get you out of this scrape?" demanded Jack, who, by this time, had let himself down by the rope which he had previously secured to the roof. "So far, master, I have managed the affair without anybody being the wiser, and it will be your own fault if you are found here in the merning when the hour for the execution arrives."

"My good fellow, I understand you not."

"You dont!" exclaimed the other; "then I'll endeavour to make myself understood. Of course I needn't ask if you would not rather live than be hung up to-morrow morning like a dog?"

"I would, indeed," answered Jonathan; "but as no choice is left I must e'en submit to my sad fate."

"Then I can only say all my trouble has been thrown away," answered Jack Rackbottle; "for I fancied it was quite possible to get you out of this place, and had made such preparations for it, that I thought it quite unlikely we should fail."

"Are you sure nobody has watched you here?"

"Quite," he replied; "for the men that were set to watch this place are now enjoying themselves over a mug or two of ale at the public house, and as for Sergeant Sam, I saw him just now taking your wife and little ones home. So we are safe for an hour at least, and in that time you may get to a place where no one will ever think of looking for you,"

"What place is there in this neighbourhood," demanded Jonathan, "where I should have a chance of eluding the strict search that would be made after me?"

"Will you be satisfied if I tell you that I know of a spot where you will be ▓▓▓ for at least a week to come?"

"I am satisfied of your fidelity, my good fellow," answered Bradford, "but am also certain that no effort would be spared to place me once more in custody."

"But you don't know yet the place where I thought of taking you."

"True, but I am certain so rigid a search would be made that an immediate discovery must follow."

"Nothing is impossible to a willing mind," answered Jack, "or I should not have found means to get into this place."

"But you may have been observed."

"I'm sure no one saw me," replied the other, "for I kept my eyes open, and when every thing seemed to be quite safe, I cut a hole through the thatched roof with a hay knife that I had brought with me. The rope you see will just serve your turn to a nicety, so that instead of dying by one, it will be the means of saving your life."

"You speak as you wish, my good fellow," answered his master, "but I have too many difficulties in the way to make an attempt which I am sure must fail."

'Won't you try to escape then?"

"Escape!—no, no, no—why should I flee like a coward when I know my own entire innocence?"

"Because innocence won't save you now that the sentence has been passed," replied Jack. "Almost all the people about here believe that you murdered the old gentleman, and only think, dear master, what a terrible thing it is to die for a crime that has been committed by some one else."

"There is at least one consolation in knowing that you believe me to be innocent of this dreadful act."

"I'm sure of it," replied Jack Rackbottle, "or I would not have taken all this trouble to get you off. You are innocent, master, and there may be some consolation in knowing that you are so, but for all that they'll hang you in the morning unless you take my advice and get away from this place as soon as you can."

"Alas! where could I hope to find concealment?"

"In the crypt under the church."

"The crypt!"

"Yes," answered Jack, "it ain't a very pleasant place I know to be in by oneself, but then you have a clear conscience of your own, and any port in a storm rather than the certainty of dying on the gallows."

"But that place among others would be sure to undergo a strict search when it is discovered that I have escaped."

"Take my word for it master, that no one will ever think of looking for you there," he replied. "Besides, the experiment is worth trying at any rate; and if you would but conceal yourself among the tombs there for a short time, I think I could manage to bring to light the man that really committed the murder you have been unjustly condemned to die for. Only think of that sir, and that you might then return to the inn to my poor misses and the dear children that must otherwise be fatherless in a few hours."

"What reason have you for supposing that the real assassin may be discovered?" asked Bradford, eagerly.

"Why, I didn't want to tell you about it just yet, sir," answered the other; "but the truth is, I've a notion that I could name the fellow that killed poor old Mr. Hayes."

"Indeed! who is he?"

"I suppose I mustn't keep the secret to myself any longer," replied Jack Rackbottle, "so I'll tell you at once that I've a strong suspicion against one of the two strangers that slept at your house on the night of the murder."

"Ha! why may they not have both been concerned in it?"

"Because I find that one is a poor simpleton that is made a mere cat's paw of by the other."

"Which one do you suspect?"

"The one that called himself Squire O'Connor, from Kilkenny," replied Jack. "There's ro guery in every look of him, and so others besides myself think, now that he is suspected, since he is thought to have committed a robbery a little while ago, at the farm-house of Mr Brown, at Frogmore."

"But they were never seen in this neighbourhood till the night when they slept at my house."

"There you are mistaken," replied Jack, "for some of the people hereabouts recollect seeing 'em lurking about the place some few days before, and it was then thought they were here for no good purpose. Besides, it's pretty well known that the chap I'm speaking of goes by two names —that is, Dan Macraisy, alias Squire O'Connor; and if that ain't a case of strong suspicion against him, I don't know what is."

"Have they been suffered to escape?" asked Bradford.

"They've not been laid hold of yet," replied the other; "but they are supposed to be still lurking about the neighbourhood, and some say they have disguised themselves in some queer way, though nobody knows exactly how. But let that be as it may, a reward is to be offered for their apprehension, so that, I dare say, they'll soon be laid hold of; and then, perhaps, we may be able to discover whether one of them was not guilty of the murder that Lawyer Dozey has so unjustly laid upon your shoulders."

"It was most unfortunate that he should have done so," answered Bradford; "and yet, serious as the consequences have been to myself, I do not believe that he was actuated by any unworthy motives. All circumstances, indeed, concurred to throw suspicion upon me; and as I was unable to show any probable grounds by which to prove that the charge was ill-founded, the jury had no other course than to return their verdict according to the evidence they had heard."

"That may be all very true, master," exclaimed Jack Rackbottle; "but you ought not to let this opportunity slip, when you have it in your power to escape, and may keep yourself out of sight till we discover who it was that killed poor old Mr. Hayes."

"Your sympathy, my good fellow, deserves all my gratitude," replied his master; "but it would be an act of madness to attempt to escape, when I know the certainty of a failure. Indeed, I have made up my mind to meet my fate with calmness and resignation, so that it may be said the bitterness of death has already passed away."

"Ah, sir!" exclaimed Jack; "but only think of the sufferings of your poor wife and the two little ones."

"Believe me, I think of them," replied Jonathan, "and for a time, the thought of their sufferings drove me almost to madness.—I have, however, seen the uselessness of repining at that which cannot be avoided, and had therefore resolved to meet my doom manfully under the certainty that my innocence will soon be proved, and that then my name will no longer be branded with shame and ignominy."

"But why not leave this place, when I have made all right for your concealment for some days to come?"

"For that I am most grateful to you," answered the convict, "but of what use would it be for me to escape, when I know that every effort will be made to discover the place of my retreat?"

"Why, at all events, it would be worth trying," he replied, "and especially when I tell you that the crypt is the last place they will ever think of searching. Indeed, nobody ever goes there, for the people here are very superstitious, and it would be no easy matter to persuade any one to go down there, even if there were ever so great a certainty of your being discovered. Then, if you like it, misses might go and see you there, and nobody need know anything about it, because I could contrive to take her when every one in the place was fast asleep, and not thinking of what was going on.'

"Would that I had known of this a little sooner," exclaimed Bradford, "for then might I have taken her advice how to act in a case of so great an emergency."

"Well," replied the other, "I wish it had been so, for I'm sure she would have persuaded you to take the only chance that I can see of escaping the fate they intend for you to-morrow. Poor creature!—they have spared her life at any rate, and I can't help thinking that ought to be the greater reason why you should do all in your power to save your own whilst there is a chance left."

"Alas! I see none."

"At any rate there can be no harm in trying."

"Except that my attempting to escape will confirm my guilt."

"I should like to know who wouldn't do the same thing if they were placed in such a situation as you are," exclaimed Jack Rackbottle. "Every man has a right to save his own life if he has only got the chance, and you have not such a bad one, if you will but follow up what I have begun."

"Yet of what value can life be when name and character are both gone?"

"Dont I tell you that I believe that it won't be difficult to fix the crime upon the right person?" asked the other. "Besides, misses, poor creature, ought to be thought of, and especially as she will be left to struggle with the world for her poor dear children."

Jonathan Bradford made no immediate reply to this, for his mind was occupied with a thousand conflicting thoughts, and his resolution began at last to give way to the homely arguments of the humble friend who had been left to him in the midst of his heavy afflictions. At length, unconscious of what he was saying, he muttered to himself—

"Heaven seems to speak to me in the voice of this honest lad, and something now whispers to me, that something might indeed be done to prove my innocence if a brief period only could be gained to collect the requisite evidence; he reminds me, too, of my wife and children, and the sufferings they must endure should they be deprived of him to whom they have to look up for the support they so much need. I will—I will attempt my escape, for something seems to whisper to my soul, that all hope has not yet abandoned me. Yes, I will obey its dictates, and trust to Heaven for that aid which alone can rescue me from my present misery and despair."

"I'm glad to hear you say that, master, at any rate," exclaimed Jack, "for whatever may come of it, the attempt is worth making; so follow me up the rope, and in a quarter of an hour I will take you to a place where, I hope, you will be safe till we have found out who it was that did the deed you have been condemned for."

Placing a table underneath the aperture which he had made in the roof, Jack Rackbottle tried the strength of the rope, in order that no accident might occur to defeat the object he had in view; and then climbing up he made a careful examination round the spot to convince himself that no one was near to watch what was going on. Then having satisfied himself that all was safe, he in a whisper called upon his master to follow him, and then, reaching down to the full extent of his arm, afforded no little assistance towards rendering the ascent of Jonathan Bradford tolerably easy and safe. This being accomplished, they both of them remained seated on the roof some few minutes while they looked about them; and when at length they were assured that no fear of a discovery was to be apprehended, Jack pulled up the other end of the rope, and let it down gently on the outside of the building, so as to afford the means of reaching the ground without noise or danger. As on the former occasion, the young man was the first to try the strength of the rope, and having succeeded in effecting a safe landing, he was immediately followed by his master, and both of them then prepared to complete a project which had so far succeeded to the utmost of their hopes.

"It's all right, you see, master," whispered Jack; "there's not a soul near the place; and if we only mind what we are about we shall reach the church without being interrupted."

"Unless any person is watching us that we don't see," answered Jonathan, in the same low tone.

"Depend upon it, there's no fear of that," returned the other; "for if we had been seen, an alarm would have been raised before now. So don't be afraid of anything. and I'll answer for it we shall get to the place we want without being interfered with."

"But if we should fail, I tremble to think of what would be the consequences to yourself, my good fellow."

"Oh, never think of me," exclaimed Jack, "for it's a good cause that I'm engaged in; and if anything wrong should happen, I shall only be sorry on your account. But we are losing time, and every moment that's wasted is only adding to your danger."

"Having gone so far, it is too late to think of turning back," replied Bradford; "though it must be confessed I already repent having yielded to your earnest solicitations."

"Then you forget your wife and family?"

"Indeed, it is on their account, and not for any selfish consideration, that I have consented to take this step," replied the convict. "Had it not been for them, I would have remained in my cell, and calmly awaited the doom to which I have been sentenced."

"And if you had done that," exclaimed Jack, "poor missis and the young ones, would soon have died of grief. As it is, however, there's every chance of your getting off, and then only think how happy that will make 'em for the rest of their days."

On a sign being given to that effect, Jack Rackbottle moved cautiously until they had crossed the road, and then entering a field they crept along under the shadow of a hedge so as to avoid all chance of being seen. In this way they at length reached the church-yard, where they again paused to ascertain that they were still unobserved. A few minutes' examination was sufficient to convince them that, so far, they had nothing what-ever to fear, and without venturing to speak another word the guide pointed in the direc-tion he was about to take, and after gliding stealthily from one tomb-stone to another they reached the wall of the chancel, from the bottom of which Jack, with very little diffi-culty, removed a large square stone, which it was evident he knew before-hand was loose. On displacing this an aperture was discovered sufficiently large to admit the passage of either of their bodies, and the guide, being himself the first to crawl into it, made a sign for his companion to imitate his example with as little noise as possible. Bradford was not long in doing this, and having passed through the opening he found himself in a place so profoundly dark that he could not see a yard in advance of him in any direction except towards the hole which had afforded the means of ingress.

"Is this the place," he asked, with a slight shudder, "where I am to find the concealment you promised?"

"Yes," replied Jack, "this is the crypt I told you of, and though it ain't quite so comfor-table as the parlour of the George Inn, it's a great deal better in my opinion than the quarter you've just left."

"Is there no other entrance than the one we come in by?" asked Jonathan Bradford in the same low tone as before.

"Oh yes," he replied, "there's a door that leads into an adjoining vault that's more than half filled with coffins, and over head is a trap-door that communicates with the chancel above. You may sometimes hear the old sexton moving about perhaps, but don't let that alarm you, for he's never so much at home as when wandering about the church that he has been connected with ever since he was a boy."

THE CELL OF JONATHAN BRADFORD AND HIS WIFE

" Does he ever come into this place?"

" Never by any chance," replied Jack, "for funerals never take place in this crypt, so that he feels no interest in coming here. However, you are sure to hear him whenever he visits the church, for the old gentleman is troubled with a terrible asthma, and his cough will always give you fair notice when it's time for you to be quiet. '

' You seem to know this place, Jack, as well as the habits of the old man you are speaking of."

No. 11.

"That's very true, master," he replied, "and it's not to be much wondered at when I tell you that as a boy I often used to come here and spend hours at a time. It was a curious fancy you'll say, but I happened to discover the loose stone at the place were we entered just now, and from that time there was scarcely a week passed but what I spent some hours here by myself."

"Then you have not the same superstitious fear that most people feel at being so near the dead?"

"I don't know what it is to be afraid, sir," answered Jack, "and somehow I had a strong notion of being alone when other boys of my own age were thinking of nothing but play."

"Did you never tell any one of the entrance you discovered?"

"Not I," replied Jack, "for if I had done that I should never have had my favourite hiding-place to myself again. So you may make up your mind that no one will come to disturb you except myself, and I shall only visit you late at night when no one's likely to see me, and just to bring what food is needful for your support."

"Don't make too sure of that, my good fellow," exclaimed Bradford, "for I'm afraid my too selfish regard for my own safety will involve you in more trouble than I thought for."

"What trouble can I get into?"

"Why," answered his master, "a full inquiry will be made into all the circumstances connected with my escape, and I see nothing to prevent a discovery of the share you have had in snatching their victim from the fate that was intended."

"I shall take care to look out for that," exclaimed Jack, "and if there should be any danger, it will be easy enough for me to come here and take up my quarters along with you."

"In which case we must both starve together."

"Oh, there won't be any fear of that, whilst Sally knows where to find us," he replied. "She's to be depended on, and the good-hearted soul would not mind risking her life for the sake of serving either her master or myself. However, I don't think anybody will ever suspect me of having anything to do with your escape, and if they don't I shall set myself about the task of looking for this Dan Macraisy, alias Squire O'Connor, who, I have no doubt, is the man that ought to have been sentenced to be hanged instead of yourself."

"Have you mentioned your suspicion to any person?"

"Not yet, sir," he replied, "but I suppose I must, for fear he should find means to escape his deserts."

"Under any circumstances," exclaimed Bradford, "you must be very careful how you proceed in this business, or your design will be frustrated, when success seems to be most certain. Besides, if this man is what you expect, he is a desperado of the first magnitude, and would not hesitate to take the life of him who first turned the suspicion against him."

"Depend upon it, master, I shall not give away a chance," he replied, "for I pretty well know the sort of chap I have to deal with, and my inquiries about him shall be so carefully managed, that he shall not know anything about what I'm doing till all is ready to clap hands on him. And when that's the case, I'll have plenty of assistance ready to prevent his escaping from justice; and then there'll be a reprieve for you at any rate, till the magistrates have looked into the affair to see whether I'm right or not."

"Upon what foundation do you suspect him?"

"Why, in the first place, I'm sure it was not you that murdered poor old Mr. Hayes," he replied.

"But that don't prove him to be the assassin."

"I know it don't prove anything," answered Jack Rackbottle, "but if we once lay hold of the fellow, there's no knowing what may turn up to prove all we want to know. A guilty conscience may force him to make a confession, or we may find something upon him that will fix him with the crime that has been falsely laid to you."

"All this is well-intended, my good fellow," exclaimed Bradford, "but I feel no hope that your exertions will serve to place me in a better position than the one I am now in. Indeed, I already regret that I left the cell without considering the whole affair more fully.

"And if you hadn't followed my advice, to-morrow would have been a bitter day for your wife and children."

"Ay," he replied, "that was the thought that urged me to take a step that I am already sorry for."

"Why should you be sorry, when you may remain here in safety till the right person has been taken?"

"Because the moment my escape is known it will be said that, if anything was wanted to confirm my guilt it was that I fled from the justice that ought to have overtaken me."

"It may be all very well for people to say so," answered Jack, "but where's the man, I should like to know, that would stay to be hanged whilst he had a chance of getting his freedom? Besides, it will soon be known that some one else besides yourelf is suspected, and then we shall see whether this Macraisy is not believed by all to be the most likely of the two to have committed the murder. Then there's something to be said for Mrs. Bradford, who will be a good deal comforted when she hears that you have contrived to escape from the fate that was intended for you to-morrow."

"She already knows my innocence," answered Jonathan, "for I was in the bar with her at the very moment when the alarm was first raised by Mr. Hayes."

"That may be," exclaimed the other, "but I should say it's all the worse for her to know that you were accused wrongfully. At any rate she'll be glad enough to hear that you have escaped from the cell; and only think how grateful she'll feel to-morrow when the fatal hour passes and she knows that her husband still lives."

"She will not be more grateful for my escape," replied Jonathan. "than I feel towards the man who has made so generous an exertion in my behalf. You may, however, rest assured that if all ends well, I shall not forget to reward my preserver in any way that he may think proper to propose."

"At any rate you'll not be taxed very heavily," exclaimed Jack, "for I shall only ask you to persuade Sally to be my wife, and then I shall be one of the happiest fellows in the world."

"I thought you were already her accepted lover?"

"So I am," he replied, "but then she takes-on so about this affair of your's, that she desires me never to say another word to her upon the subject of marriage unless you and misses get out of your present trouble. Mrs. Bradford, it is true, has been lucky enough to receive a free pardon, but I'm afraid that won't do unless you get off as well. So you see, I had my own turn to serve, though I believe I should have been just as anxious to save your life even if it had not been for what Sally has said to me. At all events, I've done my best to serve you, sir; and if you'll only remain here a little while, I may perhaps bring some news that you'll be glad to hear."

"Having gone so far I shall remain under your hands till I see the prospect you have raised up begins to fade away," answered his master. "You have therefore my permission to take any steps you please in this affair; and all I ask for in return is, that you will confide to your mistress the secret of my hiding-place."

This Jack Rackbottle faithfully promised to do; and having arranged a few more matters with his master, he left the crypt, and replacing the stone in its former position hastened back to the inn, to inform Mrs. Bradford of the glad tidings he was charged with.

CHAPTER XIII.

DAN MACRAISY AND CALEB ARE DRIVEN TO THE LAST EXTREMITY.—APPEARANCE OF AN IMMEDIATE DISSOLUTION OF PARTNERSHIP.—A REWARD OFFERED FOR THE AP-PREHENSION OF A ROBBER.—THE VAULT OF DEATH.—JACK RACKBOTTLE IS IN FULL PURSUIT.

NOTWITHSTANDING the conviction of Jonathan Bradford, and the awful sentence o death which had been passed upon him in consequence, the fears of Dan Macraisy fo his own safety were as strong upon him as ever. Caleb wondered what it could all mean, but he was answered so sharply on one or two occasions when he ventured to ask a question on the subject, that he forbore to speak about it any more, and contented himself with the determination to cut his present connection as soon as possible. But if his wonder had been already excited by the altered manners of his comrade, it was raised to a still higher pitch when Dan, with much mystery, informed him that there was some danger of their both being taken up for a robbery which had been committed a short time before, and proposed that they should disguise themselves as a couple of rat-catchers, a change which Macraisy informed him could be easily effected, as he had just purchased the clothes and necessary impliments for the trade of a couple of men with whom he had fallen in at a public-house. Caleb would have scouted this proposition but for the muttered threats of his comrade, and proceeding with him to a barn not far off, they soon transformed themselves so completely as to afford every chance of avoiding recognition. Being thus attired, they concealed the clothes they had just taken off, and then leaving the barn, strolled towards the village and entered the churchyard, as the bell was tolling heavily for some person who was about to be consigned to the earth. Dan Macraisy looked about him with an uneasy glance of one who expected every moment to be pounced upon, but Caleb, who had no such thought, only gave way to his vexation at the shifts to which they had both been put.

"This is a very pretty set out," he muttered, "to throw away one's own decent clothing, and appear as a couple of rat-catchers, when neither of us know our business, even if we were to get a job in our new line. But I'll not carry this mummery any further, for I mean to give up your company as soon as possible."

"What are you grumbling about now?" demanded the other, who had only heard a few words of what he had said.

"Why, I'm not satisfied with the way we're going on," replied Caleb. "Here am I disguised as a miserable rat-catcher just to serve your own purposes, though I hardly know what they are."

"Psha! what is it to you if I choose to travel incog?"

"You may travel incog, or in anything else you please," answered the other, "but I'm a respectable London apprentice, and have been advertised for by my affectionate master to return home, when all faults are to be forgiven."

"Nonsense! would you go and work like a slave?"

"To be sure I would, Mr. Macraisy," he replied, "for trade is honourable when it's fairly carried on, and I wish to dissolve partnership with your firm as soon as possible, and to return like the prodigal son to my worthy old master in Seven Dials."

"Then you are an ungrateful scoundrel for your pains."

"How am I ungrateful?"

"Why, after all my lessons and careful training, you have not done one clever trick since we have been together. You haven't so much as decently picked a pocket, though I've showed you how it ought to be done a dozen times. How are you ever to pay me for your board and education, I should like to know?"

"Board! why, I've been regularly starved ever since I've had the misfortune to be with you," exclaimed Caleb Scrimmidge. "An empty watch-case has as much inside it as I have; and as for your careful training, as you call it, I begin to see that I should have been a great deal better off if I had never had the misfortune to meet with you."

"What the devil have you got to grumble about?"

"Why, everything, according to my way of looking at things. Ain't people hunting all over the neighbourhood to find us? and if we fall into their hands shan't we stand a chance of being transported, or perhaps hanged?"

"Nonsense! it's only me they are looking after."

"So you'd like to persuade me," answered Caleb; "but a man is always judged by the sort of company he keeps, and I'm thinking they'll reckon me no better than yourself, when it's known we have been so much together of late. Besides, to tell you my mind plainly, Mr. Macraisy, I don't at all like the dishonest vagabond sort of life you wish me to lead."

"And why shouldn't you like it as well as myself?"

"Because it don't agree with my notions; and I don't care how soon you and I dissolve our partnership accounts."

"Ho! ho! that's it, is it, my fine fellow?" exclaimed Dan. "Haven't I sacrificed my own inclinations to consult yours in everything? Didn't I try to set you up in a respectable profession?—and ain't you now a gentleman rat-catcher on your own account? But you are ungrateful, Caleb, and all my kindness has been thrown away upon you."

"Talking about rat-catching," returned Caleb Scrimmidge, "I wonder what my friends in Seven Dials would say if they were to see me in this precious plight?"

"Do you call this a plight?" demanded the other; "why, it was the only way left us to get out of an awkward dilemma."

"Very likely," replied the other; "but the long and short of it is, I never had any genius for rat-catching; and they seem to know it, too, for when I used to try to catch the rats that swarmed my old master's cellar they seemed to know that I was afraid of 'em, and would sit grinning at me like so many apes."

"I'll just tell you what it is, Mr. Caleb Scrimmidge," exclaimed his companion, "I'm threatened with danger, and can't stand upon trifles merely to humour your cowardly notions. You know of my breaking into the farmhouse last week, and though you would not have had the courage to join me in the affair, I've a notion that you might muster up courage enough to peach, and get me into trouble. But that won't do, my boy; so in order that you may be always under my own eye, I shall not consent to a dissolution of partnership till we get clear away from this place."

"May not I leave you when I please?"

"Certainly not," replied Macraisy.

"But suppose I take French leave?" he asked.

"Why, then you'll soon repent it," exclaimed the other, "for I shall keep my eyes open; and if you attempt to leave me without my permission, I shall send a brace of bullets after you that shall lay you as nicely by the heels as if you were stuck in a bag with your heels uppermost. You have never been of any use to me, Caleb, so that I shall not be very particular if you drive me to extremities."

"How would you expect me to be useful," asked Caleb, "when I was never brought up to this sort of roguery?"

"Well, if you have never been of any use to me, you may be of some now."

"In what way?"

"Why you can read, can't you?"

"Yes, I can do that tolerably well when hard words don't come in my way; and I suppose you can do as much as that?"

"No," answered Dan Macraisy, "learning is one of those effeminate superfluities that I have always despised, except just signing my own name, which every gentleman ought to be able to do."

"Will you have the kindness to tell me what you mean?"

"To be sure I will," replied Dan, pointing towards the church-door. "Do you see that bit of paper stuck up there?"

"I do."

"Well then, just have the kindness to read me what they say on that scrap of paper, for it strikes me at this distance off I can see the name of—"

"Dan Macraisy, alias O'Connor," exclaimed the other, reading the paper as he had been desired.

"Just say that over again, will you?"

"It's your name, that's all about it," exclaimed Caleb.

"Or some other gentleman who has been blackguard enough to borrow my name for some bad purpose. But go on, my boy; read—read it all, that I may know what's in the wind."

"They don't mean me by the alias, do they?"

"Nonsense! you are not even suspected," exclaimed Dan Macraisy, "so read the paper, and let me know the worst."

"I will," replied his companion, and again advancing towards the church-door, he read as follows—

"'One-hundred pounds reward for the apprehension of Dan Macraisy, alias O'Connor, alias &c., &c.; who it is suspected broke into the farm-house of Mr. Brown, at Frogmore, on the night of——'

"Enough!" exclaimed Dan, impatiently interrupting him.

"I suppose so," replied the other, "for it's your description exactly, and the next question is how you will ever be able to get yourself out of this bit of trouble."

"Oh, easily enough if I have any luck. I must put a bold face upon the matter, and shift the affair upon the shoulders of somebody else, if I can."

"Nonsense! how can you do that, Mr. Macraisy?"

"Only wait a bit, my good fellow," replied Dan, "and you shall see how cleverly I'll manage the affair. But hark! what means that horrible sound that thrills to my very heart?"

"What does it mean?" exclaimed the other; "why it's the church bell tolling for the funeral of Mr. Hayes."

"For the funeral of Mr. Hayes!" muttered Dan Macraisy, with a start of horror which, however, was not perceived by his companion.

"Yes," he replied, "like all other dead men, he must be put under ground; and from what I heard some country people say just now, his funeral may be expected to arrive here very soon."

"Coming here!" exclaimed the other, again starting as if the intelligence had struck him with consternation.

"Ay, this is the place where they are going to bury him."

"And what men are those that I see creeping about there for all the world like thief-takers?"

"I don't know who they may be," answered Caleb, looking in the direction which had been alluded to, "but if ever I saw police-officers in my life, they are some of them. Why what in the name of fortune can they be prowling here for?"

"Why, it's me they want, to be sure!" exclaimed Macraisy, scarcely conscious of what he said.

"You, Dan? Do you know 'em then?"

"To be sure I do."

"But what can they want you for?"

"How should I know, unless it's about that unlucky robbery that you were reading about just now."

"Well then, suppose I run and put 'em on a wrong scent the other way," exclaimed Caleb Scrimmidge, glad of any excuse to get out of the company of such dangerous society.

"No, you don't do anything of the kind," retorted the other, grasping him firmly by the arm.

"Why, what ails you all of a sudden?"

"Never mind what ails me," he replied, "but the long and the short of it is, I'll not trust to you."

"What are you going to do then?"

"Hide myself."

"Where?"

"Anywhere," replied Macraisy. "This sort of a rabbit's burrow will do, I suppose, till the coast is clear."

"In there!" exclaimed the other. "Why, that's the entrance into the old vault underneath the church."

"I know it is;—but we are both of us in danger, and must hide ourselves till the danger is over."

"You can do as you like about it, Mr. Macraisy," returned his companion, "but I no more dare go into that horrid dark place than I dare put a pistol to my own head."

"Psh!" ejaculated the other, "what is there to be afraid of? I have the means with me to procure a light, and then we may be as comfortable there as any where else."

"I tell you I can't go there; so if you are obstinate about it, you will have to go alone."

"Don't provoke me with this obstinacy of yours," exclaimed Dan Macraisy, "because I'm a desperate man, and am not to be trifled with without danger to yourself. This is no time to stand upon trifles, and as it don't seem that you are to be trusted, and if you won't follow me freely, I'll drag you into the vault by main force."

"Holloa!" exclaimed Caleb Scrimmidge, "don't you think, Mr. Macraisy, you are going it a leetle bit too strong?"

"I am compelled to be resolute," he replied.

"But you might be civil, I think."

"So I will, when I find you a little more tractable," exclaimed Dan Macraisy; "but I've a notion that you mean to sell me to those officers of justice, and sooner than be betrayed by a cowardly comrade, I'll shed your heart's blood this very moment."

"Upon my life, Mr. Macraisy you have formed a very wrong opinion of me, for I had no thought of doing you any harm."

"Then why did you want to sneak away from me?"

"Only to put the officers upon a wrong scent. I meant to tell 'em to look for you in some other direction, so as to give you an opportunity of hiding yourself somewhere."

"Wherever I go, you shall accompany me," exclaimed Dan Macraisy, "so dont think to play me any of your slippery tricks. Yonder vault is the only place that I can see to suit my purpose at a pinch like this, and there we must conceal ourselves till we have an opportunity of getting clear out of the neighbourhood."

"But they are going to bury Mr. Hayes there, and only think what a horrible thing it will be, to be shut up in a vault with the corpse of a man that has been murdered."

"Humph! you didn't murder him, did you?"

"No," replied Caleb, "thank goodness my conscience is quite clear as far as that goes; but then it's not long since we were in his company, and I should fancy every minute that he was going to rise from his coffin, to—to——"

"Well, what do you suppose he would do?"

"Ah!" exclaimed the other, "that's a question that I can't very well answer; but the truth of it is I have my misgivings, and if you would but excuse my going into the vault I should take it as a very great favour."

"I dare say you would," muttered Dan, "but this is no time for trifling, and for this once I'm determined to have my own way. Ain't the bill that you just now read on the church-door quite enough to convince you that we have no time to lose?"

"We?" exclaimed Caleb Scrimmidge; "what in the name of fortune have I to do with it?"

"That's what I want to know myself," answered the other. "Of course you have iso reason to be afraid, though I have good cause to suspect that if you once leave my nght, you would not be very scrupulous about fixing me with the robbery at Farmer Brown's."

"Upon my word I never had such a thought."

"I don't care whether you had or not," replied Dan Macraisy, "but there's nothing like preventing danger when one suspects there is any, and that's why I don't intend to let you leave my sight till I know there's a good opportunity for me to get clear off. When that's the case, you and I can take leave of each other; but you had better take care of what you are about, for though you may not think it, I shall constantly have my eye upon you; and upon the first appearance of any treachery, I shall know how to get rid of a treacherous enemy."

"Do you think me treacherous then?"

"I have a very strong suspicion of it," answered Macraisy.

"And yet I never gave you any cause to think that I would betray you."

"That may be all very true," replied the ruffian, "but there's nothing like taking care of oneself in good time. So you must make up your mind to keep me company in that vault yonder, or you'll know what to expect before we part."

"Ah!" exclaimed Caleb Scrimmidge as the church bell tolled, "they have started from the house, and the funeral procession will be here presently."

"Ay," answered the other, drawing a pistol from his pocket, "the funeral will come from that direction, and the officers of justice will come from the other, ready to pounce upon their victim. Quick man, quick, or you'll have little chance of living till you get inside of the vault. Ugh! there goes that horrible bell again; so enter before I'm forced to send a brace of bullets through your head!"

Much against his inclination, Caleb Scrimmidge entered the vault with his companion; and scarcely had they disappeared when Jack Rackbottle and Henry Dornton, the lover of Lucy Hayes, approached the spot which had just become vacant. They looked round them as if in search of some one; and having satisfied themselves that the coast was clear, Jack said in a whisper to his companion—

"I can't think what has become of the chap, sir; but from what I was told before we started, I made sure we should find him here."

"Him," exclaimed Dornton; "why don't you say them, when in my opinion one is quite as guilty as the other?"

"Because I think it will turn out that only one of 'em had any hand in the murder," answered Jack.

"And which do you believe to be the guilty man?"

"Why, the fellow that goes by two or three names," he replied. "When he came to my master's house he called himself Squire O'Connor, and talked very largely about some estates he had in Ireland; but since then I've heard that his real name is Daniel Macraisy; and if we are to believe all we hear, he is the man that broke into the house of Farmer Brown a few nights ago."

"But I suppose that is a mere matter of suspicion?"

"There's nothing to be said for certain, of course," answered Jack Rackbottle; "but when people speak as if there were almost a certainty about it, it makes me believe there must be some certainty in it. At any rate I should like to know where he's to be found, because the inquiries that are going on are likely to bring something to light."

"Have you no better reason to believe him to be the murderer of Mr. Hayes, than the bare fact of his having slept in the house on the night when the crime was committed?" asked the young man.

"That's one thing, sir," answered the other; "but then it mustn't be forgot that he is supposed to be the man that robbed Farmer Brown."

"Which supposition may be a groundless one," replied Henry Dornton; "and it is too hazardous an experiment to cause a man to be arrested for a crime that we cannot bring home to him by positive proof."

"Depend upon it if we lay hold of him it will not be long before we find something more against him," answered Jack; "and for my own part I could pretty well undertake to say that it was he, and not my master, that stabbed poor Mr. Hayes in his own bed-chamber."

"Can you give any sufficient reason for laying the crime to him?"

"I'm quite satisfied about it myself."

"On what grounds?"

"Why, Sally, our chambermaid, thinks so because the bed that Daniel Macraisy was to have occupied was not slept in at all that night."

"Is that the only evidence you have to produce?"

"I don't know what you may think of it, sir," answered Jack, "but in my opinion it has a very queer look with it. He pretended to be knocked-up with fatigue when he came to the house to ask for a bed, and yet it turns out after all that if he laid down it must have been on a sofa that happened to be in the room."

"Was there any communication between his chamber and the one that was occcupied by Mr. Hayes?"

"Oh, yes, it was easily to be reached by crawling along the parapet that led from one part of the house to the other."

"And you think that was done by the person we are speaking of?"

"There's very little doubt about it."

"Was he seen anywhere near the chamber of the murdered man when the crime was first discovered?"

"I believe not; but if he got there in the way I've mentioned, it was quite as easy for him to return to his own room by the same way that he had left it. Indeed, it was

remarked by everybody that this Macasy didn't appear to have been asleep, though he wanted to make all about him believe that he had just been woke up in a fright."

"Perhaps it was your anxiety for your master that made you think the act had been committed by some other person?"

"I was not present when the discovery took place," replied Jack Rackbottle, "so I only go by what other people told me; but by all accounts it was easy enough for this chap to have got into Mr. Hayes' room, if he were tempted by the money the old gentleman was well-known to have about him."

"Alas!" sighed Henry Dornton, "this terrible calamity might have been spared us, if Mr. Hayes would only have listened to the entreaties and remonstrances of his wife. But he slighted her warning, and through it his life has been sacrificed."

"I have been told, sir, that the lady had an ugly dream, on the night before he was to leave home."

"She had," answered the young man, "and though in most cases I am inclined to place little or no reliance in such superstitious notions, it must be admitted that in this instance, the warning was especially intended for the prevention of danger. Indeed, had he remained at home but a few hours longer, in all probability his life would have been spared from the fatal attempt that was made upon it."

"But I hope, sir, you don't believe that my master had any hand in the murder of the old gentleman?"

"If we may trust to the verdict of the jury it was he who struck the blow," replied Dornton, "and so far we have nothing else upon which we can place any reliance. At all events he was found in the room immediately after the crime had been committed—the knife with which the bloody-act had been perpetrated was in his hand—and, as if to place everything beyond a doubt, the watch of the murdered man was also found in his possession. These are all serious facts against him, and, as far as I am concerned, I can see no reason to believe that the verdict which has been pronounced was an unjust one."

"Only wait a little longer sir," exclaimed Jack Rackbottle, "and it shall be no fault of mine, if I don't clear my master's character and put the saddle on the right horse."

"If your surmise be right," returned the other, "it is to be hoped your exertions may prove successful; but it must be confessed that, as far as I am concerned, I do not yet see any reason to believe that the charge already made is an unjust one."

"But when a man—like this Dan Macraisy—goes under three or four different names, it looks as if he had some reason for being ashamed of his own."

"I grant there is sufficient ground for supposing that he bears an indifferent character," answered Henry Dorton; "but I have not yet heard any reason for believing that he is guilty of the crime for which your master has been doomed to suffer the highest penalty of the law."

"Then you really believe Mr. Bradford is guilty?" exclaimed Jack, in a half reproachful tone.

"He has had a fair trial, and having been found guilty upon tolerably clear evidence, we have a right to presume that the jury came to a very proper conclusion."

"Ay, sir," returned the other; "but jurymen are liable to make mistakes as well as other people; and, take my word for it, you'll by-and-by hear and see quite enough to satisfy you that my poor master had no more to do with this murder than you or I had."

"How happened it, then, that he was found in the room when the alarm was first given?"

"I don't know how that was," answered Jack Rackbottle, "but nothing will ever convince me that he was guilty; and it shall be no fault of mine if I don't discover al about how it was done before many hours are over."

"By which time your master will be no more."

"We shall see about that," replied the other, "for I have a notion that the real murderer will be discovered in time to save poor Mr. Bradford from the gallows."

"Perhaps you are aware that some favourable evidence is about to be produced?"

"I'm in hopes I shall be able to get some before long."

"Is it such that will throw any probable suspicion upon any other person or persons?" asked the young man.

"There's very little doubt of it," replied Jack; "but at present it might be dangerous to speak one's mind too freely upon the subject, so perhaps you'll excuse my saying more about it just now. Another hour or two may very likely make all the difference, and then I daresay you, as well as myself, will rejoice at seeing an innocent man saved from the fate that is deserved by another."

"I shall indeed be very glad if clear evidence can be obtained in favour of Jonathan

Bradford," answered the young man; "and you will therefore do well to continue your inquiries into the affair till something more decisive is known. For the present, however, I must leave you, for the bell warns me that I shall soon be wanted to follow the remains of my poor friend to the grave; and when that duty has been performed, I will see you once more upon this subject."

With this the young man departed, and Jack Rackbottle prepared to prosecute the designs he had in view.

CHAPTER XIV.

THE OLD VAULT PROVES TO BE ANYTHING BUT A COMFORTABLE ASYLUM.—DAN MACRAISY HITS UPON A RATHER EXTRAORDINARY EXPEDIENT.—A WRITTEN CONFESSION.—CALEB SCRIMMIDGE FINDS HIMSELF IN A VERY AWKWARD DILEMMA.—A SUDDEN AND UNEXPECTED APPEARANCE.—MATTERS BEGIN TO WAER A MORE FAVOURABLE APPEARANCE.

WE will now follow Dan Macraisy and his more simple-minded companion into the vault where the former hoped to find a refuge till the danger of which he was apprehensive was over. But the place, gloomy and dreary as it was, recalled to his mind a thousand dark and guilty thoughts which he could not reveal to Caleb; and seating himself upon a stone, he remained for some time gloomily meditating upon the risk to which he was exposed. As for Scrimmidge, his thoughts were all absorbed in the suspicious fears with which the place inspired him; every sound, however slight it might be, alarmed him, and occasionally he uttered exclamations of terror, which were, however, unheeded by Dan Macraisy, who was to much occupied with his own uneasy reflections, to pay any heed to the ejaculations of his timid companion.

"I'll tell you what it is, Dan," exclaimed the other unable at length to suppress his fear, "this dark, ugly-looking place ain't at all pleasant, and I shall be for cutting away from it presently, so you'll have no company, unless it is the ghosts that I every now and then hear gliding about, as if they were only watching for an opportunity to pounce upon us."

"What is the fool muttering about, now?" ejaculated Macraisy, glancing fiercely at his companion, by the assistance of a lamp with which they had provided themselves.

"I wasn't muttering about anything particular," answered the other, "but it would'nt be very wonderful if I did, for this place is worse than the shades in Covent Garden on a wet day, and I dont care how soon we leave it."

"Are you frightened?"

"To be sure I am," answered Caleb, "and it would be strange if I wasn't, for I see hobgoblins grinning at us in every corner, and even if they don't trouble us, there's the officers of justice upon the look out, and we may think ourselves fortunate if we don't fall into their hands. Wh—a—t's that?" he added turning round sharply. "I could have sworn I heard a noise out yonder; and only look yourself, Dan, and see if there ain't some one peeping at us from behind that pillar at the farther end of the vault."

"Ha! ha! ha!" laughed Macraisy; "was there ever such a cowardly fool seen! Why it's only your own shadow, Caleb, that has been frightening you out of your wits. Ha! ha! ha!"

"Don't laugh, Dan—pray don't, for I'm sure something terrible is going to happen to us!"

"Not laugh!" exclaimed the ruffian, "and why shouldn't I when there's nothing to be sad about?"

"Well, now, for my part, I think there is."

"And who cares for what you may think? Hav'nt I just given the double to the gallows hunters; and don't I know that they'll never think of looking for me here?"

"Ah! Dan, Dan!" exclaimed Caleb Scrimmidge, "you fancy you've done it all very cleverly, but take my word for it you have got people to deal with that won't be easily disappointed. There's that robbery at Frogmore that they are after you for, and you'll be hanged for it as sure as a gun !"

"Psha !" returned the other carelessly ; "what makes you fancy I shall be hanged ?"

"Because I can plainly see the gallows above your head, and the rope about your neck!"

"Ha, ha, ha ! I tell you again you are a fool."

"You're laughing again Dan, but I'm thinking you'll change your tone by-and-by, when my words come true.''

"That'll never be,'' answered Macraisy, "for the hemp will never be grown that's to make a halter for my neck. Did you ever see that funny fellow Punch, in the puppet-show ?"

"Yes, very often."

"Well, dont they conspire to hang him ?"

"I believe they do."

"And don't he contrive to stick the neck of somebody else in the noose instead of his own ?"

"He does Dan, and that's the part that always makes me laugh the most. Ha, ha, ha !"

"Faith !" exclaimed Macraisy, that's a very capital joke of Mr. Punch, and won't it be easy for me to do the same thing ?"

"But how is it to be done, Dan ?" asked the other, whose curiosity began to be somewhat excited.

"Sit down here by the side of me, my dear fellow," exclaimed Macraisy, "and I'll convince you how it may be done in the easiest manner possible. Take a seat, Caleb, for though there's a great difference between us, I'm not at all proud."

Scrimmidge did as he had been directed, and having seated himself by the side of Dan Macraisy, the latter took from his pocket some writing materials and placed them on a stone before his companion.

"Now," he said, "you see this bit of paper, and this pen and the ink bottle ?"

"Yes."

"Do you know what I'm going to do with 'em ?"

"Write, I suppose."

"No," replied Dan Macraisy ; "that's an accomplishment that was quite overlooked in my education. You, however, are a bit of a scholar, and can't you, with that great ugly fist of yours, write down the words I tell you ?"

"That'll depend upon what you want me to write."

"Oh, nothing that can do you any harm.," answered Dan Macraisy. "It's only a little bit of a confession just to see how the thing will read, if I should want to make use of it. Besides, I shall not forget to reward you for it by-and-by when something turns up to put me into cash again."

"If that's all, I don't mind obliging you," exclaimed the other. "So now for it— tell me what I've got to write down, and I'll do it in the most elegant style that I'm able."

"That's all right," answered Macraisy, "so now to begin with the beginning, write down the date—June 17th, 1736——"

"Well, that's put down, Mr. Macraisy."

"I do confess."

"Go on ?"

"That I alone, did break open the farmhouse of Mr. Brown, of Frogmore.

"Hilloa !" thought Caleb Scrimmidge, "why he's going to make a confession to have himself hanged, that I may get the three hundred pounds reward for his apprehension ! At any rate, he's grateful for what I've done, and this is a handsome way of rewarding me for my trouble."

"Have you written down all that I told you last ?" demanded Dan, after a pause.

"Yes, it's all down, and I'm ready to write anything more you have to tell me."

"By the powers !" exclaimed the ruffian with pretended pity, "I'm heartily sorry that poor Jonathan Bradford is going to be hanged for the murder."

"So am I," answered the other, "but I see no help for it now that he has been sentenced."

"There's only one way," exclaimed Dan Macraisy, "and I have been thinking now that if some solitary half-starved, poor devil of a fellow, for whom nobody in the world would care a straw, would confess that he was the chap that murdered this Mr. Hayes, Jonathan Bradford and his wife might be saved from their horrible fate."

"Can it be done, do you think?"

"It can and shall be done."

"Bless my heart!" thought Caleb to himself, "he's going to make a martyr of himself for the sake of poor Jonahan and his family. Hang me if I don't begin to think he's a better fellow than I at first took him for."

"Now then, go on," exclaimed Dan Macraisy, "and write down word for word as I tell you. Go on from where you left off with this :—I did the murder that another has been tried for. I stole from the casement of my own room to the chamber where Mr. Hayes was sleeping ;—I stabbed him in the struggle with a knife which lay on the table, and hearing footsteps when the alarm was raised, fled the way I had come. Jonathan Bradford is innocent. The murder was committed by my own hands."

"'Jonathan Bradford is innocent. The murder was committed by my own hands,'" muttered Caleb, as he wrote down the words. "How uncommonly like the truth all this reads!"

"Have you finished writing down all that I told you?" asked Dan Macraisy.

"Yes, every word," he replied, "and am only waiting for you to tell me what I'm to do next."

"Sign that paper!" exclaimed Macraisy, suddenly starting up from his seat.

"Very good —who's name am I to put to it?"

"Your own!'

"Mercy on us! What do you mean, Mr. Dan?"

"Exactly what I have said ;—sign your name to that confession, or I shall compe you."

"Sign my name to a written confession of murder!"

"Yes, it must be done, Caleb, but only as a *witness*, that's all.'

"But I dont choose to do it at all though," exclaimed the other, "for what would people think if they saw my name after such words as these ?—'The murder was committed by my own hands!' I dare say indeed! A pretty fool I should make of myself if I were to put my name to such a confession as that."

"Sign it, I say!"

"It's quite impossible," exclaimed Caleb Scrimmidge, "for I have lost my pen."

"Coward! You have dropped it," vociferated Macraisy, presenting a pistol at his head. "It is at your feet,—pick it up, and sign the paper instantly."

"What will become of me!" cried the other falling on his knees. "Did'nt I hear some one coming this way?"

"Idiot!" exclaimed the other stamping his foot furiously ;—"I'll have no evasion. Sign—or you know the consequence."

"Well then," replied Caleb despairingly; "just have the kindness to turn away that pistol and I'll sign—but the sight of that ugly looking weapon frightens me so that I could'nt keep my hand steady."

"Well, I'll put it out of sight then," answered Dan Macraisy, laying down the pistol on the further end of the stone. "Now then, put your name at the bottom of that bit of paper, or in less than two minutes you will be a corpse!"

Most reluctantly Caleb took up the pen, and was about to obey the command, when footsteps was heard rushing towards them, and in an instant Jonathan Bradford had snatched up the loaded pistol, and presenting it at the head of Macraisy, exclaimed in a tone of command—

"It is you, villain, that shall sign the confession, or your life will be instantly forfeited!"

Delighted at his unexpected deliverance, Caleb Scrimmidge could not help capering about with joy, whilst Macraisy, confounded by the suddenness with which he had been detected, glared round him with terror, and muttered —

"Fiends of darkness! what does all this mean? Jonathan Bradford here?"

"Yes, monster!" exclaimed the other, almost infuriated to madness, "that Jonathan Bradford whom you would have sacrificed for a crime of which he was not guilty. The husband of a wife, the father of children, whom you would have plunged into irretreivable and everlasting infamy."

"How—how came you here?" demanded Macraisy, still almost breathless with astonishment.

"Heaven hath heard my prayers," he replied; "heaven hath sent me hither, seeking concealment from my enemies even in a tomb."

"Why hast thou come here?"

"To witness for myself," answered Bradford; "to avenge—to punish thee for the crime thou hast committed, and for which I have been sentenced to die."

"Then escape while it is yet in your power," exclaimed Dan Macraisy, "for there will be people here presently, and it will then be too late. Not a moment is to be lost!"

"It is you who have not a moment to lose," replied the other, pointing to the pen which lay before him. "Sign the paper that contains the confession of the murder, sign it instantly, or this minute will be your last! Murderer! Listen to the solemn knell of your unfortunate victim, and if, within three strokes of that awful summons, you put not your name to that confession, I swear solemnly you shall lie stretched at my feet a haggard corpse, never to rise again but in hell's eternal flames!—Sign!"

"Nay," cried the other, imploringly; "listen to me and say if I was not about to prove your innocence by means of the bit of paper you want me to put my name to?"

"Liar! cheat!" exclaimed Jonathan Bradford, furiously; "do I not know your motive? What availed it whether it was I, or your companion, or all the world did perish so that you might be secure. Hark! once the bell hath tolled, and you have not yet said whether you will do as I have bid!"

"Do but hear me, Bradford," exclaimed the assassin, in a tone of the deepest humiliation. "Ask me to do anything but that and I will obey you."

"What else need I ask of you?"

"Bid me lead you to a place of safety, and I will do so even at the hazard of my own life."

"Why should I seek safety in flight," demanded Jonathan Bradford, "when my innocence must be made manifest to all the world from the moment that confession receives your signature? Quick then, do my bidding, for I have sworn that you should clear me in the eyes of those who have been misled into a false notion of my guilt."

"I'll not be forced against my inclination," answered Dan Macraisy in a sullen tone.

"Then you will force me to do that which I would have fain avoided," returned the other. "I have said that the perpetrator of the crime should be brought to light, and as heaven is my witness I will not make my vow in vain. Hark—twice the bell hath tolled! Another stroke villain, and——"

Macraisy stood irresolute for a moment or two, but the stern, fixed gaze of Bradford assured him that no mercy was to be expected, and at length seizing the pen he wrote his name upon the paper, just as the bell sent forth its solemn sound for the third time.

"There—there, 'tis done!" he exclaimed throwing down the pen. "I have put my signature to it as you desired. I have made myself liable to be hanged for this crime, but surely, Mr. Jonathan Bradford, you'll not be so hard upon me as to go and inform people of what has been done till I have had time to escape out of the country? I hope you'll consider my wretched plight,—and you Mr. Scrimmidge. We have been old friends together, and surely you'll not turn against me when I'm in danger of coming to the gallows."

Old friends we have been, have we?" returned Caleb, rejecting the hand which had been held out to him. "I'd sooner shake hands with Old Scratch than with such precious villain as you have turned out to be. Oh! I only wish I was safe back again in Seven Dials and out of your infernal clutches."

" Fear nothing, Caleb," exclaimed Jonathan Bradford, "for I know enough to be assured that you had nothing whatever to do with this murder. For you," he added, turning towards Macraisy, " I'll not betray your lurking-place ; justice, not blood, is all that I require. Beware! The curchyard is now thronged with people, following the body of the man you murdered to his last resting-place on this earth. I go to surrender myself into the hands of those who are in pursuit of me. If you can, escape from hence whilst there is yet some slight chance left. Farewell—repent! and be assured that sooner or later, guilt like yours meets with its just punishment!"

A low murmur from without announced that the funeral procession had reached the churchyard, and Jonathan Bradford, scarcely conscious of what he was doing, rushed from the vault, leaving Caleb uncertain whether to follow him or not. At length, however, terror seemed to urge him to flight, and he was about to leave the place, when Macraisy, seizing him with a giant's grasp, exclaimed—

" Whither are you going, coward? Would you betray me into the hands of those who seek my destruction?"

" Upon my life I was not going to do anything of the kind," answered Caleb Scrimmidge, alarmed at finding himself in the clutches of a desperate man.

" What were you about to do then ?"

" I was merely going to see if there was any way of getting out of this place without being seen."

" And you would leave me here alone ?"

" Why shouldn't you be left alone after the trick you would just now have served me ?" demanded Caleb Scrimmidge. "Recollect, you were going to force me to sign my name to a confession that would have fixed me with the crime of having murdered Mr. Hayes. So, as I don't think you are exactly a safe sort of person to be with, I shall take my leave, wishing you a safe deliverance from your present troubles."

" Villain!" exclaimed Macraisy ; "you are going to set the blood-hounds on my track!"

" Indeed, you were never more mistaken in your life," he replied, " for it would be dangerous to acknowledge any sort of acquaintance with you ; and if I have but the chance of getting away from this neighbourhood without being seen, I shall do so without troubling myself to tell any one where you are to be found."

" How can I trust you," exclaimed the other, " when I know that my life is in your power ?"

" You may do so very safely," answered Caleb, " because I happen to know that I should not stand a much better chance than yourself if they should happen to catch sight of me. So of course I shall get away as fast as my legs will carry me, and all I hope is that you may be able to follow my example."

" Why not wait till we can go together ?"

" Because I don't like throwing away a chance," replied the other, " and something strikes me that the sooner I turn my back upon this place the better it will be for me. I'm known to have been travelling about with you for some time past, and as it's also certain that I slept in the same room with you on the night of the murder, there's no saying whether or not some people might take it into their heads that I had as much to do with killing poor old Mr. Hayes as you yourself had."

" And why shouldn't you run the same risk as I do ?"

" For this simple reason :—that I now begin to see you only wanted to make a cat's paw of me, and if it hadn't been for Jonathan Bradford pouncing upon us as he did, you would have made me sign a paper acknowledging that I alone was guilty of the murder."

" Fool ! I only did that to try whether you had courage enough to face any danger that might threaten us."

" Ay, ay, its all very well to tell me so," exclaimed Caleb Scrimmidge, " but fool a I am, I'm not quite so big a one as to believe all I hear. Besides I've wanted to us this partnership affair for some time, and now I'm determined to get back to my old master in Seven Dials as soon as I can. Watchmaking seems to me to be a better business than wandering about the country with nobody knows who, and from this moment I intend to stick to my business and get an honest living by hard labour."

"Stay at least till these people have left the churchyard."

"Not another moment," exclaimed Caleb, and suddenly releasing himself from the grasp of his companion, he left the vault.

"What's come over me!" muttered Macraisy, after a pause. "It seems as if I were asleep, and that my heart had altogether gone away from me. Infernal curses on that boy! I'll follow him and secure the papers he has taken away, or my knife shall rip open his heart! Merciful powers!" he groaned as the coffin and mourners were entering the church above him; "they are bringing here the body of Hayes, to deposite him in this vault! Is there no way to escape? Horror! they are lowering the coffin into this place! I am enclosed—the murderer with the murdered! No—no—no—rather than that I'll die by my own hand!"

In an instant the knife which he held was plunged into his body, and he staggered faintly into a corner of the loathsome dungeon.

CHAPTER XV.

A WOMAN PROVES TO BE MORE THAN A MATCH FOR A LAWYER—RUSTIC COURTSHIP.—JACK RACKBOTTLE STILL REMAINS FAITHFUL TO HIS MASTER.—AN UNPLEASANT RECONTRE, WHICH, HOWEVER, DOES NOTHING TOWARDS THE DISCOVERY OF THE SECRET.

PERHAPS no one in the village felt more deeply interested in the events that were oing on than did Sally the attached domestic of Mrs. Bradford, and her firm friend now that she was placed under such trying circumstances. It is true she had the consolation of seeing her mistress released from confinement; but Bradford himself had esaped from the place where he was to await the moment of his execution, and from all she heard there could be but little reason to hope that he would be able much longer to elude the search that was being made for him in every direction. Her lover, Jack Rackbottle, she felt assured knew more about the affair than he chose to admit, and being at length determined to draw the secret from him, she left the inn, and made here way towards a cross road by which he was expected to return home. Here she remainad waiting for some time, and was at length about to retrace her steps, when she was unexpectedly accosted by Lawyer Dozey, who had made himself so busy from the time when the murder of Mr Hayes had been first discovered.

"So, so," he exclaimed, "you are just the person I wanted to see, for no one is more likely than yourself to be able to tell me where Jack Rackbottle is to be found; and if you choose to give me the information I want, ten pounds shall be your reward."

"Ten pounds?"

"Ay, it's a large sum my good woman, and yet half a dozen words will serve to put that money into your pocket."

"Indeed!" exclaimed Sally; "then I'd have you to know, Mr. Lawyer, that ten thousand times the sum you have offered would never tempt me to act the part of a common spy and informer."

"Take care what you are about, or I may perhaps be obliged to do something you will be sorry for."

"What's that, sir?"

"Order you to be placed under arrest, and kept in close custody till you think proper to tell all you know about the escape of Jonathan Bradford."

"I've never said I knew anything yet."

"Ah, you deny everything, but I've been used to these sort of things all my life, and experience tells me that your lover would not have kept such a secret as this from you."

"I don't know what secret you are talking about," replied Sally, with pretended innocence.

"Well then," exclaimed Lawyer Dozey, "do you mean to swear positively that Jack Rackbottle has never informed you where he had hid his master."

THE DEEP DESPAIR OF MRS. BRADFORD.

"Lor! no, sir," she replied; "I don't suppose the poor fellow knows anything more about the matter than you or I do."

"But I happen to have pretty good authority for believing, not only that he knows where Bradford is lurking, but that he planned and assisted at the escape."

"Ah!" exclaimed Sally, "I only wish he was present to hear you say so much to his face."

"I wish he was with all my heart," replied the old gentleman; "for if ever he comes within reach of me, I'll take care not to lose sight of him again till he has discovered all he knows."

No. 13.

"And have you vanity enough to fancy you are a match for Jack Rackbottle?" she asked, eyeing the lawyer with a look of the most sovereign contempt.

"I might not be able to cope with him myself," answered the lawyer; "but there is assistance close at hand, and they would be here on my slightest signal."

"They!—who do you mean by *they?*" she asked, with some little alarm that she could not conceal.

"Why, Sergeant Sam and three or four of his men."

"Indeed!" cried Sally; "and so you have thought it necessary to employ the assistance of the military against a poor harmless fellow like Jack Rackbottle!"

"Harmless!" exclaimed the lawyer. "Do you call him harmless, when he has broken open the strong-room, and liberated a prisoner that was under sentence of death?"

"I don't know that he has done so."

"But I know he has, and so does everybody else in the neighbourhood; and we have determined to punish this lover of yours unless he at once deliver up the murderer into our hands."

"Who dare call Mr. Bradford a murderer!" demanded Sally, in a tone of indignation.

"Every one has a right to call him so," answered Lawyer Dozey, "after having been convicted of the crime by a jury of his countrymen. He has been sentenced to die for the crime, and as your lover has thought proper to aid and assist in the escape of a prisoner under the doom of death, you must not be surprised if he be transported for the term of his natural life."

"I'll be bound he's transported already," exclaimed Sally—"but it's with joy that his master has succeeded in getting beyond the reach of danger."

"Don't be too sure that he will escape altogether," replied the old gentleman, "for the place is all up in arms; and the people here are determined to keep up such a watch that he cannot leave his hiding-place without being seen."

"But suppose he happens to be already beyond their reach?" asked the female.

"We know he has not been able to get away," replied Mr. Dozey, "and there are so many eyes upon the look out that he can neither leave his lurking place nor receive assistance from his friends without the fact becoming instantly known. So it will be better for you to tell me at once all you know about the matter, or I may presently conceive it an imperative duty to order you into the custody of the people who are within call."

"What could you give me into custody for?" she asked.

"For refusing to answer my questions."

"Then you had better set about it at once," exclaimed Sally, "for if you were to ask me till this time to-morrow, not a word more would be got from me than you have already heard."

"Hasn't Jack Rackbottle told you where Jonathan Bradford has been concealed?" he asked.

"I don't suppose he knows anything at all about it," answered Sally, "and even if he does he has been wise enough not to trust the secret even to me. So all your trouble has been thrown away, old gentleman, and if you want to get any information you had better try some one else."

"You are determined then not to divulge the secret?"

"Havn't I told you that I don't know of any secret?" she asked.

"You don't mean to deny having heard that Jonathan Bradford has escaped from the strong room?"

"I've been told he has," answered Sally, "and to tell you the truth I was never better pleased in my life."

"Then your gratification will soon be at an end," he replied, "for the ends of justice are not to be so easily defeated, and I am happy to say the people hereabouts are determined to re-take him as soon as possible."

"That is to say—if they can find him!"

"And what's to hinder it?" demanded Mr. Dozey, "when there are so many persons bent upon one purpose? Besides, a large reward has been offered for his apprehension, and if nothing else would have done it, that will keep our neighbours upon the alert till we have the prisoner once more under lock and key. So now, take my advice—earn the money, and it will go towards a marriage portion for you some of these days."

"I know nothing about it, I tell you," exclaimed Sally, "and even if I did, who do you think would marry me for the sake of money that was obtained by betraying a fellow creature to death?—to say nothing of my own feelings afterwards when I might reflect upon the base act I had been guilty of."

"Nay, it is your duty to assist in bringing a just punishment upon the guilty."

"I wish you wouldn't trouble me any more upon this subject," she exclaimed, "for I have already said what I mean to do upon the affair, and you are only wasting your own time as well as mine by asking me all these questions. Ask somebody else, and I'm sure you'll be able to get quite as much information about this affair as you will from me."

"Very well," replied the old gentlemen, "I see you are determined to be obstinate, so I shall leave you for the present, and in the meanwhile I hope you will reflect upon the course it will be best for you to pursue. Remember, you are suspected of knowing more of this affair than you choose to confess, and by-and-by it may be my duty to order you into custody till you see the folly of screening a murderer from justice."

Upon saying this, Lawyer Dozey left the place, and having watched him as long as he remained in sight, Sally was about to return to the inn when her lover made his appearance from a turn in the road. Upon seeing her he hastened forward, and perceiving that something had occurred to vex her, he eagerly inquired into the cause, promising himself to give a severe drubbing to any person who might have had the temerity to annoy her. Sally, however, was not aware of this, and without hesitation she related all that had passed between her and Lawyer Dozey.

"And so the old fellow suspects that I've had a hand in setting my master at liberty?" exclaimed Jack.

"He does more than suspect you," she replied, "for he seemed almost certain of it, and I advise you to keep out of his way, for he talked of having you taken into custody and punished for having assisted a criminal to escape."

"How does he know I had anything to do with it?"

"I suppose it was all guess-work with him, Jack," she replied; "but it don't matter how it may have happened, for the old gentleman seems to have made up his mind about it, and poor Mr. Bradford—though he may have contrived to escape for a time must at last be taken and confined in the same miserable cell where he was placed before."

"Keep up your spirits, Sally," exclaimed her lover, soothingly, "for I tell you master will never be discovered if they keep up a search for the next twelve months."

"Why won't he be discovered?"

"Because they'll never think to search the place where I've put him," answered Jack Rackbotde.

"Then you have had something to do with it after all?"

"To be sure I have," he replied, "and when it's dark enough again, it's in the little thicket near the churchyard where I'll be with a stout horse that shall carry him far enough off from all his enemies. Perhaps he may have the good luck to reach the sea-side, and if he does, I'll get him over to France or Holland, and then no one will dare lay hands on him."

"Ah!" sighed the girl, "but there's poor missis——"

"Well!" he exclaimed, anxiously, "what of her? She's safe enough still, ain't she?"

"I'm afraid not," replied Sally, "for there have been several consultations going on in the house, and, from what I could make out, they think of sending her back to prison, and may be, she'll be hanged in master's stead."

"Nonsense! that's not English law."

"I'm glad to hear it," exclaimed Sally; "but the lawyer, and the rest of 'em have been whispering so much that I don't know what to make of it. However, you ought to kr.ow best, and I'm glad to hear you say they can't do anything with Mrs. Bradford through her husband making his escape."

"No, no, she's all right enough."

"But what do you think will happen to poor master?"

"Why, I expect he'll get clear off," answered her lover; "for the law is catch me, hang me, and it strikes me they won't find Mr. Bradford in a hurry. However, don't you go and fret yourself any more about it, for take my word all will go well; and master, as well as misses, will spend many a happy year yet, though matters do look a little cross just now."

"But do you think they'll be able to prove master's innocence?"

"I'm sure of it."

"Ah! but how is it to be done?"

"Easily enough if we only set about it the right way" replied Jack Rackbottle. "I feel certain that master never did commit the crime of murder on any one, much more on an old gentleman that came into his house as a guest."

"That's just exactly what I think about it."

"Who can have any other notion?" he asked. "No, no, the thing won't bear thinking of, for everything is clear and straightforward enough, and if time only can be gained, the whole truth will come out."

"And you still think the murder was committed by the two strangers that slept in the house that night?"

"I don't think they both had a hand in it," replied Jack; "but the one that called himself Squire Connor is a queer sort of fellow; and I feel pretty certain that we shall be able to prove by and by that he did it. At any rate, he and his companion have been missing ever since; and one of 'em is pretty well known to be the chap that broke into the house of Farmer Brown, at Frogmore."

"Can't anybody tell what's become of 'em?" she asked.

"Just at present they keep out of harm's way," answered Jack Rackbottle; "but it's almost certain they are still lurking about the premises, and if so we shall he sure to have 'em."

"And even if they should be caught, what proof have we that either of them did the murder?"

"We've none at present," he replied; "but only let us lay hold of 'em, and then leave it to me to bring forward proofs against the fellow that I suspect."

"You mean Squire Connor?"

"Yes, or whatever his name may be," answered Jack, "for I think we shall very soon find out that he has more names than one to travel with. The moment he came to the house I thought what a suspicious looking chap he seemed to be, and when Mr. Hayes talked before him of the money he had brought to pay for his new estate, I fancied to myself how foolish it was to say so much before a couple of strangers. And so it turned out, for the poor old gentleman was stabbed to the heart for the sake of the gold that had tempted the murderer. But I say, Sally, who the deuce are those chaps yonder, that are coming this way?"

"Why," she replied, "I declare if it ain't Lawyer Dozey and the four or five soldiers that he talked about just now, so depend upon it there's mischief in the wind."

"What the plague can they be wanting here?" exclaimed Jack Rackbottle. "However, we shall soon know, for they are coming towards us as fast as their legs can carry them. Now, sir," he added, as they came up to the spot where he and Sally were standing, "who is it you are looking for?"

"You," exclaimed Mr. Dozey.

"Me!"

"Ay; do you pretend not to know what our business with you is?" asked the lawer.

"I don't know what you can want with me."

"Then, in as few words as possible, we have come here in search of a villain."

"Villain!" exclaimed Jack. "Come now, don't you call people out of their names, or there'll be a quarrel between us presently."

"You are insolent, fellow!"

"I'm not insolent, that I know of," answered Jack Rackbottle. "But I suppose you are chopfallen because there's to be no execution, after all the trouble you've taken. Ha—ha—ha! I'm glad poor Mr. Bradford has managed to get off."

"Scoundrel!"

"Don't call me ugly names," exclaimed Jack, "or perhaps I may return the compliment in a way you won't like."

"And I shall do something that you won't like," returned the lawyer, and then making a sign for the soldiers to advance, he added, "Sergeant Sam, this is the fellow I was looking for. Arrest him in the king's name, and convey him to a place where he'll be safe till the time comes for his examination."

The men immediately closed round him.

"Arrest me!" exclaimed Jack Rackbottle, indignantly. "What for, I should like to know?"

"For aiding and abetting in the escape of the condemned prisoner, Jonathan Bradford," answered the lawyer.

"Who dare say that I have done anything of the kind?" demanded the other endeavouring to force his way through.

"*I* have dared to say it!" answered Mr. Dozey; "and if these men suffer your escape it will be at their own peril. You are now legally in custody, and those who have the care of you are responsible for your safe keeping."

"I'll tell you what it is, Mr. Lawyer," exclaimed Jack, "if such fellows as you never put their roguery into a worse purpose than helping a poor condemned fellow-creature to escape from hanging, may be Jack Ketch would'nt meet with quite so many customers. So put that in your pipe and smoke it, old gentleman, for it isn't every day that you hear a bit of good truth."

"And this shall cost you dearly," replied the enraged lawyer, "for I have only performed my duty, and yet am to be scoffed at and insulted as if I had been guilty of some crime!"

"Oh, pray sir, don't send him to prison!" cried Sally, wo now became seriously alarmed for her lover.

"I'll not hear a word in his favour," exclaimed the lawyer. "I'll be deaf to the voice of mercy—so away with him, soldiers, and guard him well; for if he should escape, I will report you all at head-quarters."

"Have mercy on him, pray!" again cried Sally, half maddened by her terrors.

"Ask *mercy*, and *pray* for me!" exclaimed Jack; "and why should you do so? I've done no harm that I know of. May be he thinks to frighten me; but he shan't do it, though. I know what I know, and it's devilish little the wiser they'll be for it, I can tell 'em. So, hold up your head, Sally, and don't ask for mercy, because I look for that from better than any of the people I see here."

"You are insolent, fellow," said the lawyer; "but I may find means to bring you to your senses before long. The law must be obeyed, and if you won't make a full confession by fair means, we must try what force will do. So now tell me what has become of Jonathan Bradford, and, instead of punishment, I'll take care that you shall receive a handsome reward."

"A reward!—and do you think I'd accept of money to betray a man that I know is innocent?"

"But a jury has pronounced a contrary opinion," answered Mr. Dozey; "and as there is every reason to believe that the murder was committed by Bradford, it is your duty to assist in bringing upon him the doom that has been pronounced."

"Humph! suppose I don't know where he is to be found?"

"You do know, sirrah."

"Very well, have it your own way, Mr. Lawyer; but you can't make me say anything against my inclination."

"At all events, I can take you before a magistrate, and have you committed to prison."

"What for?"

"For assisting the escape of a criminal."

"Who, besides yourself, says I have done so?"

"I'm not bound to answer all your impertinent questions," exclaimed the old gentleman. "It is sufficient that I have good reasons for believing that you are concerned in the escape of Jonathan Bradford, and I shall not let you out of my custody till you have given a satisfactory reply to my questions.'

"You'll have no other than I have already given."

"So you may say now," answered Lawyer Dozey, "but I rather think we shall hear a very different story when you have been in prison a little while. That will try you a bit, my boy."

"And what right have *you* to send him to prison?" asked Sally.

"I am not going to answer your impertinent questions," replied the old gentleman testily. "It is enough that I take so much authority upon myself, and if he don't like the idea of confinement, he knows very well how he may avoid it."

"If all people got their deserts, Mr. Dozey, I wonder where you would have been before now?" she exclaimed.

"Take care what you are saying, young woman," returned the other, "or perhaps I may consider it my duty to order you under arrest for attempting to prevent the course of justice. If I do wrong, I am answerable for it to others, but in this instance I happen to know that I am perfectly in the right."

"But you don't happen to know that I helped poor Mr. Bradford to get out of the clutches of his enemies," replied Jack.

"Ay, but there are pretty good reasons for believing that you did though," answered the old gentleman, "and I am justified in keeping you in close custody, till we can get together sufficient evidence to prove the fact. It is certain that escape could not have been made without assistance, and there is no one else that we know of who would have run such a risk for the sake of a man who has been condemned to death for the perpetration of a barbarous murder."

"Any one ought to do it, if they believe, as I do, that the man has been unjustly convicted," answered Jack Rackbottle. "However, I'm not going to say anything that you may afterwards bring against me; so, if you have made up your mind to send me to prison, do so at once, and then you'll see that I can bear confinement, without being coward enough to say a word that would get a poor persecuted man into farther trouble."

"Then you are determined not to confess where Jonathan Bradford is concealing himself?" said the lawyer.

"I've quite made up my mind not to say anything."

"In that case I have only one course to pursue," exclaimed Lawyer Dozey. "So let him be led away, sergeant, and remember, if he should make his escape you will have to answer for it."

Sally again pleaded for her lover, but her entreaties were all in vain. Jack Rackbottle was forced to accompany the guard, and the only regret he felt at it, was that he would thus be deprived of the power of giving any farther assistance to his master. At length Sally, perceiving that she could be of no use, made her way towards the inn to inform her mistress of the misfortune that had befallen her lover.

CHAPTER XVI.

JONATHAN BRADFORD BECOMES UNEASY AT THE STATE OF UNCERTAINTY IN WHICH HE FINDS HIMSELF INVOLVED.—HE MEETS WITH ANOTHER STAUNCH FRIEND, WHO GIVES HIM INTELLIGENCE THAT INCREASES HIS ALARM. — THE INTERVIEW IS INTERRUPTED BY THE ARRIVAL OF A THIRD PARTY.

NEVER did time appear to hang so wearily as that which passed whilst Bradford was waiting for the return of his faithful friend, Jack Rackbottle. He could not in any way account for the delay, for his messenger had promised to come back immediately with news from home, and a thousand harrowing fears passed through his mind as one thing after another convinced him that some mishap had occurred either to his wife or to him who had gone on his errand. Sometimes he even ventured so far as to approach the verge of the thicket in which he had found concealment, to see if his deliverer was yet returning, but each time he was doomed to the bitterest disappointment. Not a soul was within sight, and he became more and more convinced that the few friends who yet remained faithful to him had fallen into trouble through his escape. He therefore determined at length to surrender himself at once, and was just leaving the thicket for that purpose, when Sally, who we have seen leave her lover on his way to prison, passed near the place, on her return to the inn. Bradford paused, and would have turned back, qut the female had perceived him, and running eagerly towards the place where he was standing, she earnestly entreated him not to quit his present concealment, lest he should be discovered by those who were searching for him. Almost unconscious of what he was doing, the fugitive retraced his footsteps, closely followed by Sally, and desiring her to take a seat beside him, he eagerly inquired after his wife, for whose safety he was so painfully alarmed.

"Ah!" she exclaimed, with a sigh, "your's is a sad, melancholy home now, sir, for everything is at sixes and sevens, and poor missis is fretting herself to death lest you should be found before we have time to prove your innocence."

"Do people then still believe that I committed the murder?" he asked.

"I'm afraid they do," answered Sally, "for thas ill-natured old lawyer won't hear a word that's said in your favour, and he has just now taken poor Jack Rackbottle to prison because he has taken it into his head that he helped you to escape."

"Console yourself as far as he is concerned," exclaimed Bradford, "for a few hours will enable me to prove that he committed no fault in giving me that liberty of which I had been unjustly deprived."

"Who is to prove it?"

"I will do so myself," he replied.

"You?"

"Yes, Sally, I am innocent, and can therefore have nothing to fear, even from the malice of my worst enemies,"

"Ah, it's all very well to think so," answered the female, "but people hereabouts have made up their minds that you did the murder, and nothing but the most positive proof will ever serve to convince them that you had no hand in it."

"And that positive proof I shall be able to bring forward."

"What! can you convince them that poor old Mr. Hayes was murdered by somebody else?"

"I can."

"Has the man, whoever he was, confessed the crime?"

"I cannot, just at this moment, enter into all the particulars," replied Jonathan Bradford; "but I have discovered beyond all doubt by whom the deed was committed, and I have reason to believe that these heavy afflictions of mine will be speedily brought to an end."

"Then, hadn't I better run home and comfort my mistress with this good news?" asked Sally, eagerly.

"You can do so if you please," answered her master, "but unless my hopes deceive me, I fancy she will know all quite as soon if you leave everything to take its own course. In a short time everything will be ready for the discovery I have to make, and when that is the case, I shall fearlessly seek those who have been loudest in their accusations against me, and then will I bring forward such evidence as shall completely clear my name from the infamy that has first made me a convict and then a fugitive."

"May I ask why you don't clear yourself at once?" she asked.

"It is a question that might be easily answered," replied Bradford, "but the reason will so soon be made manifest, that there is hardly any occasion to enter into an explanation of my motives just now. I may, however, tell you that the murderer is still lurking about this neighbourhood, and I believe his conscience has been so far roused that he will soon come forward voluntarily to confess his crime, and release me from all further suspicion."

"Why not go before a magistrate and accuse him of it at once?" demanded the female.

"Because by so doing I should most likely defeat the purpose have in view," answered Bradford. " The man of whom I speak, has long been a hardened, desperate villain, and if I were to accuse him, he would be almost certain to deny his guilt, and I have no other proof of it than his own confession, which can only be obtained by leaving him to his own remorseful conscience."

" But suppose he should escape?"

" That, I think, is scarcely possible, for I understand a reward has been offered for his apprehension for a robbery that he is supposed to have committed in this neighbourhood."

" Ah!" cried Sally, as a sudden thought struck her. " Then you are speaking of the strange traveller that slept at our house on the night when the murder was committed."

" Ay, one of the two men who came together."

" Then Jack Rackbottle was right, for he has said all along that he was sure one of 'em did it."

" Which one did he suspect?"

" The man that called himself Squire O'Connor."

" He was right then in his surmises," answered Bradford, " for that man has confessed in my own hearing that he murdered Mr. Hayes, and afterwards escaped from the room before any of us had time to get there. I and my wife were unfortunately discovered near the dying man, and suspicion falling upon us, we were immediately accused of a crime of which both were perfectly innocent."

" Then wouldn't it be better for me to go at once to Lawyer Dozey, and tell him that the murderer has been discovered?"

" No," replied Bradford, " as things have gone so far, I can now wait with patience till the time comes for a full development of this mystery which had so nearly proved fatal to me. The assassin is so surrounded that he cannot escape, and I will remain where I am till the moment arrives when the truth must come out. This day will witness the termination of the sufferings I have so unjustly endured, and afterwards I shall have the satisfaction of knowing, that my innocence is acknowledged even by those who are now loudest in condemning me as the perpetrator of this foul deed."

" That may be all very well to look forward to, sir," answered Sally, " but how will it be if in the meantime they should find out where you are hiding yourself?"

" It can matter but very little," he replied, " for my deliverance from danger is now certain, and even though I may fall into the hands of those who are in search of me, it will only serve to bring the affair all the sooner to a termination."

" But that old lawyer will never believe the crime was committed by any one but yourself."

" You are mistaken," answered the master, " for Mr. Dozey, though somewhat obstinate in this instance, is actuated by no other than the best motives. The circumstances against me were certainly very strong, and much as I have suffered through his mistaken zeal, I must do him the justice to say, that he has not been urged by any feelings of animosity against myself. In short, I believe no person will rejoice more than himself at my escape, if once convinced that I have been unjustly accused."

" I've told him, at least a dozen times, that you had nothing to do with it," answered Sally; " but he only flew in a passion, and said I knew nothing at all about it "

" That was because he thought you were unnecessarily interfering in the matter and raising up a feeling in my behalf which I did not deserve."

" Then it shows what an obstinate old fellow he must be, for my word ought to be as good as his any day."

" So it is, Sally, but Mr. Dozey has unfortunately made up his mind upon the subject, and nothing but the most positive proof will convince him that he is wrong. That proof, however, I now have, and my future life, I hope, will be unclouded as it used to be."

" It certainly ought to be so," answered Sally, " for you have had trouble enough of late, and it is high time you should know what rest and quiet is. Let the guilty alone suffer, for it's a shame and a hardship that people should be in peril of their lives when they have done nothing at all to deserve it."

"But you forget," exclaimed Jonathan Bradford, "that all of us are liable to misfortunes in this world."

"I know that," she replied, "but it's rather too much to be in danger of the gibbet for doing nothing."

"True," answered Bradford, "but you forget that I have every reason to be grateful for escaping from the danger. In a few hours my innocence will be known, and then will come the reward for all the misery I have been obliged to endure."

No. 14.

"Ah!" exclaimed Sally, "how happy it will make poor missis, when she hears that your character is cleared, and learns that all your troubles, as well as her own, are at an end."

"For which good news you can prepare her when you return home."

"I must be very careful how I do it, though," answered Sally, "for this is more than she expects, and the sudden news of your safety might be of serious consequence. To be sure she may have heard the good news from somebody, and I hope she may, for I should break my heart if anything I said were to make her ill."

"That is impossible," answered Bradford, "for the confession of the real murderer is known only to his companion; and he, I rather think, is too much alarmed for his own safety to remain any longer in this neighbourhood, now that he has discovered the sort of man he has been associating with."

"Don't you think it would have been as well to have had them both taken up?" asked the female.

"Why should we commit such an injustice, when one of them has confessed that he alone committed the murder? The other has, very unfortunately for himself, fallen into bad company; but there is every reason to believe that he sees his folly, and will be glad enough to return home as soon as he can."

"And do you know, sir, where this Mr. O'Connor is hiding himself all this while?"

"I know pretty near the place."

"Then why not let me go and send the officers after him?"

"Because I have witnessed his terror, and do not wish to be the one to betray him into the hands of his enemies," answered Bradford.

"Don't you think he deserves hanging, then?"

"I am sure he deserves the utmost punishment the law can inflict," he replied, "yet I would prefer that he should be captured through the means of any other person than myself. I have little reason to pity him, Sally; but his horror and remorse are so great, that for the life of me I cannot endure the thought of sending him to prison, whose doors would close upon him for ever. You, however, know all the circumstances, as far as I can at present divulge them, and it is therefore in your power to convey consolation to your mistress, by assuring her that the troubles which threatened to crush us are almost at an end."

"Ah! but do you think she will believe me, sir?"

"She knows you to be faithful and zealous in our behalf," answered Bradford, "and you are at perfect liberty to tell her in private that you have seen me, and heard from my own lips a solemn assurance that all danger is at an end."

"Won't she wonder at your not returning home, now that you say your innocence can be proved?"

"Say I have a reason for it," exclaimed Jonathan Bradford, "and she will wait with patience till I can return home,, and explain why this course has been preferred."

"Very well, sir," answered the female. "I'll lose no time in performing your errand; but I hope it will not be long before you follow me home, for missis will be more anxious than ever for your return, and there'll be no persuading her to stop in the house when she hears that there's no longer any fear of your showing yourself."

"Tell her I will be at home as soon as possible."

"I will, sir; and I'm much mistaken if we shan't have everything prepared to give you a glorious reception."

Overjoyed at the unexpected turn which affairs seem to take, Sally took leave of her master, and made her way out of the thicket, in order to convey to her mistress the cheering intelligence with which she had been entrusted. Restless and uneasy, however, Bradford paced up and down the pathway, thinking over the events which were upon the eve of transpiring, and occasionally looking forth from his hiding-place to see if any one was approaching the spot. In this way nearly an hour passed, and he was about to seat himself once more upon the green bank, which had before served him for a resting-place, when footsteps were heard approaching, and upon looking round, he perceived a young man, whom he did not remember having seen till that moment. Startled by this unexpected sight, he seemed as if preparing to make a retreat into the thickest part of the copse, when the young man, addressing him by name, declared in friendly accents, that he was there rather as a friend than as an enemy.

"You know me, it seems," exclaimed Bradford.

"I do."

"And yet intended not to lay hands upon me?"

"I am one of those few friends," answered the young man, "who have believed you to be innocent, in spite of the evidence that has been produced against you."

"May I ask your name, sir?"

"It is Henry Dornton."

"I remember; you are about to become the husband of Miss Lucy Hayes, the daughter of the gentleman who was unfortunately assassinated in my house?"

"The same."

"And you believe me innocent, in spite of the circumstances that appear so strong against me?"

"Had I not thought so," answered Dornton, "I should not have omitted to bring others here in order to secure you."

"You knew I was in this place, then?"

"I did; for passing by, an hour or two ago, I saw you when cautiously looking out to observe whether any one was approaching. You saw me not, and I purposely abstained from seeking an interview till I could do so without a chance of running you into further danger."

"May I ask the purpose of your visit?"

"Yes; it was to offer you my services, in case they might be needed."

"To escape?"

"Ay;—you surely do not wish to remain here?"

"Only for a short time longer," answered Jonathan Bradford, "and then I hope to be able to produce such evidence of entire innocence, that no one shall dare accuse me of this murder."

"Do you know who is the guilty man?"

"I do."

"Then why not denounce him at once, and thus clear your own character without any unnecessary delay?"

"All shall be explained in good time," replied Bradford: "but at present you must be content with knowing that I have motives which I do not think it necessary to explain at present."

"But others may discover your retreat here as easily as I have."

"I am aware of that; and they may drag me forth like a felon. Happily, however, I have now the means to disprove all that has been urged against me, so that even Mr. Dozey shall be forced to admit that he has cruelly wronged me by his suspicions."

"That he has done so, nobody can be more convinced then myself," replied the young man; "but he has been urged rather by his anxiety to obtain justice against the murderer of his friend, than any malice towards yourself. Only make your own innocence manifest to Mr. Dozey, and no one will be more prompt than himself to render all the atonement that may be necessary."

"I have never blamed him for what he has done," answered Bradford, "but, on the contrary, have admitted that the circumstances against me were so strong that he had every right to believe the crime had been committed by me. I was found in the room at the moment after the alarm was raised—the very weapon, still reeking with the blood of the victim, was clutched in my hand—and the agitation I betrayed, all went to confirm the suspicion that the blow had been struck by me. The accusation was made—I have been tried, and found guilty—and by a most unlooked-for circumstance have been enabled to leave the place from which escape was supposed to be impossible."

"Had you not done so," observed Henry Dornton, "you would ere now have paid the penalty for a crime of which you are innocent."

"That I have escaped is, indeed, marvellous," exclaimed Bradford; "and it seems to me like a special Providence guarding me against an unmerited punishment."

"Know you what has become of the real criminal?"

"I only know that he is full of remorse," answered Jonathan, "and there is reason to believe he will surrender himself up to justice, rather than drag out a miserable existence, under the constant dread of being taken up for the offence. He is already a prey to the most dreadful mental anguish, and it is probable that before now he has surrendered himself up into the hands of those who are in search of him for another crime of which he has been guilty."

"Do I know the man?"

"You may have heard of him," answered Bradford, "but he has been in this neighbourhood only a few days, and most likely would have made his escape before now, but for the look-out which has been kept up in consequence of a burglary he is supposed to have committed."

"Are you sure he has not found means to get away?"

"I have every reason to believe that he has no thought of making such an attempt," answered Jonathan Bradford, "for I saw him not long since; and, judging from the wildness of his manners, I have reason for believing that he will yield himself up to justice, and confess his crime to others as he has already done to me."

"I know not what your motive may have been," observed Henry Dornton, "but it appears to me that you should before now have dragged him before a magistrate, and denounced him as the murderer of Mr. Hayes."

"Such was the course I once thought of pursuing," answered the other, "but knowing the uncertainty of finding the ruffian, I was fearful of throwing myself into the hands of my enemies, till able to produce the villain for whose crime I have been tried and condemned."

"Trust the task of finding him to me," exclaimed the young man, "and I'll never give up my project till it has been brought to a successful termination."

"Nay," answered Bradford, "let us wait a short time longer, and I believe all that we desire will be accomplished, without either you or I taking any part in the affair."

"You rely then upon his conscience urging him to make a full disclosure of all he knows about it?"

"I have no doubt of it, for he has already confessed to me, and there is every reason to believe he intends to make a more public disclosure."

"Not if he can find means to get away from the neighbourhood."

"Which will be an utter impossibility," replied Jonathan Bradford, "for all the people in the place are upon the look out for him, on account of the burglary at Frogmore farm; a large reward has been offered for his apprehension, and, as it is strongly suspected that he is still lurking hereabouts, so close a watch will be kept that it will be impossible for him to get away without detection."

"That will depend upon circumstances," replied Dornton, "for if he keeps close in the retreat he has found, he may in time get away without anybody being aware of it."

"You forget that he has no one to assist him, and therefore must starve for want of sustenance."

"Has he no money to bribe those who might be disposed to afford assistance if he can pay for it?"

"I have reason to believe that he has left himself without means," answered Bradford; "for, though robbery was no doubt the motive that induced him to commit the murder, the alarm was given so soon that he had no time to secure any of the property of the person whose life he had taken."

"And suppose they should discover you before they secure the man of whom you speak?" asked Henry Dornton.

"That is what I am most anxious to avoid," answered the fugitive, "for as I have been tried and convicted, the moment for my execution would be hurried, in order to prevent a repetition of the escape I have once made."

"Why not leave the neighbourhood then?"

"Because that would look like an admission of my guilt,"

"Then at least allow me to do as I have already suggested. Let me go before a magistrate, and declare my belief that the actual assassin has not yet been taken into custody, and depend upon it I will leave no measures untried to secure the villain for whom you have suffered such unmerited wrong."

"Wait till to-morrow," exclaimed Bradford, "and if he has not been taken into custody by that time, I may perhaps be induced to take other steps. I however believe it will not be long before he surrenders himself; and if such should be the case, I can then leave this retreat with a name and character pure and without reproach."

"That may be all very true," answered the other, "but I'm afraid the man you speak about may find means to get away, and you will then be left here to answer for the crime he has committed."

"Nay," he replied, "I have placed my reliance in heaven, and am content to abide the result, whatever it may be. For your kind intentions, my young friend, I am deeply indebted, and there is a something which assures me that I shall live to acknowledge the generosity you have displayed towards me when almost all the world besides had turned against me."

"What I have done," answered the young man, "has resulted from a conviction in my own mind that you have suffered much sorrow needlessly. Nor do I stand alone in that opinion, for even the widow of the murdered man, and she has looked carefully into the whole case, believes that the blow was not struck by your hand."

"There is some consolation in that," exclaimed Bradford, "for I thought she, beyond all others, would look upon me as the wretch who had brought sorrow and desolation upon her. It is true I know my own innocence, but that only added to the bitterness of my own thoughts, since I felt that I should be judged harshly by the world, and there was besides the harrowing reflection that my name would be for ever branded with infamy. It seems, however, that I was mistaken, and that there were some few who were not to be inflamed by the general outcry."

"And from what you have told me," replied Henry Dornton, "even those who believed you guilty of this foul deed, will soon acknowledge the wrong they have inflicted. You will, therefore, still have something to congratulate yourself upon, since it will be a gratifying reflection by-and-by, to see that prejudice has been completely vanquished by the force of truth and reason."

"That," answered the fugitive, "will depend upon whether I am able to conceal myself till after the assassin has made his confession to others besides myself."

"Would it not be better to face your enemies boldly at once, and denounce the man for whom you have suffered so much?"

"I have thought of doing so," replied Bradford, "but I know not how it is that I have felt hitherto afraid of doing so. I will, however, reflect further upon that subject, and perhaps may act upon the suggestion you have thrown out. You, it seems, are my friend, Mr. Dornton, and as the only favour I may perhaps ever crave from you, I would ask you to see my wife, and console her with an assurance that I may yet be restored to her with a name as unblemished as ever it was."

"The request is one that can be easily granted," exclaimed the young man, "and you may rest assured that I will lose no time in faithfully carrying out your wish. I will now hasten back to your house, and inform Mrs. Bradford of all that has passed in this interview."

He pressed the hand which had been held out to him, and having repeated the promise, bade farewell to the fugitive, and immediately hurried away to execute the task he had taken upon himself.

CHAPTER XVII.

CALEB SCRIMMIDGE IN A BIT OF A QUANDARY.—HIS RETURN TO THE VAULT, AND THE INTERVIEW THAT TAKES PLACE BETWEEN HIM AND HIS FORMER ASSOCIATE.— THE GEORGE INN, AND WHAT TRANSPIRED THERE.

WHEN Caleb Scrimmidge left the vault after the confession which he had heard from the lips of his companion, his first thought was to make his escape from the neighbourhood with all possible despatch. A little reflection, however, served to open his eyes to the true position in which he was placed, for, simple-minded as he was, he saw that suspicion was as likely to be fixed upon himself as upon Dan Macraisy, and he knew that a flat denial would be of no use, when it was perfectly well-known to every one, that he had been for some time the associate of the man who was soon to be charged with the murder. These considerations made him pause, and then his mind was again busily occupied in devising the best scheme for avoiding the dangers with which he was threatened on every side. If he ventured to leave the place ever so stealthily, there was every certainty of being taken by some of the numerous persons who were acquainted with the intimacy which had subsisted between him and Macraisy, which would of itself be sufficient to warrant his detention, till inquiries could be made into the share he might have had in the fearful tragedy, which was then occupying so much attention. That step was therefore to be abandoned for the present, at least, and it now became a consideration whether he should return to the vault, and share the danger with his companion, who he was almost sure would make a bold effort to avoid the peril which his situation involved. Even here there were difficulties in his way which he was afraid to encounter, but his case was so urgent that, after some little reflection, he determined to run the risk, and, having first looked about to see if any one was watching him, he made his way towards the ancient church, whose grey tower was seen rising above the trees at no great distance off. At length, having reached the spot, and again satisfied himself that no person was near, he removed the stone and crept through the opening which gave admission to the vault of which we have already spoken. Once there he crept over the fragments with which his path was strewed, and, at length, by the faint light of the lamp which was still burning, discovered Dan Macraisy, who was now recovering from the long fainting fit which had succeeded the wound which he had inflicted on himself.

"Holloa! What the devil is the matter now?" exclaimed Caleb, as he saw him in a sitting posture leaning for support against one of the massive pillars which supported the vaulted roof. "What ails you, Dan? Surely you have not attempted to commit suicide?"

"I have," groaned the other, "and would have made another attempt but that the knife is beyond my reach, and I am so weak from loss of blood that I am not able to reach it."

"And what did you do it for?" exclaimed Caleb, kicking the weapon away with his foot. "Are you tired of your life, or are you afraid of being in this place alone, after the crimes you have been guilty of?"

"I have met with horrors here that I litttle thought to experience," replied Macraisy. "They have lowered the dead body of my victim into this vault, and his bleeding form now lies within a few yards of me. I would have fled, but death stared me in the face on every side, and at last, as my only refuge from these terrors, I sought death by my own hands."

"And have not been able to meet with it?"

"No," replied the miserable wretch, "I must still live, and each moment I fancy I hear the approaching footsteps of those who are seeking my place of retreat."

"Then though you were not afraid of committing a murder, you are too great a coward to meet the consequences?"

"Ay," muttered the other, "you dare insult me in my helplessness, but would not have ventured to have uttered one such word had I been able to protect myself. But beware how you wrong me, Caleb, for rage may yet lend me sufficient strength to hurl vengeance upon those who come to triumph in my downfall."

"Come, come, don't let you and I make a quarrel over it," exclaimed the other, "for I'm in as much danger as you are, and for the life of me, I don't know which way to get out of it."

"Haven't you the free use of your limbs?"

"Yes, but what's the use of that, when I shall stand as hard a chance as you do if they lay their hands on me?"

"Fool! Can't you tell them you had nothing to do with the murder?"

"Yes," answered Caleb, "I can tell 'em so, but the question is whether they'll believe a word I have to say."

"But you have heard my confession, and I dare say mean to make use of it," exclaimed the other.

"Perhaps that's what I ought to do," he replied; "but somehow I don't much fancy turning informer, even though I know you deserve to be hanged, as much as any fellow that was ever sent to the gallows."

"That may be," returned Dan Macraisy with a groan, "but I would have spared myself the pain of being made a public spectacle of, if my arm had not failed in doing its duty. Curses on the ill-directed blow, for had my aim been true, my heart would have ceased to beat long before now."

"Don't you think then it is better to live a little while and repent?"

"Repent!" exclaimed the ruffian; "you little know how much I have to repent, or you would not talk so lightly about it. But why talk of that when the bare thought of the past is a torture, that you and others like you cannot imagine?"

"But you are recovering, and may yet escape."

"How can I escape when my limbs are too weak to support me?" he asked. "I have tried to stand upright on my feet, and fell, as you see me, at the first step I attempted to make."

"That may be," answered Caleb, "but you will gain strength presently, and then, perhaps, with the assistance of my arm we may be able to reach the high road, where we shall meet with a coach, or some other conveyance that will take us to London, and if once we get there, you surely have friends that will give you shelter, till there's an opportunity of crossing over the water."

"I know not a soul," answered Macraisy, "that would not betray me for the sake of a reward."

"Barring myself," exclaimed his companion; "for though I hate the crime you have been guilty of, I'll not turn round against you when I see that everybody else has done so."

"Do you mean that?"

"I do."

"Then you are a better fellow than I took you for," answered Macraisy, "and if it hadn't been for this wound, I should have had some hope of getting out of this infernal scrape. But it's no use talking now, Caleb, for I'm fixed here; and the best thing you can do, will be to go and tell the first person you meet with where I am to be found."

"What should I do that for?"

"For the sake of the reward, to be sure."

"Then, once for all, I'll have nothing to do with it."

"And why not," demanded Dan Macraisy, "when you may as well have it as anybody else?"

"Because money got that way would never do me any good," replied Caleb; "and even if it did, I should be sorry to earn it by giving up a fellow-creature to the gallows."

"But I have no wish to live, tortured as I am by this wound."

"Don't you think that may be healed?"

"Perhaps it might," answered Dan. "but who can heal a conscience that suffers all the torture that mine does? No, no, 'Caleb, I have thought it all over while I've been lying here, and would rather perish at once than live another hour. Besides, I've been reflecting a good deal about that Jonathan Bradford; and if he should be hanged for a crime that was done by myself, it would only be adding another murder to the deeds I have already committed."

"You repent what you've done, then?"

"I do; but what's the use of that when I know it's too late? Didn't this hand of mine strike the blow that killed Mr. Hayes?—and can my soul ever know rest after such an act as that?"

"It was bad enough, there's no doubt," answered Caleb Scrimmidge; "but for all that, I think it would be worth while to try and escape."

"Escape is impossible, I tell you."

"What, if I give you a little of my assistance?"

"No assistance can be of any use now," replied the other, "for I have lost much blood, and am too weak to walk a dozen steps, even with the help you could give me. Jonathan Bradford, however, may yet be saved; and, if you would save me from a still further crime, go and declare to the first magistrate you can meet with that he is innocent of the deed he has been tried and condemned for."

"That he has himself stated already," exclaimed Caleb; "but he can't find any one that will believe him."

"But you, at any rate, can declare that you were present when I confessed the crime he has been charged with."

"I've already said I'll have nothing to do with that."

"And why not, when you can do as you please about saying where I am to be found?"

"That, to be sure, may make some difference," replied the other, "though, to confess the truth, I would rather not have any hand in the matter."

"Perhaps you are afraid of being suspected as my accomplice in the murder of the old gentleman?"

"I didn't give that a thought," replied Caleb, "though now you mention it I shouldn't wonder at all if they did suspect something of the sort, for we slept in the same room at the George that night, and they would hardly believe the murder could have been committed by one, without the other knowing something about it."

"And yet it was so," exclaimed Macraisy, "for I can swear that you had no more hand in it than Jonathan Bradford himself. So away with you, Caleb, and see if you can get that man out of the horrible dilemma I've helped him into."

"Won't you be afraid of being left by yourself in this vault?"

"I'm afraid of being here even when you are with me," answered Dan Macraisy, ' but anything will be better than dying with the knowledge that I have suffered another to be hanged for my crime. Had the blow at my own heart just now been struck as I intended, you would have found me dead instead of bewailing a crime that its no longer in my power to prevent."

"That may be all very true," exclaimed the other, " but it strikes me, Dan, that it would have been much better to have tried to make your escape instead of giving yourself all this pain, till you saw no other way of getting out of the clutches of the people you are afraid to face."

"Till now I never knew what fear was," returned Macraisy, "but you don't know what it is to have the blood of a dying man crying aloud for vengeance. I would have laughed at the notion till now, but the reality has worked a great change in me."

"I suppose then you don't mean to make any attempt to get yourself out of this awkward plight?"

"What can a helpless fellow like me do?" he asked. " I feel too weak to crawl out of this infernal dark hole, and the question is whether it won't be better to give myself up at once."

"You ought to know best about that," exclaimed Caleb, "but of course I needn't say what the consequence of it will be."

"I know all about that."

"And you are not afraid of the gallows?"

"There's nothing I'm so much afraid of as living to endure the torture of a guilty mind," answered Dan Macraisy. "The image of the murdered man will ever be before me, and can anything be more horrible than the remorse I must feel for a deed that, sooner or later, must be brought home to me? You can, therefore, tell the blood-hounds of the law where to find me, and say also they may come fearlessly, since I am unarmed and too weak to offer resistance."

"It shall not be I who betrays you," exclaimed the other, " for I couldn't find it in my heart to betray you to the gibbet, though I don't know but I may tell some of the people hereabouts, that Jonathan Bradford is not guilty of the crime that he has been tried for."

"Then you must tell them who murdered Mr. Hayes, or they'll not believe what you say."

"Very likely I must," answered Caleb, "but I'll try to make them believe that you have got clear away from the neighbourhood."

"Which they'll do as they like about believing."

"At any rate they shall get nothing more out of me," he replied, "so stick close to the place where I have you, Dan, and when I come back again it shall be to see whether something can't be done towards getting you away from this part of the country. You shall have some brandy, my boy, and if that don't put some strength and spirits into you I don't know what will."

Whilst he was saying this he placed Macraisy in a more comfortable position, and

No. 15.

then once more crept out of the vault to carry into effect his well-intended but somewhat ill-advised project into effect. Having first made a careful survey to ascertain whether anybody was lurking about, he issued from the small aperture by which he had entered, and then making his way across the churchyard, pursued the path over the fields which led towards the place which he was about to visit. In a quarter of an hour he arrived at the George Inn, and entered it just as Sally had related to Mrs. Bradford the interview she had just had with her husband. Both of them seemed to be confounded by the unexpected appearance of one of the men who had slept in the house on the night of the murder; and Sally, uttering a slight scream, exclaimed—

"Ah! misses—misses!—here's one of the ruffians come back to finish the bad work they've began."

"What do you mean, young woman, by calling me a ruffian?" demanded Caleb Scrimmidge indignantly. "Have I ever done anything to deserve being called such a name by you?"

"Where is your companion?" asked Mrs. Bradford, who by this time had recovered some little degree of composure.

"Don't ask me about *him*, ma'am," replied Caleb, "because I shall not answer any questions that have nothing to do with the business that brought me here."

"Do you know who committed the murder?"

"That's another question that I can't answer at present," exclaimed Caleb Scrimmidge, "but it may be some consolation to hear me say that your husband is innocent."

"Of that I was already certain."

"Very likely," he replied, "but your being certain would'nt be enough to save him from the gallows."

"Can you throw any light on this horrid affair?"

"If time is given me I may be able to do so," answered Caleb, "but at present all I can say is that something will soon come out to set this matter in a right light."

"Then it's clear you know something more about it than you are willing to admit," interpose Sally.

"Young woman, you know nothing about it," he exclaimed, "or you would not suspect a poor innocent fellow like me of committing a murder."

"Did'nt you come here with that other stranger and sleep in the double-bedded room on the very night of the——"

"Yes, yes, that's all right enough," interrupted Caleb, "but I know nothing of the crime that had been committed till I woke next morning."

"Then pray what more do you know of it now?" asked Mrs. Bradford.

"I have only a clue," answered Caleb Scrimmidge after a pause, "but its very likely that may lead to something of importance if you will only have a little patience."

"Patience!" sighed Mrs. Bradford. "Do I not know that my husband is at this moment in extreme peril?"

"So he is, but matters won't last long as they are, and a few hours may serve to put everything to rights."

"Then, why not tell me whether the murderer is within reach of those whose duty it is to take him into custody?"

"Only have a little patience and you shall know all," exclaimed Caleb Scrimidge; "cases like this, Mrs. Bradford, must be dealt with very cautiously, or justice is defeated. So, leave everything to me, and when the proper time comes, I'll prove beyond fear of contradiction that your husband has been unjustly convicted."

"I know all that already," she sighed; "but, alas! nothing but positive proof will save him from a dreadful death."

"And why can't he keep out of the way of his pursuers till the truth of the case can be made clear?"

"Because so close a watch is kept round the neighbourhood that it is impossible for him to remain concealed much longer."

"A few hours will be enough," answered Caleb; "and by that time I expect to be able to give all the information that will be required."

"Do you know where to find the person who calls himself Squire O'Connor?" demanded Sally.

"No—n—no," stammered Scrimmidge; "how should I know anything of a man that has left the place?"

"It is said, that he is still lurking somewhere near."

"Who says so?"

"People that are like enough to be right," answered Sally; "and I rather think you could throw a great deal more light upon this affair if you had a mind to do it."

"Nonsense; don't you see how anxious I am to save an innocent man from punishment?"

"You would make us believe so," she replied; "but I've a notion that it's only done to turn away our attention whilst the murderer gains an opportunity to escape. You know it was that Squire O'Connor, or Dan Macraisy, as some people call him, that killed the old gentleman."

"How should I know anything of the kind when I tell you I was asleep all the night that it took place?"

"Couldn't you guess by his manner that he was guilty?"

"Lor' bless you!" exclaimed Caleb Scrimmidge; "is it at all likely he would let out the secret?"

"It appears, at all events, that you are not inclined to do so," answered Mrs. Bradford, "and it will therefore remain for us to trace out this dark deed as well as we can. Others, besides myself, suspect the man they call Dan Macraisy, and no trouble shall be spared to discover the place where he has secreted himself."

"Then they'll have to look for him a long way off," exclaimed Caleb, attempting to mystify the affair.

"At all events," answered Sally, "our people here are not likely to be misled, and it will be time enough to look a long way off when they have convinced themselves that he is not skulking somewhere in the neighbourhood. And here comes some one that will look pretty sharply after him, and after you, too, if you don't tell all you know about your companion."

Just at that moment, Henry Dornton was seen passing the window, and Caleb, unwilling to subject himself to a more rigid examination, hastily bade them good-day, and left the house just as the young man was entering it.

"I have come to bring you good news, Mrs. Bradford," exclaimed Dornton, "and to assure you, that within a very short time the real assassin of Mr. Hayes will be in custody."

"Alas!" she sighed, "will it not be too late to save him who has been unjustly condemned to die?"

"There is every reason to believe that all will turn out favourably," answered the young man, "for Bradford is still safe in his place of concealment, and it is supposed the murderer cannot much longed avoid detection."

"Is he known?"

"To your husband he is."

"And the villain is one of the two men who slept here on the night of the murder? In short, the man who accompanied the person who just now left this place?"

"I know nothing for certain," answered Henry Dornton, "but he is very strongly suspected, though your husband, who I have just seen, will not at present name the person who he himself believes committed the crime."

"You have seen my husband you say?"

"I have."

"Does any person besides yourself know where he is to be found?"

"I think no one, except your servant, and she is too faithful to betray a secret of such importance."

"Yes," exclaimed Sally, "there's another person in the secret, and that's Jack Rackbottle, but he would sooner suffer his right hand to be cut off than get his master into trouble. Poor fellow! they've taken him into custody on the bare suspicion that he assisted

Mr. Bradford to escape, and if they keep him locked up for the rest of his life, I'll be bound they'll never get a word out of him."

"Why has not my husband fled from this neighbourhood whilst there was a chance of doing so?" asked Mrs. Bradford.

"Because he thinks it would appear like a tacit admission of his guilt," replied the young man. "Besides, he now possesses the means for fixing the crime upon the right person, and is only waiting for some opportunity that has not yet been explained to me."

"Can I not go and see him?"

"It would be most ill-advised to do so," answered Dornton, "for you would be most certainly watched, and that would lead to a disastrous result which it is unnecessary for me to explain. From what has been said, there appears to be every prospect of a more happy termination than was expected, and I think we cannot do better than let your husband follow out his own plans."

"Alas!" sighed Mrs. Bradford, "you seem to have forgot the prejudice that exists against him."

"That some few persons have expressed their belief of your husband's guilt I am well aware," answered the young man. "But even the most prejudiced will acknowledge the wrong they have done him, when the truth comes to be properly explained."

"And even if they don't, I fancy it will matter very little," interposed Sally, "for there's plenty that will be his friends by-and-by, and for my own part I wouldn't give a thankye for the good opinion of people that turn their backs upon another the moment he has fallen into trouble. As for that Lawyer Dozey, if I was master, I'd never have another word to say to him for the mischief he has done."

"You must not judge Mr. Dozey too harshly," returned the young man, "for though he certainly has taken a very active part in this affair, he was no doubt actuated by what he conceived to be an imperative duty. Nay, even your master himself, who has suffered more than anybody else, acquits him of all blame in the course he has thought proper to pursue."

"But two innocent people might have been hanged through him."

"Very true, and we have reason to be thankful that such a termination is not now likely to take place. In a few hours all will be satisfactorily explained, and then Mr. Bradford will be once more restored to the happiness he so well deserves."

'You think then," sighed the wife, "that he will never look back with regret to the misery he has passed through?"

"The remembrance must undoubtedly sometimes pass through his mind," answered Henry Dornton, "but there will still be the consolation left of knowing that he has regained the good opinion of the world."

"That's all very true," exclaimed Sally, "but it's not very pleasant to know that one has suffered without deserving it."

"But will he not have about him those that he loves?"

"Ay," exclaimed Mrs. Bradford, "and it shall be my anxious and constant endeavour to banish from his thoughts the recollection of the sorrows he has endured. Time, too, will I have no doubt have a favourable effect upon him, and when his friends smile upon him as they used to do, he may perhaps feel that his situation is not so terrible a one as it might have been."

"And with his wife and children about him he will soon be as happy as he was," observed the young man. "There will be the care of his business, too, to occupy his attention, and that will serve in no slight degree to chase away thoughts that will but be a source of grief and affliction to him."

"Think you his friends will respect him much as ever?" asked Mrs. Bradford, in a tone of doubt.

"I should think their friendship not worth having if they do not," he replied, "for when innocence is once clearly proved, there can be no excuse for the coldness and neglect of those who have made professions of their esteem. For my own part I have not known your husband long, but I sincerely pity him for the misfortunes that have so undeservedly fallen upon him, and will henceforth do all in my power to show the world that there is at least one person, who is willing to be ranked among the number of those who regard him with respect."

The arrival of some customers at the Inn here put an end to the conversation, and whilst Mrs. Bradford was attending to their orders, Henry Dornton left the place for the purpose of seeking out Lawyer Dozey who he was so anxious to convince of the fatal error into which his suspicion had led him.

————

CHAPTER XVIII

A PURSUIT AFTER THE FUGITIVE.—LAWYER DOZEY AND CORPORAL SAM HOLD A COUNCIL TOGETHER.—PROSPECTS OF A SUCCESSFUL TERMINATION OF THE SEARCH.—AN ATTEMPT IS MADE TO TRIFLE WITH THE FIDELITY OF JACK RACKBOTTLE.—PERIL AGAIN THREATENS MRS. BRADFORD.

THOUGH at present very few persons suspected Dan Macraisy of the murder which had created so great a sensation, it was known almost to a certainty that he had been guilty of a burglary at Frogmore Farm, and the whole neighbourhood was in a state of commotion and anxiety for his arrest. That he had not yet been able to make his escape from the place was certain, because a sharp look out had been kept up from the moment when his guilt had been rumoured about, and the large reward offered for his apprehension had set every one on the alert to earn the attempting bait. Corporal Sam was one of the most active in the pursuit, and having mentioned the subject to Mr. Dozey they both proceeded to the vault beneath the church where it was rumoured the fugitive had been seen. Their search was, however, too late, for Macraisy, having somewhat recovered from the effect of his self-inflicted wound, had contrived to crawl forth from his hiding place, and sought refuge in a neighbouring hovel, where he concealed himself beneath a quantity of straw till an opportunity should offer itself for getting beyond the reach of danger.

"The bird has flown if ever he has been here," exclaimed the corporal, "and hang me if I know where we can look for him next."

"Why should we be wasting our time about him when there's matters of more importance to think of?" demanded Dozey. "The fellow seems to have changed his quarters ; but there's Bradford still lurking about, and we ought to think of taking a murderer before we go hunting after a fellow who must sooner or later fall into the clutches of some of the many people that are in pursuit of him. But I see how it is, corporal, you are thinking more of the reward than of the duty we owe the public."

"I don't know much about that," answered the soldier, "for it seems we should be only throwing away our time and trouble, now that people begin to fancy that Bradford had no hand in the murder."

"And do you believe all that a parcel of foolish people choose to say ?"

"Not exactly ; but if he is guilty, it's not likely he would remain in the neighbourhood after having contrived to give us the slip."

"So you may fancy," answered Lawyer Dozey ; "but I'm very much mistaken if he goes away without attempting to see his wife. We must, therefore, keep a good look-out, and I'll answer for it we have him before many hours are over."

"And supposing we do?" asked the corporal, "what will they do with him?"

"Send him to the gallows, to be sure."

"Whether he deserves it or not, I suppose?"

"How can any reasonable man entertain a doubt upon the subject?" exclaimed the old gentleman. "Hasn't he been convicted by a jury after a fair trial?—and isn't that quite enough?"

"It would be, if it were impossible for people to make a mistake," replied the corporal; "but I have heard of mistakes being made before now, and there's a good many that begin to have a notion that Jonathan Bradford had nothing at all to do with the murder."

"How happened it, then, that he was found in the room while poor Mr. Hayes was still in the agonies of death?"

"He says he went there immediately upon hearing cries for assistance."

"Ay, ay," answered the old man; "that excuse may do for some folks, but for my own part, I am not to be so easily deceived by such a story, and would rather believe the evidence of my own senses, seeing him as I did, standing by the side of the murdered man, with the instrument of assassination still in his hand. Besides, he could not explain anything in a satisfactory manner, and I am therefore still of opinion that he deserves the fate he has been doomed to."

"But if more time were given he might still be able to prove that he had nothing to do with the crime."

"Humph, then you must assist in looking after him."

" I'd much rather look after that other chap," answered the corporal: "for it's pretty certain he has committed a robbery upon one of the farmers in this neighbourhood, and I have received orders to capture him with as little delay as possible, because it's thought something of importance may come of it after he is taken."

"Psha! who has put that foolish notion into your head?"

"The man you lately ordered to be arrested."

"What, Jack Rackbottle?"

"I believe that's his name, but whether it is or not, you know the chap I mean, and he said plainly enough, that he suspected Dan Macraisy to be the person who committed the murder."

"And can't you understand why he said that?"

"No."

"Then I'll tell you,—he want's to clear his old master, and don't care upon whose shoulders he throws the blame. The scoundrel has already endeavoured to defeat the ends of justice by assisting the prisoner to escape, and now he would complete what he has begun by directing suspicion upon some other person."

"Don't you think Macraisy had anything to do with it?"

"How is it likely when he was not in the room at the time I found Jonathan Bradford and his wife there?"

"That's a question more easily asked than answered," returned the corporal. " He may have escaped immediately after the act was committed, and as Bradford and his wife were the first to go to the assistance of the old gentleman, they were at once suspected of having made away with him."

"Depend upon it you are deceived," exclaimed Lawyer Dozey, "for the case has been proved as clearly as possible, and there were few persons in the court, I believe, who were not satisfied with the verdict of the jury. Bradford knew the old gentleman had a large sum of money in his possession, and there can be no doubt that the gold tempted him to perpetrate the diabolical deed."

"And yet, I have heard that he has always till now borne a very excellent character among his neighbours."

"That may be," answered the other; "but this is by no means a solitary instance of a man suddenly becoming exceedingly wicked and doing that which no one would ever have suspected them of before. Be that as it may, however, I am determined never to relax in my endeavours till that fellow, Jonathan Bradford, is again placed under safe custody."

"And where are we to look for him?"

"In every place that is likely to afford him a refuge," answered Mr. Dozey. " He may perhaps be concealed in his own house; and, in order to try whether that is the case, I shall order Mrs. Bradford to be again taken into custody."

"What good do you expect to get by that?"

"Why," answered the other, "it is well known he loves his wife very dearly, and the moment he finds she is in danger he will surrender himself up, in order to effect her deliverance."

"Humph!" muttered the corporal, "your plan may be a very ingenious one; but it strikes me as being about as cruel a notion as ever entered the mind of a man. Mrs. Bradford is innocent, or she ought not to have been set at liberty, and I don't see why she should be taken up again, merely because her husband has been lucky enough to escape."

"As for that," exclaimed the lawyer, " everything is fair when you want to lay dolh of a great criminal."

"But it's doubtful whether Bradford is a criminal."

"Those who doubt it are fools," answered Dozey, "for I who have paid more attention to the matter than any other person, am quite satisfied that my first suspicions are perfectly correct. And if anything were wanted to prove the truth of my conjecture, it is to be found in the fact of the accused man having taken the first opportunity that offered to escape."

"And who wouldn't have done the same thing," demanded Corporal Sam, "when he saw that nothing else could save him from the gallows? Nor can I see how it proves anything against him, and, for my own part, I should not be sorry if he manages to keep himself out of sight till the real murderer has been discovered."

"Then, I suppose you will not assist me in looking for him?"

"I'll not go so far as to say that," replied the soldier, "because I'm bound to afford my aid when lawfully called upon to do so; but, if I may venture to give a word of advice, I should say that the best thing we can do, will be to look first of all after this Dan Macraisy."

"Pshaw! he is only a robber, and the other has been guilty of a far more serious offence. Besides, one knows well enough that he cannot escape; and it will be time enough to look for him when Jonathan Bradford is once more safe under lock and key."

"But how are you going to find out where he is?"

"By asking Jack Rackbottle."

"Who, I suppose, will not be likely to betray his old master, even if he knows where he is to be found."

"That remains to be proved," exclaimed Lawyer Dozey, "for imprisonment will even bring him to his senses; and he will have no chance of being restored to liberty till he has given the information I require. I intend, therefore, to see him immediately, and ascertain how far we may rely upon his services."

"He'll be a fool to say anything so long as he is a prisoner."

"I expect to find him obstinate," answered Mr. Dozey, "and therefore will take him to the George Inn, where we shall have an opportunity of questioning him, in the presence of Mrs. Bradford. He is obstinate so far, but may be brought to his senses when he finds that we are determined to leave no measures untried till the culprit has been restored to the custody of those he has escaped from."

"Do you want me to go with you to this Jack Rackbottle?"

"Yes, for he may escape unless you and two or three of your soldiers have him in charge."

"But he may not choose to say anything to throw light upon the affair you are so anxious to discover."

"In that case he'll run the risk of being shut up in a prison for a very considerable period."

"Which he may not mind if he is determined to remain faithful to his old master."

"His old master is a covicted murderer, and therefore deserves no commiseration or assistance."

"I'm afraid you are rather prejudiced against this Bradford," exclaimed the corporal, "for it seems to me that he may be innocent, and if so it would be cruel to hurry him to the gallows till an opportunity has been given to fix the crime on the right person. A few hours may bring strange things to light, and for my own part I hope nothing will be seen or heard of the fugitive till after it is known whether Dan Macraisy had any hand in the murder."

"Perhaps you know where Bradford is?"

"I know no more about it then you do," answered Corporal Sam.

"And if you did it seems you would keep the secret to yourself. However, I would advise you to be careful how you act, for I shall keep a watchful eye upon you, and shall announce the fact to your commanding officer if anything should happen to confirm my suspicion."

"Do you suppose I had any hand in his escape?"

"No," replied the old gentleman, "I acquit you of all blame there, but you must also give the assistance that may be required, for the man we seek cannot be far off, and our exertions, if made at once, may lead to the result I anticipate."

"You think then that he will remain in a place where there's no chance for him to escape?"

"I certainly think so," answered the old gentleman, "because there are strong motives why he should not yet leave the neighbourhood. A short time, however, will serve to prove whether my expectations are well founded; and if Bradford should be taken through your means I will myself take care to reward you."

"I'm obliged to you Mr. Dozey," exclaimed the corporal, "but in my opinion it would be much better to look after the other chap."

"What, Macraisy?"

"Yes," he replied, "we have good reason for believing that he is a thief, and may therefore suspect him to be the man that committed the murder Mr. Bradford has been tried and sentenced for At any rate, he ought to be looked after, and then if he confesses the crime we shall have the consolation of seeing an innocent person restored to his home and family."

"We'll think of that by-and-by," exclaimed the old gentleman, "for the greater crime demands our attention sooner than the first one. I am not vindictive in pursuing this course; and if it should after all be proved to the satisfaction of the world that he has been unjustly subjected to the prosecution, no one will be more ready than myself to make reparation for any injury he may have suffered. So now accompany me to the cage, and assist in conveying Jack Rackbottle to the inn, where we will make one more effort to prevail upon him to confess where his master is secreted."

Seeing that it would be useless to offer any further remonstrance, Corporal Sam and his men followed Mr. Dozey to the village, where the latter obtained admittance to the strong-room, leaving the soldiers on the outside till their services should be required. Jack, not at all alarmed at the situation in which he found himself, received the lawyer with as much apparent unconcern as if nothing particular had occurred; and after a slight nod of recognition, inquired if anything had yet been heard of his unfortunate master.

"At present he has succeeded in eluding our vigilance," replied Mr. Dozey; "but as we have every reason to believe that he is still in the neighbourhood, he is only uselessly delaying a capture that must shortly take place."

"And what would be done with him if he is caught"

"Why, in that case, our first duty will be to place him in safe custody, where he will remain till we have communicated with the proper authorities."

"Who I suppose would order him to be hanged?"

"Most likeely they would," answered Mr. Dozey, "for as the time named for the xecution has already passed, there will be no necessity for any further delay. And its cannot be denied that he deserves his fate, you, Jack Rackbottle, ought no longer to conceal from us the place where he is to be found."

"And who has told you that I know the place where he is to be found?" asked the other sharply.

"Nobody has asserted anything of the kind as a fact," replied the lawyer, "but it is pretty generally rumoured that you assisted him in his flight, and it is therefore the object of my present visit to caution you against keeping the secret any longer."

"You may caution as much as you please," exclaimed Jack, "but I know best what to do, and no one shall ever persuade me to betray a man that has always been kind to me."

"Then you admit knowing where he is?"

"I admit nothing of the sort."

"Come, come, my good fellow," exclaimed Lawyer Dozey, "this is no time for

trifling I can tell you, for we are determined that the ends of justice shall not be defeated, and all who aid in shielding a criminal from the law, will be made to feel the consequences of their own rashness. I speak to you as a friend, and my advice is that you look to your own safety, by delivering up a murderer to those who are in pursuit of him."

"So I would if I knew him to be a murderer," answered Jack, "but as I have good reason to believe him as innocent as you or I are, I will not say a word that will get him into trouble."

No. 16.

"If you are so positive of his innocence, why not say at once whether you suspect anybody else?"

"Because Mr. Bradford will do that when the proper time comes, and then you'll be ashamed of yourself for having caused all this persecution upon one that never deserved it."

"But I acted upon the strongest evidence."

"I don't blame you for what was done in the heat of the moment," replied Jack Rackbottle, "but you have had plenty of time for reflection since then, and I don't see why those two men that slept at our house on the night of the murder were not to have been suspected as well as anybody else."

"They were neither of them in the room when I entered it."

"Very likely not, but there was plenty of time to escape after the fatal blow was struck, and it ain't to be supposed they would stay after the house was alarmed by the old gentleman's cries."

"I see you are determined to see this affair only in a light favourable to your master," exclaimed Lawyer Dozey, "the case, however, has undergone a most careful consideration, and after hearing all the evidence, the jury would come to no other conclusion than that the prisoner was guilty of the crime charged against him. The same opinion prevails also everywhere else, so that if I am mistaken I have the consolation of knowing that I do not stand alone in my opinion. His anxiety to escape, too, adds considerable weight to our former suspicions, and I therefore cannot conceive why you so obstinately adhere to your own ill-supported prejudice."

"It may be all very well to argufy the matter to suit your own notion," answered Jack, "but by-and-by you'll hear something that will bring you round to my way of thinking."

"If you know anything why not reveal it at once?"

"Because I have been told by Mr. Bradford himself to leave everything to him."

"When did you see him last?"

"Humph! that's a question I would rather not answer."

"Will you tell me then if he intends to surrender himself up?"

"I think it's most likely he will; but that must depend upon whether he can do so safely."

"In other words," exclaimed Mr. Dozey, "you expect he will be able to fix this crime upon somebody else?"

"Exactly so."

"And I suppose you are thinking of the two men who slept at the George Inn on the night of the murder?"

"I only suspect one of them."

"And that is the man known as Dan Macraisy?"

"Ay, or Squire O'Connor, or anything you please."

"You are mistaken then," answered the lawyer, "for, worthless as the fellow is, I feel quite confident in my own mind that he is entirely free from this crime."

"Ah," exclaimed Jack Rackbottle, "but I've a notion you'll change your opinion by-and-by if you can only lay hold of the fellow. But no, he is suffered to go at large, though he knows a great deal more than you imagine. But never mind, time will prove all, and then perhaps you may be sorry that you were in such a hurry about accusing other people."

"I can assure you that nothing would afford me greater satisfaction than to be convinced of your master's innocence," answered the lawyer, "though it must be confessed I am as far from believing it as ever."

"Then you are still determined to look for him?"

"I am, and you must assist me."

"*Must*? We shall soon see about that."

"At any rate you must accompany me back to the George Inn, and if you still refuse to give the desired information, I shall feel it my duty to order Mrs. Bradford once more into custody on suspicion of harbouring a fugitive from justice."

"Why you don't mean to say, that you are going to be so cruel as that?" exclaimed Jack Rackbottle.

" Extreme cases like this require extreme measures," answered Mr. Dozey, "and I am forced to adopt a scheme that I believe is the only one that will lead to the discovery. Bradford is, I know, warmly attached to his wife, and I have no doubt he will at once come forward to deliver himself up when he hears she is in custody. '

" And don't you think the scheme a confoundedly bad one, when a wife is to be made the means of bringing her husband into trouble ?"

" It may be so, but I have no alternative."

" Then for the first time since I've been here, I'm sorry that you have deprived me of my liberty."

" Why ?"

" Because, if I had been free, and knew as much as I do now, I would have let Mr. Bradford know of your devilish plans."

" So, then," exclaimed the old gentleman, " you know where to find him readily, do you ?"

" I have never altogether denied it," answered Jack Rackbottle ; " but it's not likely I was going to tell you anything, when I know what sort of fate my poor master might expect. However, there's one consolation, things won't turn out as you wish, and by-and-by you'll get nicely laughed at for the trouble you've thrown away."

" Never mind how I'm laughed at," exclaimed Lawyer Dozey, " for when a man is performing his duty, it matters very little what the world may say or think about him. At all events, you must go with me, for I have Corporal Sam and two or three soldiers to assist ; and if you won't go by fair means, we must try what a little force will do. And hark ye, sirrah !—if you say a word in the presence of Mrs. Bradford to spoil the business I have undertaken, you shall afterwards have sufficient reason to repent it."

The old gentleman then opened the door, and beckoned for the corporal to come to his assistance. The soldier obeyed, but with evident reluctance ; and seeing no other alternative, persuaded the prisoner to offer no resistance. This, however, was not needed, for Jack Rackbottle had already made up his mind what course to pursue; and all being in readiness, he left the place under a military guard.

CHAPTER XIX.

UNAVAILING EFFORTS TO PROCURE EVIDENCE.—ANOTHER ATTEMPT IS MADE WHICH PROVES EQUALLY FRUITLESS.—APPEARANCE OF THE FUGITIVES.—UNFORTUNATE TESTIMONY AND ITS RESULTS.—A VOLUNTARY SURRENDER.—REMORSE AND CONFESSION OF THE CULPRIT.

DURING their progress towards the inn, Jack Rackbottle maintained a determined silence, and all the efforts of the lawyer were thrown away upon the man he had thought to frighten into a confession of the place where his master had secreted himself. The honest-hearted fellow was determined to suffer anything rather than betray the secret which had been entrusted to him ; and by the time they had reached the space in front of the George Inn, the old gentleman found himself as far as ever from the object he had in view. The corporal and his men, however, were ordered to stand on one side in case their assistance should be needed; and then the lawyer once more addressing himself to Jack, pointed out the uselessness of endeavouring to defeat the ends of Justice; and made great promises of his future favour and protection in the event of his making the required disclosure.

" I'll tell you what it is, Mr. Lawyer," exclaimed Jack Rackbottle, at length breaking silence, "you think, maybe, to frighten me into opening my mind upon this subject ; but it won't do. I know what I know, but it's devilish little you'll be the wiser for it, I can tell you."

" Then you prefer going back to prison, where you will have to remain till you think proper to tell all you know about this affair ?"

" Your threats won't get anything out of me," answered the other, " so you may as well spare yourself the trouble of asking any more useless questions. My master is safe enough where he is; and as for my mistress, you'll get no information from her, so I would advise you not to ask her any questions."

"She must take the consequences then."

"What consequences?"

"Why she will be immediately conducted to the county-prison, there to await the further orders of government."

"And what are you going to do with me?"

"It will be for others to decide what punishment you are to receive," answered Mr. Dozey; "but, at all events, you can expect no quarter, after the obs'inacy you have manifested."

"I shall get as much as I ask for," returned Jack, carelessly.

"Have you reflected that it is probable you may be transported for having assisted in the escape of a convicted murderer?"

"He may have been convicted," answered the other, "but he is no more guilty than you or I."

"That is not the question," exclaimed Mr. Dozey. "He has been convicted upon what appears to be satisfactory evidence, and you will be punished for the share you have had in his flight."

"It's all very well to tell me so," answered the other, "but big words will get nothing out of me, I can tell you. Don't throw away your precious time, Mr. Dozey, for I have spoken out my mind freely and boldly, and I would say just the same if the king himself were to question me upon the subject."

"You will change your tone before long, sirrah."

"So you may fancy," answered Jack Rackbottle: "but I've made up my mind what to do, and you'll be just as likely to get the secret out of a milestone as out of me."

"Yet for all that, Jonathan Bradford will not be able much longer to hide himself from our search."

"I don't know that he'll need to do so much longer," answered the other, "for he is only waiting till the proper time comes, and then he'll not be afraid to show himself to you or anybody else. However, yonder comes my poor mistress, looking sorrowful enough, as she well may; so I hope, for humanity's sake, you won't do anything to add to the misery she already feels."

The person of whom he spoke now approached them, and inquired why the military had been brought so near the house?

"I should have thought, madam, such a question was quite unnecessary," replied Mr. Dozey. "You are, of course, aware that your husband has escaped from custody? and as it was thought most likely he had sought refuge in his own house, I have brought these people to assist me in making a search."

"The doors, as you see, are open for you," replied Mrs. Bradford; "but before you commence, I declare most solemnly that the person you seek has not been here since that fatal night when he was dragged away to answer an accusation of murder."

"Have you seen him since his escape?"

"I have not."

"You may have spoken the truth," exclaimed Lawyer Dozey, "but there is a strong case of suspicion, and as only one course remains open to me, I must place you under arrest till others, whose authority is superior to my own, have had an opportunity of investigating the case thoroughly."

"If this be said to intimidate me," she replied, "the attempt has been made in vain. I am ready to accompany you to prison, and will not utter a word of complaint at the harshness of your proceeding, so long as I know my husband is free."

"Be assured it is impossible he can be so much longer."

"Yet I dare hope for the best."

"Hope for nothing," answered Mr. Dozey. "If found, he will not easily escape again, for these soldiers, as you see, are armed, and their orders are to fire upon him, rather than permit a condemned criminal to elude them. If, therefore, you know aught, I counsel you for your own sake, not to trifle any further with those who are but performing their duty."

" Do not dare, sir, to insult the feelings of a wife !" she exclaimed resolutely. " 'Tis for him and for himself that I suffer : for myself, nothing. You have now heard my answer, and I am willing to accompany you to my prison, since it must be so."

" Don't do anything of the kind," interrupted Jack Rackbottle, "for missus don't know where her husband is, though I do, and if any body ought to be shut up in a prison, it's myself."

"Faithful fellow ! Be sure Heaven will reward the noble services you would perform," exclaimed Mrs. Bradford. " You, however, shall not suffer in our cause, for rather would I perish in a dungeon than suffer such fidelity to meet with a punishment that is deserved only by the guilty."

" If you are determined to be obstinate it will be no fault of mine, whatever may happen," he replied. " Every chance has been offered you ; and since my well-intended advice has been neglected, you must now go with these men to the prison, where you will have to remain as long as your husband continues to evade our pursuit."

"Stay !" exclaimed a voice suddenly from behind, " for Jonathan Bradford, whom you seek, is here to surrender himself rather than see his wife dragged away to a dungeon that she merits not."

"Ah !" cried Lawyer Dozey, turning to the soldiers ; " let him be seized, for this is the fellow of whom we were in search."

" Fellow !" exclaimed Jonathan, fiercely ; " I have never deserved the name, and will bear it no longer. Look up, my dear wife," he added, producing a written paper from his pocket. " Look up, gladly and proudly, for this contains the proof of my innocence. Here, read this confession of the real assassin, and then join with me in thanks to Heaven for the mercy that has been bestowed upon us. Read it, Mr. Dozey, and then admit how cruelly I have been wronged by the vile calumnies you have assisted to heap upon me."

" Eh, what's this ?" exclaimed the lawyer, glancing over the paper which had been placed in his hand. " What's this I see ?—The confession of the murderer of Mr. Hayes !—Signed ' Daniel Macraisy !' "

" Exactly so," interposed Jack Rackbottle ; "so now you see that I was right, for that's the name of one of the men that slept at our inn on the night when the poor old gentleman lost his life."

" That may be all very true," observed the lawyer, " but we must not give an opinion in too great a hurry, for this document may after all be a forgery."

" A forgery !" exclaimed Bradford.

" Ay ; have you any witnesses to prove that it is genuine ?"

" I have the person who was present when the confession was written, and signed by the man whose name is signed."

" Let him be produced."

" Caleb, stand forward !" exclaimed Bradford, and scarcely had the words been uttered, when the person he had named presented himself.

" Is this your witness ?" asked the lawyer.

"It is."

" Humph !" muttered the old man, eyeing Caleb from head to foot ; " this is a very important affair to decide upon, and, to confess the truth, your witness does not appear to be respectable enough to be credited, even upon his oath."

" What's your objection to me?" asked Scrimmidge.

" I have already stated it. Besides, I see you are one of the two men that slept in the house on the night when the murder was committed, and therefore your evidence must be received with suspicion,"

"So ! I'm not respectable, ain't I ?"

" Your appearance is not so at any rate, and I shall therefore decide upon rejecting it as worthless."

" This is very pretty treatment," exclaimed Caleb, indignantly, " but I'd have you know that I am a respectable watchmaker's apprentice from Seven Dials, and though I was fool enough to run away, I mean to run back again as soon as I can."

"What do you know about the document?" asked the old gentleman, after having again perused it.

"Why I know everything about it, to be sure," answered Caleb. "I was standing close by Dan all the while he was telling me what to write down, and terribly frightened Macraisy looked too, as well he might when we come to think of everything."

"How do you know he was frightened?"

"By his hand shaking, as you may yourself see, if you only notice how crookedly he has written all the letters of his name."

"And pray wha reason had he to be frightened?"

"Reason enough I think," answered the other, "for Mr. Bradford stood over him all the while, and thretened to blow out his brains with a loaded pistol that he held in his hand, if he didn't put his own signature at the bottom of the paper."

"'Tis as I suspected," exclaimed Mr. Dozey. "Force has been use to compel this man, Macraisy, to sign his name to the document, and therefore the confession being extorted, is of no use. Your evidence is quite conclusive, young man, and has clearly proved all that had before suspected."

"But just now you said I was not worthy of belief."

"What I may have said just now and may think at present are two very different things," answered the old gentleman. "There seems to be no doubt of your having spoken the truth, and upon your word I see every reason to place the fullest reliance."

"Have I been doing any mischief then?"

"On the contrary you have performed a very serviceable part, and it shall be my care to see that you are properly rewarded for it. A malefactor has been convicted by your evidence, and justice will now fortunately overtake him."

"What the deuce does all this mean?" demanded Caleb Scrimmidge, completely bewildered by what he had heard. "I came here to give my evidence in favour of Mr. Bradford, and now it seems you are going to turn it all against him."

"You have nothing to reproach yourself with on that score," answered Lawyer Dozy, "for a conviction had already taken place, and as the prisoner has now surrendered himself, nothing remains but to take care that punishment speedily follows."

"Punishment! why he is innocent."

"Don't deceive yourself with any such notion," exclaimed the lawyer, "for his guilt has already been clearly proved, a conviction has taken place, and as everything is prepared, the sheriff will consider it his duty immediately to attend the execution of the criminal."

"Alas!" cried Mrs. Bradford, falling upon the neck of her husband; "all hope has now fled for ever!"

"Yes," he replied with a groan of anguish, "it is in vain that I struggle any longer against my inflexible destiny. The web in which I am entangled cannot be shaken off! Death claimes me, and the victim must needs yield to his dreadful fate!"

"Nay," she cried. "if that must needs be, I will at least share the fate with you. Take me with you, Jonathan, for life has become a heavy burden to me—a dream—a curse. I will therefore forsake it—father,—children—all—rather than be left to mourn the sad destiny of one who was so dear to me."

"No," exclaimed Bradford, hoarsely. "I will at least be spared the shame of dying as a murderer on the scaffold. I am innocent of the crime charged against me, and fear not to quit life even though it may be by my own hand. I am armed, wife, and though I would not willingly injure another, I will defend myself, and, if need be, turn the weapon against my own life."

Thus saying, Jonathan Bradford suddenly drew a brace of pistols from beneath his vest, and presented them at those who were approaching to secure him. The lawyer saw not a moment was to be lost, and addressing himself to the soldiers, he ordered them immediately to arrest their prisoner.

"No one shall arrest me," exclaimed Bradford resolutely, "for I am a desperate man and ready to die rather than submit to meet the doom of a felon. I am ready to die as a man should, but it shall not be by the halter! Now then, soldiers, do your worst,—fire at my unprotected heart, and my last words shall be uttered in blessings for the mercy you have showed me."

The unhappy wife still clung to the bosom of her husband, and the soldiers, with levelled muskets, were preparing to despatch their victim, when Henry Dornton, with frantic cries, rushed wildly forward to his rescue.

"Hold !" he exclaimed, throwing himself between the soldiers and the man they were about to immolate. "Jonathan Bradford is innocent of the crime of murder! The real assassin has been found and will presently be here to confirm the words I have spoken."

"What does all this mean ?" demanded Lawyer Dozey, quite perplexed at the sudden interruption. "Who says Bradford is innocent after the proof we have had of his guilt ?"

"I say so," answered the young man ; "and if further evidence is wanting, it will presently be supplied by the wretched criminal who has already acknowledged his crime."

"Who is the person you speak of ?"

"One Daniel Macraisy, who lodged at the George Inn on the night when the deed was perpetrated."

"There, I told you so!" exclaimed Caleb Scrimmidge. You said a little while ago I was not respectable enough to take my word, and this unfortunate man would have been hanged if the chap who did the murder had not have been discovered just in the nick of time."

"Is Macraisy in custody ?" demanded Lawyer Dozey, without paying any attention to what had been last said.

"He is."

"And he admits the crime ?"

"He has made a full confession," answered Henry Dornton, "and appears to be full of remorse for the dreadful crime he has acommitted."

"Did he make no attempt to escape ?" asked Jonathan Bradford.

"He would have been troubled to do so," answered the young man, "for he has attempted to commit suicide, and was found lying completely exhausted near the door of a hovel where it is supposed he had fled for refuge. At first it was supposed he was dead, but after some little care had been bestowed upon him, consciousness returned, and the blood which was flowing from his wound having been staunched, he is now likely to recover sufficiently to take his trial."

"And of course he'll swing for it," observed Caleb Scrimmidge.

"If all we have heard be true, there can be little doubt of that," replied Mr. Dozey. "But now, young man, it is necessary to ask you a few questions. Pray how did it happen that you were seen associating with a man who we have reason to believe is both a robber and a murderer ?"

"We met by accident," answered Caleb. "I had been foolish enough to run away from my master, and a day or two before we came to this place I fell in company with this Dan Macraisy, and as he seemed to be a decent fellow, I agreed to travel in company with him."

"Do you happen to know anything about the robbery that took place at Frogmore farm ?"

"Nothing more than Dan Macraisy told me after it was all over."

"Did he admit having a hand in it ?"

"Yes; and he says he did it all by himself," replied the other. "So now, as I have got so well out of what might have been a very awkward dilemma, I shall get back to soon as possible to London, and earn my living in future as an honest watchmaker."

"You must not be in too great a hurry about leaving us," exclaimed Lawyer Dozey, "for it appears your evidence at the examination of the prisoner will be important, and you must remain here till this Daniel Macraisy has been committed for trial. You may then leave us for a time, but must return again before the day fixed on for our next county assize. Of course I mean if the news we have just now heard proves to be correct."

"A very short time will serve to convince you of that," answered Henry Dornton, 'for when I came away the prisoner's wound was nearly dressed; and when that was finished they were going to bring him here."

"Then my husband is again free?" cried Mrs. Bradford, who had now recovered from the speechless amazement into which the recent and sudden announcement had thrown her.

"Matters begin to wear a more favourable aspect it must be admitted," answered the lawyer; "but the news requires the fullest confirmation, before Bradford can be released."

"Is he, then, still suspected?"

"On the contrary," answered the old gentleman, "I begin to suspect my charge against him was ill-founded; and if so, no one can regret more than myself the alarm and agony I have occasioned him and his family. I, however, believed I was only performing a solemn duty; and even those who have been most injured will admit that there were strong grounds for the suspicion I entertained."

"I do admit it," replied Jonathan, "and am deeply impressed with gratitude for the services that have been rendered me by a faithful servant. But for him I should not have escaped from prison, and ere this discovery was made, the laws would have added one more victim to those who have already been made to suffer for crimes of which they were innocent. To him I owe my life; and the first use I make of my liberty shall be to establish him in some business in which his own industry and zeal will support him."

"Here comes the real assassin, I suppose," exclaimed the lawyer, as a crowd of people was seen approaching, two of whom, with difficulty, were supporting a man that they led between them.

"Yes," exclaimed Dan Macraisy, who had heard the latter words, " I am indeed the real murderer. The gold was too great a temptation for me, and I killed Mr. Hayes, to possess myself of it."

"Then how was it that the money was not touched?" asked Mr. Dozey.

"Because I was disturbed too soon," he replied. "The old gentleman called for assistance, and when I heard you and others hastening to the room, I made my escape as quickly as I could."

"Did anybody take a part in your crime?"

"Not a soul."

"Then you entirely acquit this young man, Caleb Scrimmidge, of any participation in it?"

"I do," answered Macraisy. "We occupied together the double-bedded chamber, and when my companion was asleep, I opened the window, and creeping along the tiling, entered the chamber of Mr. Hayes, and did that which I have now to suffer for."

"Are you sure that this young man was not watching you?"

"How could he do that when I drugged his drink, and he went off into a sound sleep? But why need I tell you anything more, when the paper I have signed will tell you all about it? It's enough that I confess my own guilt; and if my aim had but been a true one, I should not have been here to tell you of the crime I have been guilty of."

"You seem to be a penitent," observed Mr. Dozey, "and yet how nearly had you suffered another to be punished for your own dreadful act."

"Ay," answered Dan Macraisy; "and I never once thought of saving him by a confession, till they lowered the murdered body of my victim in the very same vault where I had sought concealment. Ah! what a moment of horror was that!—It seemed as if all the fiends of hell were surrounding me, and preparing to drag me to the place of punishment that I had hardly ever before thought of. The terror of the moment drove me mad, and in the frenzy that then possessed me, I made the attempt which has made me the hapless, miserable wretch you now behold me."

"And still," said Lawyer Dozey, "you made one last effort to escape from the neighbourhood."

"I did," replied the assassin, "but could only crawl to a hovel, where I concealed myself beneath some straw, in the hope that I might by-and-by have strength enough to get beyond the reach of danger. But though I remained some hours there, I still felt weak through loss of blood, and could only reach the place where they afterwards found

ns, as they at first supposed, dead. Then, all hope having forsaken me, and remembering the confession I had already given into the hands of Jonathan Bradford, I determined to make a clean breast of it, and acknowledge to the world that I was the real murderer. And now, what mercy have I to expect, since the blood of the victim can only be appeased by the blood of him who shed it."

"And you mean these people to understand," exclaimed Caleb Scrimmidge, "that although we were in company together, I had nothing to do with the murder of Mr. Hayes?"

No 17.

"I have already said that you were asleep when I left the room to go on my deadly errand."

"And perhaps you'll tell them also that I had nothing to do with the robbery at Frogmore Farm?"

"Let it suffice that I alone was concerned in it."

"Then as there's no charge against me," exclaimed Caleb addressing himself to Mr Dozey, "I suppose I may return to Seven Dials as soon as I please?"

"You must not leave us till your evidence has been given before a magistrate," answered the old gentleman.

"And when will that be?"

"As soon as this man has sufficiently recovered from his wound to be able to have an examination. Probably a week will be sufficient to effect that, and after your depositions have been read over, you may return home till the trial comes on."

"If I had thought to have lived to be dragged into a felon's dock, I would have made a second attempt against my miserable existence that should have been more certain than the first was," exclaimed Dan Macraisy grinding his teeth with rage. "But it is impossible I can survive, for my body is feeble through loss of blood, and I shall yet perish otherwise than by the hangman's hands."

"Don't be too sure of that," returned Caleb, "for crime always meets with its reward, and the gibbet will be your lot after all, in spite of what you may think of dying of your wound. Not that I want to make you more unhappy than you are, old fellow, though it was your fault that people had begun to think I deserved hanging as much as yourself."

"Whatever his faults may have been, let us spare our reproaches now," interposed Jonathan Bradford. "That he has been guilty of a most heinous crime we have his own confession to prove, and it will therefore become us as Christians to soothe rather than disturb the few days that may remain to him in this world. Let him then be conveyed to prison without delay, in order that he may be promptly attended by those who will devote all their care to the healing of the wounds not only of his body, but of his mind also."

"If you mean the priest and the surgeon I want neither of them," answered Macraisy sullenly. "I would perish as I am, for on the one hand I wish to escape the gallows and on the other I would avoid the canting of your parsons, who I have never had anything to do with since I first knew what crime was."

"Listen not to his blasphemous ravings," exclaimed Lawyer Dozey, "but convey him at once to the strong room lately occupied by Jonathan Bradford. He will there receive all the medical assistance he requires, and to-morrow, after the examination is over, he will be sent to the county jail, to await his trial for the crime which conscience has at length forced him to confess. And see that a watchful guard is placed over him, corporal, for if he should be suffered to escape, the consequences will fall heavily upon yourself, and the men under you."

Having issued this command, the old gentleman followed Bradford and the others into the tavern, and Dan Macraisy, faint through loss of blood, was supported between a couple of the soldiers to the cell where he was to pass the night.

CHAPTER XX.

ADMITTAL OF DAN MACRAISY TO PRISON.—A COUPLE OF VISITORS ARRIVE AT THE GEORGE INN.—DOUBTS AND APPREHENSIONS.—A WELL-CONCOCTED STORY LULLS THE SUSPICIONS OF THE HOST, AND THEY ARE ADMITTED INTO THE HOUSE AS GUESTS.

THOUGH still suffering greviously from his self-inflicted wound, Dan Macraisy was taken the next day before a magistrate in order that an examination might be made into the charge that had been brought against him. Though evidently half repenting the admission he had made in a moment of remorse, he still avowed that he alone was the perpetrator of the crime which had been committed, but at the same time expressed his satisfaction that death would remove him ere the period could arrive when the law's dread functionary would be sent down to dispatch his victim. He listened with apparent indifference to the evidence that was given in support of the declaration he had himself made, excepting only when Caleb Scrimmidge was brought forward to add his testimony to that which had been already given. During the time the latter was under examination, the eyes of the prisoner flashed with fury, and it was no small relief to Caleb when he was at last allowed to remove himself to a greater distance from the man into whose company fate had so unfortunately thrown him. Immediately on the removal of the last witness, Macraisy resumed all his usual appearance of cool indifference. Being asked at the end of the examination if he had any questions to ask or observations to make, he replied in the negative, adding that, after all the trouble they had been taking to send him to the gallows, he should yet deprive them of the gratification they anticipated. The depositions were then read over to the various witnesses ; and having been duly signed by them, the commitment was ordered to be made out, and within an hour afterwards Dan Macraisy, under a sufficient guard, was conveyed in a post-chaise to the county prison.

Matters now went on as usual at the George Inn, and Jonathan Bradford saw to his satisfaction, that everybody treated him with the same kindness and respect as before the unfortunate circumstance which had nearly terminated in a death of shame. The house was perhaps more than ever thronged with customers—some coming thither through curiosity and others through kindness, but none of them ever alluding to a subject that they knew must be painful to him. Jack Rackbottle still remained with his master till the period should arrive for his marriage with Sally, and no one felt so happy as he did now that their troubles were past and over. Though not required to follow his old vocation, he still remained at his post, and would have done so till the end of his days had it not been that Sally's interest as well as his own required that he should start in some business in which the exertions of both might tend to their mutual benefit. Thus a month passed away, and the period fixed for the assizes at Oxford arrived and the fate of Dan Macraisy was to be decided by a jury of his countrymen. At length the long-looked-for moment came ; the prisoner was placed at the bar, and after a patient inquiry, that occupied nearly the whole day, a verdict of " Guilty" was returned, and sentence of death pronounced upon the culprit. Macraisy was then removed to the infirmary belonging to the prison, on account of the weakness which still remained in consequence of the wound which he had inflicted upon himself. Late on the following afternoon, the London coach stopped opposite the door of the George Inn, and two strangers dismounting from it, directed their way towards the house, but were met midway by Jack Rackbottle.

"Can we have a bed here to-night, my good fellow ?" inquired one of them of the boots.

"Don't know, I'm sure, sir," replied Jack, eyeing them suspiciously.

"Is the house full of company, then ?"

"It's not exactly full," answered the other, "but I don't know whether there's a bed to spare for all that."

"Where's the landlord ?"

"In-doors, waiting upon his customers."

"By-the-by," said the first speaker, glancing towards the name on the signboard, "this inn is kept, I see, by one Jonathan Bradford—is it the same of whom so much has been talked lately in connection with a barbarous murder that was committed ?"

"Yes."

"And, I believe, it was afterwards discovered that he had no hand in the dreadful affair ?' observed the stranger.

"The charge was a false one," replied Jack Rackbottle; "and the man that did the deed has since confessed, though yesterday he pleaded 'Not guilty,' and gave the judge and jury all the trouble he could, as if the foolish fellow thought there was a chance of getting out of the scrape."

"Are you sure he was convicted?"

"Oh, yes, I'm quite sure of that," replied the boots, "for I was one of the witnesses on the trial, and never left the court till I heard sentence of death pronounced upon him."

The two strangers exchanged glances of peculiar meaning, and then the one who had hitherto acted as spokesman inquired the name of the person who had been tried?

"Dan Macraisy," he replied.

"And you say he has confessed the crime?"

"Oh, yes, he did that a month ago," answered Jack; "but I don't suppose he would have opened his mind quite so freely, only that he had made an attempt against his own life, and it was supposed at the time that he could not have got over the wound. But he did, though, and on Monday he'll be hanged; and then the world will be rid of a most desperate villain."

"Then, no time is to be lost," whispered one of the men to his companion; but perceiving that Rackbottle was narrowly watching them, he added—"He is to be hanged on Monday—eh? And the people hereabouts, I suppose, think he richly deserves his fate?"

"I don't think there's a soul pities him," answered Jack, "for it's well known that he deserves his fate; and the people are all the more enraged against him because he had almost suffered another person to be hanged for his crime."

"Was he ever known in this neighbourhood before?" asked the stranger.

"I believe not," answered Jack, "but he seems to have done a great deal of business in a short time, for he has also confessed that he committed a robbery at a farm close by, so that it will be a good riddance for us all when he is out of the way. He seems to be a regular bad 'un, though I dare say he has some friends and acquaintances who will be sorry for his fate."

Jack Rackbottle looked very hard at the two strangers as he made this latter remark, and the men immediately proceeded towards the house, at the door of which they saw Jonathan Bradford standing as if watching them.

"Don't you think I had better first run and ask master if he can accommodate you with beds?" asked Jack.

"Why should you do that when we can ask him the question ourselves?" returned the man who had hitherto remained silent. "Besides, it seems the house is not quite full, and surely we can be lodged here for the short t me we are going to stay."

"Oh, you are not going to make a long visit then?"

"Certainly not; we intend to leave here the first thing in the morning."

"You are on a tour of pleasure then, I suppose?"

"Humph!" exclaimed the first speaker, "you seem to be rather inquisitive my friend. However, we need make no secret of the purpose that has brought us here, so, to confess the truth we have come this journey for the purpose of seeing the city of Oxford, of whose fame we have heard so much."

"And yet you have stopped some miles before you reached the place, though the coach would have carried you right on!"

"That is because we have a friend to call upon on the road, and intend to walk the remainder of the distance. To-morrow night will be soon enough for us to reach Oxford, where we intend to remain some few days."

"Then of course you'll go and see Dan Macraisy hanged?"

"We have no inclination to witness such a sight," exclaimed the stranger who had first spoken, "and my friend, as well as myself, would rather walk twenty miles another way than go and see an unfortunate fellow-creature strangled by the executioner."

"But who can pity a rascal who has committed a horrible murder for the sake of the gold the old gentleman had in his possession?"

"Let everybody enjoy his own taste," answered the other, "but as far as we are concerned we should rather not be present at so revolting a sight. The man may be guilty as you say, but it will be sufficient for us to know that the law has been satisfied and the crime revenged. As for the unfortunate culprit, he will die, and perhaps in a month hence his name will hardly be remembered."

"But the murder will though," exclaimed Jack Rackbottle, "for it has been ordered that he shall be hanged in irons on the common so as to act as a warning against crime."

"Bah! what have we to do with all that?" demanded the other, impatiently. "We have not come down here to talk about crimes or criminals either; so run to your master and say we want to speak to him on business."

Jack went as he had been desired, and the two men looking after him with signs of suspicion, watched his countenance with evident tokens of suspicion whilst he was speaking to his master.

"I don't much fancy that chap, George," muttered the first speaker to his companion. "He seems to have his suspicions about us, and we must mind what we are doing or this affair will get blown before we have a chance of helping poor Dan Macraisy out of his present difficulties."

"It will be your fault if any mischief should happen, Harry," returned the other, "for I was altogether against coming down on such a mad errand, when it was as clear as possible that we hadn't a chance of saving him from the fate they've sentenced him to."

"How do we know till we've tried?"

"Why, at any rate, we may be sure that he'll be watched night and day till he's swinging on the gallows."

"Psha!" exclaimed the other, "I have made up my mind to a good bold effort, and Harry Borer is not a man to give up when he has once taken it into his head that he'll serve an old pal; Dan Macraisy has always proved himself to be one of the right sort, and as he would have done his best to serve either of us if we had got into the same scrape, it's only fair that we should try if there's no way to slip his neck out of the halter. However, if you are afraid of going on with what we've begun, you had better go back to London at once and leave me to finish the job by myself."

"Do you think I'm a coward, then?"

"I never thought so before," answered Harry, "but you seem to be afraid of the man we were just now speaking to, though he is too much of a fool to suspect either who we are, or what the business is that has brought us down to this part of the country."

"I don't know that," exclaimed the other, "for there's a good deal of whispering going on between him and his master, and as they look towards us very hard every now and then, I suppose we are the subject of their conversation."

"The host, I suppose, is considering whether he shall be able to accommodate us with a night's lodging."

"It's much more likely that he's considering whether he oughtn't to give us into custody."

"Nonsense," returned Harry, "tha landlord looks like a good-natured fellow enough, and I'll be bound he's already made up his mind that we shall not want a place to shelter us."

"Perhaps he may think the parish cage good enough."

"And suppose he should," exclaimed Harry, "ain't we both well armed? though nobody would think it by the look of us; and wouldn't you and I be able to defend ourselves against a dozen or two of fellows if we should be put to it?"

"Hush! They are coming this way," whispered George, "so mind what you say, or we may find ourselves in queer-street before we have time to put ourselves on our guard."

By this time Jonathan Bradford had approached pretty near them.

"I understand, gentlemen," he said, "that you wish to take up your abode under my roof to night. My house, however, is nearly full of visitors, and I am therefore sorry to say you will be obliged to proceed on to Oxford before you are likely to find the accommodation you require."

"Who told you we were going to Oxford?" demanded George, in a tone of considerable alarm.

"My man," answered the host, "and I suppose he must have learned the fact from your own lips."

"True," answered Harry, "I believe we did say something about paying a short visit there, but it will be impossible for us to reach so far to-night, and we shall therefore take it as a favour if you will give us the accommodation we require for one night. Indeed, I don't see why you should refuse us ; according to your own showing, the house is not yet quite full.''

"Ay," answered Bradford, "but those who are to sleep here are all known to me, and I have sworn that I will never again allow a stranger to pass a night in my house."

"Why is that ?''

"You have perhaps not heard of it," replied the landlord, "but a murder was not long since committed here, and suspicion fell so strong upon me that it was by a mere accident that I escaped suffering the extreme penalty of the law. From that circumstance I never since afforded a lodging to any but those who are known either to myself or my friends.''

"Surely you don't suspect persons of our appearance ?''

"I should be sorry to injure you by a thought," replied Bradford, " and no doubt the representations you have made are in every respect correct. In short, I feel inclined to break my resolution in this one instance, and if you will wait here a few minutes I will inquire within whether my wife can prepare a room for your reception.''

"Ah !" exclaimed Jack Rackbottle, who was standing near, "there can be to great harm in that, for I shall sit up and watch all night, and shall give an alarm in a moment if there should happen to be any occasion for it.''

"You suspect us then it seems ?'' observed Harry, as the landlord turned away toward the house.

"I don't know much about that," replied Jack, "but we live in queer times, and things had so nearly gone against my master a little while ago that it makes one a little sharpish. Not that you two gentlemen need take any offence, for I should have done just the same if any other persons, unknown to us, had been going to pass the night at our house.''

"Yo are right to be careful," exclaimed Harry, "but you will find that your care was not required, for in the morning we shall take our departure for Oxford, and probably on our return we may call again and spend some few days under your master's roof.''

"And you won't go to see Dan Macraisy hanged ?''

"Certainly not.''

"Well you have not much curiosity, then," exclaimed Jack, " for I have made up my mind to see the end of that fellow, and shall take the trouble to walk all the way to Oxford on purpose to see the execution of the murderer.''

"Perhaps he may not be executed," observed Harry.

"How !" exclaimed Jack ; "what do you mean by that ? Do you suppose there's any chance of his escaping, then ?''

"No," laughed the other, "I don't think that's very likely, unless he has some devilish clever fellows to assist him. But it seems he has inflicted a very severe wound upon himself, and I was thinking he might die before the moment of execution arrives.''

"If that's all," exclaimed Jack Rackbottle, "he's not very likely to escape the gallows, for he has almost recovered from his wound, and will be well enough to be hanged when the time comes.''

"Why have they put him in the infirmary, then ?''

"Because he seemed to be rather exhausted after the trial was over," answered the Boots ; "and it was thought he would be as safe in one place as in another if a good guard was placed over him. So there he'll remain till Monday, and then the world will be rid of as big a villain as ever swung from the gallows. But I suppose you never saw the fellow, so you don't feel the same sort of ill-will that I do against him.''

"No, no, I know nothing about the man, of course," said George.

"But I should think you must have heard about the murder he committed in our house ?''

"Oh, yes, it has made a great noise in town.''

"And he has a great many friends and companions in town, I dare say ?''

"No doubt of that," answered Harry, "for London is a large place, and contains people of all sorts. But this man, if I recollect the circumstances rightly came from Ireland?"

"I believe he did," answered the Booth, "for he talked very largely about his great estates there, and introduced himself to my master as Squire O'Connor, or I don't much think either he or his companion would have found a lodging at our house."

"Who was his companion?" asked Harry.

"Oh, a poor fellow—one Caleb Scrimmidge by name."

"Had he any hand in the murder?"

"No."

"How do you know that?"

"Because Dan Macralsy confessed as much, and that I'm thinking may be the only good action he ever did in his life."

"And what has become of this Caleb?"

"He's somewhere about, I believe; but to-morrow he sets off for London, and I dare say will not be in a hurry to leave it again after the fright he has met with here. But yonder I see master coming this way, so you'll soon know whether you can sleep at the George Inn to-night, or will have to pad the hoof all the way to Oxford."

"Well, gentlemen," said Bradford, who now approached them, "I am glad to tell you that my wife has at once undertaken to provide the accommodation you require. A double-bedded room is now being got ready for you, but it must be understood to be only for one night, for to-morrow Mrs. Hayes, the widow of the unfortunate gentleman who was murdered, will, with her family, occupy three or four of my rooms, previous to taking possession of the Manor House, which had been purchased just previous to the death of her husband."

"I wonder she is not afraid to sleep in the place where so dreadful a fate befel her husband," exclaimed Harry.

"Why the truth is, she has but little money with her," answered Jonathan Bradford, "for the estate has been paid for since the death of her husband, and there will, therefore, be no such temptation as there was in the former instance. Besides, Dan Macralsy is secure enough in Oxford Castle, and it is to be hoped there are few other persons in the world who would be guilty of so dreadful a crime as the one he is about to lose his life for."

"True," replied Harry, "and as you have been once deceived by a customer, it is not very likely you'll be taken in a second time."

"If master is, I shan't be," exclaimed Jack Rackbottle, "for I know pretty well how to distinguise between an honest man and a villain, and if any of the queer sort of customers should come here again, they had better look out, for it's not at the George Inn that they'll be very likely to find a lodging."

"I'm glad to hear you say so," observed Harry, "for it's a proof you have a tolerable good opinion of me and my friend here."

"At all events," returned Jonathan Bradford, "it is my fortune to have an honest faithful servant in my employ, for Rackbottle, not satisfied with having been the principal means of saving my life, is determined to preserve me against all danger in future."

"That's true enough, master," he replied, "and if I had my own way, I'd not leave your service at all. But Sally has consented to become Mrs. Rackbottle, and as soon as we are spliced, I suppose we must bid good-by to the inn, in order to start in some little way on our own account."

"Which, for your own sake I shall not oppose,' exclaimed Bradford. "However, we will now go in-doors, for I daresay these gentlemen will be glad to rest after their journey; and, with a house full of customers, I have so many things to do, that my presence in the bar is immediately required."

Whilst speaking, the host, followed by the two strangers, went towards the inn, and the latter, at their own request, were shown to a parlour that was used only for private parties.

CHAPTER XXI.

JACK RACKBOTTLE'S INTERRUPTION, AND THE TERROR INTO WHICH HE IS THROWN. —A WELL-TIMED EXCUSE.—THE TRAVELLERS RETIRE TO REST, AND JACK TAKES UPON HIMSELF THE TASK OF KEEPING WATCH OVER THEM.

The two adventures were supplied with a bottle of wine, and when they were left to themselves to discuss the possibilities and probabilities of rescuing their old comrade in vice from the fate which hung over him, the faith of Harry Borer seemed to be much stronger than that of his companion, and he argued that as they were each supplied with a brace of pistols, besides carrying with them an additional brace for the use of Dan Macraisy, should they be fortunate enough to liberate him, they could withstand any ordinary attack from his jailors, and be likely to prove the victors. Each of them drew his weapons from his pocket to examine them. Harry whispered "Hush!" as a step was heard in the passage, and before they had time to conceal their weapons the door was opened, and Jack Rackottle entered the room.

"Did you call, gentlemen?" he asked, with apparent simplicity.

"No, dolt," replied Harry, dropping his handkerchief over the pistols, "we did not call; but as you are here, you may as well bring us in another bottle of wine. But what the devil are you staring at, fellow?—Do you see anything to alarm you?"

"I saw some pistols on the table," replied Jack, "and was wondering what need there is to travel with such things."

"Know you not that the roads are infested with highwaymen?"

"They used to be," he replied, "but we haven't had any of 'em this way for a good many weeks past. Besides, arms are not wanted by gentlemen when they travel, because they can stop at any public-house they please before the daylight is at an end, and then there's no fear of meeting with robbers."

"That may be all very true," exclaimed Harry; "but my friend and I sometimes don't think of seeking a place to sleep in till after dark; and for our own safety, we think it right to carry arms with us. Does it strike you, my good fellow, that there is anything remarkable in that?"

"Not particularly," replied Jack Rackbottle; "but I thought that——"

"We must needs be a couple of highwaymen, I suppose?"

"No, not exactly that," he replied, "because master was just now telling some of his customers in the other parlour that he is sure you are a couple of real gentlemen, and of course it ain't for me to think differently from him."

"That's spoken like a sensible lad," exclaimed Harry, "for I am easily roused in a passion; and if anything disagreeable should occur through your babbling tongue, I should revenge myself in a way that you little expect."

"You mean, I suppose, that I mustn't say anything about seeing those pistols?" observed Jack.

"Exactly so."

"Then I'll be mum."

"But at the same time let it be understood," replied Harry, "that we have no other motive for secrecy than that we don't want to give rise to suspicions that might give rise to disagreeable misapprehensions, as to who and what we are."

"That is to say, you don't want our people here to take you for anything but gentlemen?"

"That's it, my good fellow," replied the other. "We are travelling the country for our pleasure, and do not wish to be troubled by the impertinence of a parcel of people, who have nothing whatever to do with us or our concerns."

"I see; you wish to reach Oxford as soon as possible?"

"That we certainly do," answered George.

"And a mighty fine place you'll find it," replied the other; "for there's plenty of colleges and churches to look at, besides the castle, which is now used as the county jail, and——"

"Is the castle a very strong place?" asked Harry.

"I rather think it is."

"Have you ever heard of a prisoner being able to make his escape from it?"

"Are you sure he was convicted?"

"Oh, yes, I'm quite sure of that,' replied the boots, "for I was one of the witnesses on the trial, and never left the court till I heard sentence of death pronounced upon him."

The two strangers exchanged glances of peculiar meaning, and then the one who had hitherto acted as spokesman inquired the name of the person who had been tried?

"Dan Macraisy," he replied.

"And you say he has confessed the crime?"

"Oh, yes, he did that a month ago," answered Jack; "but I don't suppose he would have opened his mind quite so freely, only that he had made an attempt against his own life, and it was supposed at the time that he could not have got over the wound. But he did, though, and on Monday he'll be hanged; and then the world will be rid of a most desperate villain."

"Then, no time is to be lost," whispered one of the men to his companion; but perceiving that Rackbottle was narrowly watching them, he added—"He is to be hanged on Monday—eh? And the people hereabouts, I suppose, think he richly deserves his fate?"

"I don't think there's a soul pities him," answered Jack, "for it's well known that he deserves his fate; and the people are all the more enraged against him because he had almost suffered another person to be hanged for his crime."

"Was he ever known in this neighbourhood before?" asked the stranger.

"I believe not," answered Jack, "but he seems to have done a great deal of business in a short time, for he has also confessed that he committed a robbery at a farm close by, so that it will be a good riddance for us all when he is out of the way. He seems to be a regular bad 'un, though I dare say he has some friends and acquaintances who will be sorry for his fate."

Jack Rackbottle looked very hard at the two strangers as he made this latter remark, and the men immediately proceeded towards the house, at the door of which they saw Jonathan Bradford standing as if watching them.

"Don't you think I had better first run and ask master if he can accommodate you with beds?" asked Jack.

"Why should you do that when we can ask him the question ourselves?" returned the man who had hitherto remained silent. "Besides, it seems the house is not quite full, and surely we can be lodged here for the short time we are going to stay."

"Oh, you are not going to make a long visit then?"

"Certainly not; we intend to leave here the first thing in the morning."

"You are on a tour of pleasure then, I suppose?"

"Humph!" exclaimed the first speaker, "you seem to be rather inquisitive my friend. However, we need make no secret of the purpose that has brought us here, so, to confess the truth we have come this journey for the purpose of seeing the city of Oxford, of whose fame we have heard so much."

"And yet you have stopped some miles before you reached the place, though the coach would have carried you right on!"

"That is because we have a friend to call upon on the road, and intend to walk the remainder of the distance. To-morrow night will be soon enough for us to reach Oxford, where we intend to remain some few days."

"Then of course you'll go and see Dan Macraisy hanged?"

"We have no inclination to witness such a sight," exclaimed the stranger who had first spoken, "and my friend, as well as myself, would rather walk twenty miles another way than go and see an unfortunate fellow-creature strangled by the executioner."

"But who can pity a rascal who has committed a horrible murder for the sake of the gold the old gentleman had in his possession?"

"Let everybody enjoy his own taste," answered the other, "but as far as we are concerned we should rather not be present at so revolting a sight. The man may be guilty as you say, but it will be sufficient for us to know that the law has been satisfied and the crime revenged. As for the unfortunate culprit, he will die, and perhaps in a month hence his name will hardly be remembered."

"No one would ever try to do so, I should think."

"It's impossible to say how that may be," exclaimed Jack, "for when a fellow finds himself in an awkward dilemma, there's no saying what he wouldn't do for the sake of getting out of it. There's that fellow Dan Macraisy, for instance, would have a try if they only gave him an opportunity."

"What makes you think of Dan Macraisy more than any other person?" asked Harry eagerly.

"Only because as he's going to be hanged it would be worth his while to run the risk of breaking his neck another way by clambering over the wall."

"I should think he would never be fool enough to make such an attempt," observed George, directing a look towards his friend.

"Impossible," returned the other, "It would be madness to attempt it, and especially as he appears to have been very much weakened by loss of blood."

"That's very true," exclaimed Jack, "but most people think that life's worth saving and as he's sure to be hanged if he stops there till Monday morning, he'd find strength enough to climb the wall I'll be bound if they'd only give him the chance."

"Which they'll not do," observed Harry, "and therefore we are only wasting time by talking about a thing that is not likely to happen. The fact is, he is safe in their clutches; and when the time comes they'll carry the sentence into execution."

"I hope they will."

"And so do thousands of others besides yourself. For my own part, however, I don't care much about it, for if a poor devil can escape the hangman's hands, I think he deserves to get clear away for his trouble."

"But this man is a murderer."

"Very true," replied Harry. "I daresay he is a bad fellow; but what have you or I to do with that since he has never done anything to injure either of us?"

"Ay," replied Jack Rackbottle, "but my master had a narrow escape of being hanged instead of him."

"Then he ought to consider himself all the more lucky for having got off when he supposed it was all over with him."

"Upon my life I don't see the force of that argument," returned the other, "for Dan Macraisy owns to having committed the murder, and I don't see why he shouldn't suffer for it as all other assassins do. But you seem to take part with this fellow, though everybody else are glad that he's going to suffer."

"You mistake in supposing that I have any wish for him to get off," replied the other. "I only say that if he were to do so by any bold effort of his own, he would deserve to get clear away, and I, for one, should not be sorry for it."

"Then I should, for it is likely enough he would come back here some night and murder all the family."

"Psha!" exclaimed Harry, "only let him once get on the outside of those walls, I'll be bound he would not stay in England longer than he could help. But what's the use of talking about such an affair when it's not likely they would suffer him to escape even if he should attempt it."

"It's not very likely, I know," answered Jack Rackbottle; "but for all that I shall not feel quite easy till I have seen the last of him next Monday."

"Then you are determined to go and see the execution?"

"Yes, that I will, if I have to walk every step of the distance between here and Oxford and back again."

"But suppose you should be disappointed after all?"

"I hope that wont be the case," he replied, "for if ever he should get loose again there's no saying what mischief would come of it. He's too bad ever to mend, and the chances are that he would kill other people by way of revenging himself for what has been done against him."

"Then you think he would be fool enough to remain in a country where he never would be safe?"

"I don't think he would stop if he could any how get way," replied Jack Rackbottle; "but as they would not give him a chance of doing that, I'm afraid he would commit other murders, and I don't think my own life would be very safe, as I happened to be one of the witnesses against him."

"You may make yourself quite easy about that," returned Harry, "for he's not likely to escape from prison, and you will therefore, I dare say, have the satisfaction of seeing him hanged on Monday next. My friend and I shall be in Oxford on that day, but neither of us will be present at the execution. So now go and fetch the wine we have ordered, and when that is out we shall be ready to go to bed. But remember, don't chatter to any one about the pistols you saw on the table just now."

"But are you sure it's all right?"

"To be sure it is. If any wrong was intended, do you suppose we should have been such fools as to let you see that we have arms?"

Jack Rackbottle either was, or pretended to be, quite satisfied with this latter argument; and, leaving the room, he returned within a few minutes afterwards with the wine.

"There's the money for what we've had as well as our bed to-night," said Harry, throwing a guinea on the table, "and the change you may keep to yourself. But mum's the word, you know; so keep a quiet tongue, my boy, and all will be well."

"Do you think that fellow is to be trusted?" exclaimed George, as the boots again disappeared.

"To be sure he is," answered the other; "did'nt you see how eagerly he pocketed the bribe? and if that ain't enough to keep him quiet, why we shall have to go upon another track, that's all. But don't you get drinking too much of that wine, old fellow, for we shall want cool and clear heads to-morrow and I only ordered the stuff to give us an air of respectability here, and remove any suspicion that might have been formed against us."

"As you please," replied George; "but I thought the wine was too good and too dear to be wasted."

"Psha!" exclaimed the other, "what's the use of thinking of the expense when we've an old comrade to save from the gallows? Let's only get Dan Macraisy clear off, and when he's beyond danger we'll have a roistering night together, and you shall drink as much as you please without my interfering with you. There's nothing like sobriety when business is to be done, for many a good job has been spoilt through getting drunk over-night; and it would be a sorry reflection for us afterwards if Dan were to be scragged through our taking a glass or two of wine more than we ought. So put the bottle aside, and let's to-bed; and in the morning we'll set about our work in a business-like way."

George made no reply to this, though he cast a longing glance towards the bottle. It was in vain, however, for Jack now appeared in answer to the bell which had been rung; and mounting the stairs, the two adventurers retired to-bed.

CHAPTER XXII.

CONCLUSION.

The following morning, Henry Borer and his companion breakfasted at Jonathan Bradford's, after which they commenced their journey in the direction of Oxford. When they had proceeded some distance they called at a roadside inn to partake of refreshments, and found that the all-absorbing topic of conversation related to the coming execution. A countryman that was speaking hoped that the culprit would not be reprieved, as he really deserved the punishment he was about to undergo.

"It's to be hoped all don't think alike," returned Harry Borer; "for I have heard before now of men being hanged when they were not guilty, and it's only fair that one criminal now and then should escape to make up for it."

"Well," exclaimed the farmer, "it's a good thing to know that this chap hasn't a chance of escaping."

"Are you sure of that?"

"I only go by what other people have told me; but it seems that Macraisy wounded himself when he thought that there was no way of getting out of the neighbourhood; and as he has not recovered yet, it's out of all reason to suppose that he can baffle the people that have been set to watch him."

"But," answered George, "his case is such a desperate one that he may try for all that."

"What do you know about it?" asked Harry, with a look of anger at his companion "This man, I dare say, knows better than we do, and if the chap is hanged, what does it matter to us?"

"You need'nt say *if* he's hanged," exclaimed the farmer, "because he's almost certain to die as to-morrow comes, and we shall have the comfort of knowing that there's one villain less in the world than there was."

"Ay, ay, that't true enough," interposed the landlord, "he'll swing sure enough, and, for my own part, I shouldn't mind if there were more executions in the year, for they bring plenty of grist to the mill, and to-morrow, when the job's over my house will be so full of customers that I shall hardly know how to serve 'em all. There's nothing like a hanging match to bring plenty of people together; and if we may judge by the lots of strangers that have arrived in the town already, I should say that Oxford will have more visitors this time than were ever seen in it before."

"And perhaps all their trouble may be thrown away," observed Harry; "for it's not unlikely that no execution will take place."

"Do you think, then, there's a chance for him to escape?" asked the countryman with surprise.

"I don't suppose they would suffer him to get out of prison alive," answered Harry 'but you said just now that he was suffering from a wound, and I was thinking it would be better for him to die of that than to be brought out to swing for the gratification of a gaping multitude."

"Ay," exclaimed the landord; "but it's the example that I think most of; for if it wasn't for the lesson the gibbet teaches us, there would be no end of murders. Besides, this fellow has shed the blood of a fellow-creature, and its only fair and just that he should be made to pay the penalty of his crime."

"With all my heart," replied Harry Borer; "let the man die, if he deserves his fate; but I'm not ashamed to say, that if it were in my power to save him, I would do it."

The people looked at him with amazement; and, finding that his words had brought more attention upon him than he wished for, he added in a different tone—

"Not, mind you, that I would do anything by force or violence; but I mean if I had any influence with the judge that tried him, I would see if something couldn't be done to save one victim from the gallows. I should do it upon the principle that the law is not justified in taking away life."

"Neither was Dan Macraisy when he murdered the poor old gentleman for the sake of his money," observed the host.

"There you are right enough," answered Harry; "but unfortunately money is too often a temptation that's not easily to be resisted; and perhaps if this Mr. Hayes had not gone about with so much gold in his pocket, he might have been alive at this moment, and the people of this city would have been spared a sight to-morrow that will end in sending a good many light-fingered coves to prison—for thieves find nothing more profitable than a good crowd assembled at an execution. However, we've nothing to do with that, for I, at any rate, shall not be there, because my business in this city will soon be over; and then I and my companion will be glad to get away as fast as we can."

"Do you wish for a bed here to-night?" asked the landlord.

"That's more than we can say at present," answered Harry. "My friend and I are going out presently to look after an old acquaintance of ours, and a good deal will depend upon whether we happen to meet with him."

"What part of the city does this acquaintance of yours live in?" asked the landlord.

"We hardly know the exact spot," replied the other; "but we have been told it's not very far from the prison."

"Rather a suspicious neighbourhood," observed the landlord, with a chuckle.

"That's a very good joke of yours," returned Harry Borer; "but the man we seek is a very decent sort of a fellow in his way, for all that, and our object in coming here is to do him a service."

"Does he expect you?"

"I dare say he does," answered Harry, "for he happens to be in a lit le trouble just now, and he knows we wouldn't forsake him just when he stands in need of our services. But it's time we should be attending to our business now," he added, "for we are sure to find him at home; and perhaps we may return here by-and-by to see if you can accommodate us with a bed."

The two strangers then drank off the remainder of their ale, and rising from their seats, left the house; and passing over Magdalen Bridge, proceeded up the High Street towards the Corn Market, occasionally looking back to see if any one were watching or following them. All, however, appeared to be safe, and they then made their way to the castle, where Macraisy was awaiting his doom, and beneath the walls of which they saw a man looking up towards the inner buildings which towered above, as if his attention were occupied with some particular object.

"This seems to be a strong place," observed Harry, addressing him with a view of obtaining some information.

"So they say," answered the man, "but for all that I was thinking just now how easy it would be for the man they are going to hang, to make his escape, if he did not mind running a little risk."

"Nonsense! How would that be possible?" demanded Harry, with an eagerness that he could not conceal.

"Why you see that light yonder, just above the wall?"

"I do, what of it?"

"Nothing particular," replied the man, "but the room where you see the light is the infirmary, and as the prisoner is there, be could easily drop down from the window on to the top of the wall, and then a piece of rope would let him down as nicely as possible. I hope he won't think of it though, for I've come fifteen miles to see the execution to-morrow, and I don't want to have all my trouble for nothing."

"You need not be afraid of that," answered Harry, "for I suppose the prisoner is pretty well guarded."

"Oh, yes, there's people with him, I dare say, but if they should drop off to sleep, only think how easy it would be for him to cheat Jack Ketch of his right."

"And are you going to watch here all night?"

"Not I," replied the man; "I only strolled this way out of curiosity, and am now, going back to my lodging, to get a few hours' sleep. So I shall wish you good night and if you take my advice, you'll be out early in the morning, so as to make sure of a good place."

The man now went away, and as soon as he was beyond hearing, Harry whispered to his companion—

"This is better than we could have expected, for we now know where to look for Macraisy; and if good luck only favours him, our trouble in coming down here will not be for nothing."

"But they'll take care not to let him escape."

"How do we know that?" demanded the other. "Perhaps they may think he's safe enough and may take a nap on the strength of it, so that Dan will have an opportunity to drop down from the window on to the wall, as the man said just now. If he can only do that, we shall not have much trouble to assist him to the ground, and then we must be off towards London as fast as we can."

"Then why not get our rope ready, in case he should make an attempt?" asked George.

"I'll do that directly," he replied, and throwing off his coat and waistcoat, he unwound, from his body, a quantity of small but very strong cord, which he again wound up in a coil, and placed near him to be in readiness when required. wall

"This will answer the purpose," he said, "if once he should be able to reach the ure A moderate degree of strength will throw one end to him, and if he makes that sec he can slide down, and his escape may then be looked upon as certain."

"Ah!" replied George, "that's easily enough said, but those that have been set to watch him must be sleepy fellows if they can't keep awake to look after him the few hours he has to live. They'll look sharp after him depend on it, and we shall be lucky if some of the people here don't lay hands upon us, on suspicion of being here for no food purpose."

" How can they suspect us any more than any one else?"

" Because we are prowling about the prison walls, and they may want to know what business we have here."

" Well, and can't we have an answer ready for 'em? We are here because it suits our humour, and let 'em make whatever they can out of that. But look up yonder! the window opens, and one of the bars is moved away as if it had been filed through beforehand. Now some one appears, and—and—by all that's lucky, its Macraisy himself?"

"So it is," whispered the other, " but how can we let him know that we are here to assist him?"

" This," replied Harry Borer, and immediately he gave a peculiar whistle, which was recognised as a signal by all those who belonged to the fraternity. A slight motion of the hand informed them that the sound had reached the person for whom it was intended, and presently afterwards Macraisy was seen to creep between the remaining bars, and place himself upon the window-sill, where he remained a few moments as if to steady himself, and then let his body gradually slide down whilst he kept a firm hold above. Having thus brought his feet exactly over the top of the wall, he hung perfectly stationary, and then relaxing his grasp, came down with his legs close together and his arms extended to ballance himself against the wall. This was managed with so much care and precision that he alighted in safety, and then turning himself round, he threw himself upon his hands and knees and crawled along till he reached the place where the rope had by this time been thrown over the summit of the wall. This he secured round a brick which projected three or four inches, and having ascertained that all was secure, let himself down by the rope to the spot where his comrades were waiting to receive him.

" By jove!" he whispered, " instead of dying by a rope, as was intended, it's a rope that has saved me."

" Don't be too sure of that just yet," returned Harry, " for you'll not be safe till we get some few miles beyond this confounded city. So follow silently, and if anybody should come in pursuit, George and I have arms to protect ourselves with."

" Can't you spare me one of the pistols?" he asked.

" Yes," replied the other; " take this, but mind, it must not be used till there seems no other way to escape. If we are pursued we must run for it, and make for the nearest place that seems likely to afford a shelter till the danger is over. If we should chance to be separated, let each make his way to London as soon as possible, and our meeting place can be at the old quarters in Drury Lane."

Whilst speaking thus, they were hurrying through various back streets where, though they were met by several persons, no one suspected the purpose for which they had chosen that unfrequented way. At length they reached the outskirts of the city a little beyond Christ Church meadows, where they were obliged to pause, in order to determine which would be the safer direction for them to take. The most secure seemed to be a path which led towards the village of Iffley, but scarcely had they proceeded a hundred yards, when the loud halloing of many persons was heard behind. This was enough to convince them that the pursuers were upon their track, and dashing aside from the path, they made towards a wood that rose darkly on the left. For a time they still had hopes of escaping, but at length to their consternation they found themselves upon the bank of a river. To turn back was certain destruction. Whilst Harry and George dashed into the stream to reach the other side, Dan Macraisy placed his back against a tree, resolving to perish by his own hand rather than be taken back to the prison where a horrible fate awaited him. In a few moments more the pursuers were within a short distance, and making with all speed towards the spot where he was standing. All hope therefore, was at an end, and just as the foremost man was making a spring to clutch hold of his prey, the report of a pistol was heard, and Dan Macraisy, uttering a loud cry of agony, sunk dead upon the earth. The body was immediately conveyed back to the castle by some of the men whilst others went in pursuit of the two accomplices. All, however, was in vain, for the two fellows had a long start, and those who had followed, returned some hours afterwards with the intelligence that all trace of the villains had been entirely lost.

www.ingramcontent.com/pod-product-compliance
Lightning Source LLC
Chambersburg PA
CBHW082012170626
46817CB00009B/3072